COGRILL'S MILL

Jack Lindsey

Copyright © Jack Lindsey, 2005

The right of the author to be identified as copyright holder of this work has been asserted in accordance with the Copyright, Designs and Patents Act, 1988.

ISBN 987-0-9549621-2-8

First Published in Great Britain in 2005
This paperback edition published in 2009

Published by:

Peatmore Press,
ENGLAND

http://peatmore.com

A catalogue record of the book is available from the British Library

All rights reserved. No part of this publication may be reproduced, stored in a retrieval system, or transmitted, in any form or by any means, electronic, mechanical, photocopying, recording or otherwise, without the prior permission of both the publishers and copyright owner.

This book is sold subject to the condition that it shall not, by way of trade or otherwise, be lent, resold, hired out or otherwise circulated without the publisher's prior consent in any form of binding or cover other than that in which it is published and without a similar condition including this condition being imposed on the subsequent purchaser.

This is a work of fiction and all characters, firms, organisations and instants portrayed are imaginary. They are not meant to resemble any counterparts in the real world; in the unlikely event that any similarity does exist it is an unintended coincidence.

This book is also available in e-book format, details of which are available at http://peatmore.com.

For Rebecca and Alexander.

INTRODUCTION

I have told stories since childhood and longed to see them published. I use to scribble away in lined exercise books and then tapped away on a portable mechanical typewriter in a bid to seem professional. This practice continued when first I left my home near Bristol to study applied biology in Essex and persisted sporadically throughout my career as a professional microbiologist.

Work on Cogrill's Mill began in 1985 using an old Amstrad CPC 464 computer when personal computers were regarded more as a toy than the everyday tool they are now. Then the text was transferred to an early PC and the novel completed ten years later. In 1996 I took a nine-month break from the laboratory where I worked to look after my two small children while my wife concentrated on her job and studied for a nursing degree. During that time I submitted my manuscript to over a dozen literary agents and some publishers. Although it was rejected many times I was encouraged by the comments I received, so much so that I decided to take the novel forward myself and formed Peatmore Press to publish and promote it online as an E-book.

The first draft and the bulk of the story were completed in the 1980s, a time before computers, mobile telephones and digital cameras were in everyday use, so the tools used by the characters particularly in the field of photography reflect those of the day.

This first issue was received positively and gained some good reviews. Buoyed by these and recognising that the electronic format was still in its infancy and little used, I chose to embark on this paperback edition. The bulk of the text remains unaltered from the E-book but I have endeavoured to correct some typing and grammatical mistakes and one small continuity error missed in the earlier edition. The setting and the story remain the same.

Jack Lindsey

Everything flows and nothing stays.

Heraclitus (c.535–c.475 BC) Greek philosopher. *Cratylus* (Plato)

CHAPTER 1

George Cogrill was uneasy. It was a bright sunny day in June and it was his birthday, but he had received a summons from his aunt. No matter what the weather, or the occasion, his aunt always made him feel uneasy and a summons from her could not be ignored.

As he trudged along the drive towards Gleefield Manor, the sense of foreboding intensified. But he was determined to put on a brave face. After all, she might simply want to give him a present and wish him happy birthday. But nothing ever seemed simple or straightforward where his aunt was concerned.

The Manor towered in front of him like a medieval castle. Poplar trees lined the driveway and a spacious lawn stretched out either side. He reached the great house, rang the bell and the heavy oak door was opened by a bent old man in black suit and dark grey waistcoat.

A long dark shape rocketed out from behind the old man and up at George's chest. It was a black Labrador, who then proceeded to dance about George on its hind legs, trying to lick his face.

"Good afternoon, Master George," creaked the old man in a broken voice. "Many happy returns of the day."

"Thank you, Gumage," said George. He rubbed the dog affectionately behind its ears. "Hello, Winchester!" Then without taking his eyes from the dog he asked, "Is my aunt at home?"

"She is in the withdrawing room, sir. I'll show you straight in."

George followed him across black and white checked tiles into a vaulted room with faded flower-patterned wallpaper, Winchester trailing at his heels. Glossy photographs adorned the walls, not of landscapes or hunting scenes, but sepia pictures of racing motorcycles, their leather-clad riders hanging from saddles as they rounded corners or crouched across dark fuel tanks. His aunt was sitting in a high-backed armchair. She was wearing a grey woollen pullover and green corduroy trousers. Iron-grey hair fell down to her shoulders. A book was on her lap. She looked up as they entered.

"Master George, My lady," croaked Gumage gravely. "Shall I bring some tea?"

She regarded both of them seriously. A pair of wire-framed spectacles hung from a chain around her neck. "No thank you, Gumage. Master George won't be staying long."

Gumage's face remained impassive. "Very good, My lady," he said and left closing the door behind him.

Winchester stalked over to the empty fireplace and lay down on the purple rug. A signed smiling photograph of Geoff Duke, in flat cap with goggles pushed above the peak from his 1950s racing heyday, stood in pride of position on the mantelpiece.

"Well, Aunt Jane," said George, "you wanted to see me."

"Yes, I did." She looked at him sternly and made no move to bid him to be seated. George hovered by the door feeling uncomfortable.

"You have been a great disappointment to me, George. Today you are thirty years old and have achieved absolutely nothing with your life. You have not married and have never had a job. Your father left you property, a large amount of money, and you have achieved precisely nothing with it. You lounge about that broken-down mill. Just precisely what do you do all day?"

"Well, Aunt. I look after my orchard, I do some gardening, I go fishing ..."

"Gardening and fishing!" His aunt snorted, shaking her head vigorously. "Those are hobbies not occupations. And watching apples grow is hardly work. You are just wasting your life."

George protested. "But I don't need any occupations. I have enough money and live quite comfortably."

His aunt sighed. "There's more to life than simply living comfortably," she said. She looked at him sternly. "Now what you don't know is that although your father left you all his money, the cottage and that confounded mill, there are certain conditions attached. And I, as his executor, mean to make sure that they are carried out." She paused for dramatic effect and then said, "It was a condition that you should have achieved something worthwhile in your life by the time you were thirty or you would forfeit your inheritance."

"I don't understand, Aunt," said George, puzzled. "What do you mean?"

"I'll spell it out for you, George. There was a clause in your father's will that you should have achieved something worthwhile by the time you were thirty. And by worthwhile it is stated that you should be earning a decent living and perhaps have got married and were raising a family.

"But that's not fair!" cried George. "I was never told!"

"That was also a condition. Your father wished that any achievements you made would not be motivated by greed. Since I consider that you have not made any worthwhile achievements, or got married, you stand to forfeit the remainder of your inheritance."

George started to protest again but she held up her right palm, silencing him. "However," she said, "all is not completely lost. Your father, himself, was on occasions not always motivated by good intentions. Indeed before you were born he succeeded in cheating his then business partner, a one Victor Gloam, out of a considerable amount of money which, shamefully, your father unscrupulously used to establish the basis of his own wealth. I have therefore taken it upon myself to propose that you find Victor Gloam and bestow on him half of what your father left you. You can then perhaps claim that you have after all achieved something worthwhile. You may then at least be able to keep the other half."

"But that won't leave enough for me to live on!" George protested.

"I realise that," said Aunt Jane raising her hand again to silence him, "which means that you will also have to get a job." She pointed a finger at him and added, "If you succeed in all these things you may then inherit my money when I die. Otherwise, your father's money and mine will all go to providing a comfortable home for Winchester." She nodded her head to indicate the large black Labrador asleep on the rug. "I promised my dear sister when she died shortly after your birth that I would see that you would be brought up properly. I also mean to see that some of your despicable father's deeds are repaid."

"But how will I find Victor Gloam? My father died years ago. Gloam might also be dead."

Aunt Jane nodded her head sadly. "Don't remind me. I remember your father drowning in a vat of Buzzbee's gin while undergoing negotiations to buy the distillery. Such a disgrace." She shook her head and said, "However, I digress. Shortly after he was swindled Victor Gloam disappeared and was never heard of again. But! Two months ago I noticed an advertisement in the Mucklesbury Gazette for V. Gloam, Photographer, Weddings and Portraits, Tidburn. I could hardly believe it. All these years and he's living in a neighbouring town just twelve miles away."

She took a newspaper cutting out of the book and handed it to George who stared at it dumbly. "Well off you go now," she snapped, "and I don't want to hear from you again until you have found Victor Gloam and given him half of all you own and half your income."

George was dumbfounded. He was still in a daze after Gumage had shown him out and closed the great door behind him. He stood for a while on the gravel drive and then slowly made his way back the way he had come. As he walked, he determined to resolve the matter as soon as possible. His aunt was very wealthy and if she kept her word, which she always did, it was probable he would stand to lose much more in the longer term than if he failed to carry out her instructions.

He set off quickly towards the village of Mucklesbury and there caught the quarter past nine bus to Tidburn. The journey across the country lanes took approximately three quarters of an hour and then all too quickly he arrived at his destination. He had already decided not to search too hard for 'V. Gloam Photographer'. He would briefly scan the main streets and then return to his aunt's with the news that the establishment could not be found. It was therefore with great dismay on stepping down from the bus in Tidburn high street that the first shop sign to confront his eyes was that of V. Gloam.

He stood glumly on the pavement and stared at the shop window. It contained prominently displayed photographs of weddings as well as portraits of an assortment of people, children and domestic animals. He agonised for ten minutes and then with great determination strode to the door, opened it and walked inside.

A bell sounded as it swung shut behind him. The shop was deserted. In front of him was a small counter, behind which was a stack of filing cabinets. He approached the counter and looked around him. More photographs, similar to those in the window, adorned the walls. To the left of the counter a small door led to a back room and to its right, a wooden flight of stairs led upwards. There was a clatter of feet on the stairs and a very pretty golden-haired girl descended. She stepped behind the counter. "Can I help you?" she asked in a polite soft voice. Her eyes were bright blue and her smile sparkled.

George was mesmerised by her beauty but he managed to summon up some words. "I ... I wish to speak to Mr Gloam," he stammered.

"There is no Mr Gloam," she replied.

George was confused but he blustered on. "The sign says V. Gloam."

She nodded, still smiling. "That's me ... Victoria Gloam."

"I was looking for Victor Gloam," George continued.

"Victor Gloam was my father. He died two years ago."

George felt a surge of relief. "Oh really," he breathed. Fate was on his side again.

The girl's smile changed to a frown. "Well there's no need to look so pleased about it," she said.

George's face reddened. "I'm extremely sorry, I didn't mean ..."

"What did you wish to see my father about, Mr ... er ... um? What did you say your name was?"

"Oh, er ... um ... Smith," replied George and added hastily, "I was asked to look your father up. I'm sorry to have troubled you, good-bye!" He turned quickly for the door.

"Good-bye, Mr Smith!" Victoria Gloam called after him.

Once outside, George hurried across the road to a telephone box. Life was pleasant once more. He could hardly contain himself. He snatched open the door, grabbed the telephone receiver and quickly dialled his aunt's number. His call was answered by the butler. "Hello, Gumage," said George, "is my aunt there?"

"I will see if I can find her, Master George."

Some moments passed and then Aunt Jane's harsh voice sounded at the end of the line. "Hello, George," she said.

"Hello, Aunt Jane!" George said breezily. She would be pleased that he had acted so speedily and successfully. "I'm calling from Tidburn!"

"Oh yes."

"Yes." Then George remembered to lower his voice and tried to sound not so joyful. "I'm afraid Victor Gloam is dead." There was silence at the other end of the telephone.

"Did you hear me, Aunt Jane?" asked George

"I heard you, George."

"So I can't give him half my inheritance."

"I realise that, George."

"Well, I thought I ought to let you know as soon as possible. Now I had better be going as I am phoning from a call box and I haven't much change. Good-bye, Aunt Jane."

"George!"

"Yes, Aunt Jane?"

"Did he leave any family?"

George felt his heart sink. "Family, Aunt Jane?"

"Yes, George, a wife, children."

George began to stammer. "I'm ... I'm not sure."

"What do you mean, you're not sure?"

"I'll ... I'll have to check."

"Well make sure that you do, because if there are any relatives then they're entitled to get what should have gone to Victor Gloam. Is that clear, George?"

"Yes, Aunt Jane," said George sadly. "Good-bye."

"Good-bye, George."

George slowly put the receiver down. Well that was that. He would have to see the girl again. It was now clear that his quiet comfortable life would definitely change. Well, it could not be helped. He crossed the road and entered the shop once more.

The interior was empty but, as the doorbell tinkled behind him, Victoria Gloam's voice sounded from behind the closed door of the back room. "Can you wait a few moments?" she called. "I'm in the dark room!"

George stood and once more peered about him. Then, as he waited he thought it might be a good idea to find out more about her and so he decided to take a quick look upstairs. If she came out while he was up there he could claim that he had misheard her. Anyway he had not much else to lose. He had already lost half his inheritance. He quickly tiptoed up the wooden staircase.

The landing was closed off by a mauve curtain which he pulled back to reveal a long spacious studio. At the end of the studio was an area surrounded by photographic lights, reflectors and tripods. In front of these stood a slim dark-haired handsome young man smoking a strong-smelling French cigarette. He was completely naked.

"Oh ... I'm ... um extremely sorry," said George.

The young man seemed unconcerned. "Hello," he said, "are you looking for Vicky?"

George nodded glumly.

"Well she's in the dark room. The film jammed in the camera. She won't be long."

"I'll wait downstairs," said George. He hastily retraced his steps and arrived at the foot of the stairs just in time to see Victoria Gloam emerge from the back room with a camera in her hand.

"Oh, hello, Mr Smith!" she exclaimed.

George looked behind him. "Mr Who?" he asked.

"Mr Smith," she repeated.

George swallowed hard. "Actually, my name's not Smith."

She raised her eyebrows. "It's not?"

"No. It's Cogrill."

"Cogrill?"

"Yes. Did your father ever mention it?"

She shook her head.

"Do you have any other relatives?" he asked

"No. My mother died when I was very young."

George sympathised. "So did mine. I was brought up by my aunt."

Victoria Gloam grew impatient. "Look, Mr Cogrill, what's this all about?"

"I've been told to give you some money."

"What money?"

George took a deep breath. "Rather a lot of money," he said. "About five hundred thousand pounds."

The young man's voice called from upstairs. "Hurry up, Vicky!" he shouted. "I'm getting cold!"

"Be quiet, Justin!" she called, "I won't be long." She turned to George. "Did you say five hundred thousand pounds? Are you serious?"

"Yes. That's right."

"But why?"

"Because I've been told to by my Aunt Jane," said George.

"Your Aunt Jane?" she asked.

"You're also entitled to some property."

"What property?"

"A half share of an old water mill. There's a cottage as well."

"I don't understand."

"Vicky!" came the call from upstairs.

"Look," said George, "it would probably be best if I came back later or better still if you contact Aunt Jane."

"Yes, all right," she said feeling rather stunned

"I'll write down her address and telephone number for you. Do you have a pencil and paper?"

She pushed a ballpoint pen and a pad across the counter towards him. George took the pen and hastily scrawled on the paper. Then he put the pen down and looked up at her. "I'd better be going now," he said. "Good-bye, Miss Gloam."

She looked at him blankly. "Good-bye, Mr Cogrill," she said.

CHAPTER 2

Aunt Jane opened wide the throttle of her 750 cc, Triumph Bonneville motorcycle and the great machine accelerated out of a corner and over the brow of Mucklesbury Hill. It plunged down the hill at breakneck speed with Aunt Jane braking fiercely at the bottom and then leaning hard over to the left so that the motorcycle swung into the drive of Gleefield Manor, narrowly missing the hedge on the opposite side of the road and the edge of the cliff above Mucklesbury quarry. A red Austin Mini stood in front of the great house. She applied the brakes once more and skidded to a halt on the loose gravel.

Gumage was standing on the front porch. The black Labrador, Winchester, was at his side. The old butler descended the stone steps and approached her reverently. Winchester sat down on his haunches and watched.

"Your visitor has arrived, my lady," creaked Gumage. "I have taken the liberty of showing her into the withdrawing room and have taken her some tea."

"Thank you, Gumage," said Aunt Jane, dismounting from the motorcycle. "I know I'm late but it was such a nice day I decided to take the road across the downs. The Bonneville ran beautifully but I think the carburettor requires further adjustment."

Gumage took the motorcycle from her. "I will see to it, my lady," he said and wheeled it towards the garage. Winchester stepped down from his position on the porch and followed him.

Aunt Jane took off her crash helmet and entered the house. Then she quickly climbed the stairs to her bedroom to divest herself of her motorcycle leathers. Ten minutes later she descended, clad more suitably in a blue dress and mauve cardigan, and entered the drawing room.

Victoria Gloam was sitting on the sofa. In front of her on a small low table stood a tea pot, two cups with saucers and a plate of biscuits. She made to rise on Aunt Jane's entry.

"Good afternoon, Miss Gloam," said Aunt Jane. "No, please, don't get up. I'm sorry to keep you waiting." She sat down beside her on the sofa, took the cosy off the teapot and felt the pot with her hand to check that it was still warm. "Would you like another cup of tea?"

"No, thank you," the girl replied.

Aunt Jane poured herself some from the pot. "Now then," she asked, "what was it you wanted to see me about?"

The girl took a deep breath and began. "I was given your name by a rather strange man who visited my shop a few days ago," she said. "He said that you told him to give me five hundred thousand pounds. Then the next day this cheque arrived." She opened her handbag, took out the cheque and showed it to Aunt Jane. The cheque was for five hundred thousand pounds and signed by George Cogrill. "I'd like very much to know what this is all about," she said.

Aunt Jane took a sip of her tea and then put the cup back down on the table. "Well, Victoria," she said, "may I call you Victoria?"

"Most people call me Vicky."

"I shall call you Victoria," said Aunt Jane and began to explain. "George is my nephew – his father was married to my younger sister. Your father and George's father were business partners until George's father cheated your father out of a considerable amount of money. He became very rich and left all his wealth to George, his only surviving heir. Since George has done nothing worthwhile with it, I have decided that he give half of it to you, seeing as you are your father's only surviving heir."

Vicky stared at her wide eyed. "And George agreed to this?" she asked incredulously.

"George always does what I tell him to do," said Aunt Jane.

"Oh."

"Tell me," asked Aunt Jane, "what do you plan to do with the money?"

"Oh," said Vicky excitedly, "I would like to expand my business, I'm a photographer. I studied photography at Art College and my father ran a small photographer's shop in Tidburn, which I took over when he died." Her eyes lit up. "I'd like to buy a big studio and do fashion photography, employing only the best models."

"And where would you like this studio to be?"

"Oh, I don't mind really. But I suppose in the country is best. I could do lots of countryside locations. Yes, in the country is definitely best."

Aunt Jane smiled. "I think I know the very place," she said.

"You do?"

"Yes, it belongs to George, but by rights at least half of it belongs to you. I t's an old water mill."

"It sounds perfect. But I couldn't deprive George of his home."

"Oh, he doesn't live there," said Aunt Jane. "He lives in the mill cottage. In fact he hasn't done much to the mill at all. It is simply wasting away, very much like George himself. Pop in and see it before you go home. It's only a few miles down the road. If you like it, I'll speak to George about it."

"Thank you," said Vicky, "I think I will take a look."

"Good," said Aunt Jane with satisfaction. "If you have any trouble with George just refer him to me"

Vicky smiled. "I will," she said. She rose and added, "Now I must be on my way. Thank you very much for your help."

"Don't mention it, my dear," said Aunt Jane and got to her feet. "I'll show you out. You know your father was such a nice man. I'll do all I can to help you. George and his father were such disappointments." She shook her head. "Such a pity."

She showed the girl out the front door. "Is that your car?" she asked, indicating the red Austin Mini.

"Yes," replied Vicky.

Aunt Jane gave the car a look of disdain. "Oh well, I suppose it's economical," she said.

Vicky appeared surprised at the comment. You don't like Minis?" she asked.

"Oh, I suppose they do suit some people," said Aunt Jane. "I myself prefer motorcycles."

"Motorcycles!" exclaimed Vicky and then added, "I did see someone arrive on a motorcycle through the window. Was that you?"

"It certainly was," said Aunt Jane. "They are such exciting machines, so exhilarating! I only ride British motorcycles of course. These Japanese and continental machines are much too inferior. I have two Triumph Bonnevilles, a Norton and an old BSA."

"Oh," said Vicky, 'but motorcycles are a little dangerous, aren't they?"

"No, not if you know how to handle them properly," said Aunt Jane, "and there aren't many things that I can't handle properly."

"Oh," said Vicky. She opened the door of her Mini and then paused. "I can probably afford something bigger now," she remarked thoughtfully. "Good-bye, Lady Gleefield. And thank you!" She got in the car, closed the door and drove off.

Vicky turned the car left out of the drive and followed the road down into the valley. It was a lovely day and there was hardly a cloud in the clear sky, which was now beginning to tinge with orange as the day was drawing to a close. She rounded a bend and then for the first time beheld the old water-mill with its smaller attendant cottage. Both were nestled snugly in the hillside. The sight was so picturesque that she stopped the car for a better view.

The mill was built largely of wood painted white, which was faded and peeled by the wind and rain. The roof was made of grey slate. Bright green ivy clambered all over it and flowed out on to the grassy knoll on which it was built and covered the adjacent stationary wheel as it leant out over the bank into the clear fast-flowing River Muckle. The cottage was of red brick, with the same grey slate roof, and was again covered with ivy. The front door and windows were painted a faded peeled yellow and the surrounding garden was a mass of spring flowers interspersed with small trees and shrubs. At the back of the house there was a large orchard of apple trees and, as it was spring, each tree was covered with white apple blossom.

Vicky sat and stared in wonder for several minutes. Then she started the car and drove up to the hedge that surrounded the garden. Two gates were set in the hedge. "The Old Mill Cottage" was carved at the top of the smaller of the two, which led to the cottage. The larger one was inscribed with the words "The Old Mill" and obviously led to the mill. She stopped the car in front of the larger gate and got out. She could see an angler standing on the bank below the great wheel, casting his rod across the sparkling water. It was George Cogrill.

She opened the gate and started up the path towards him. "Hello," she said.

"Hello," he replied reeling in his line.

"I got your cheque," she said.

He reached out to the end of the line and inspected the feathered fly, which served as bait, but did not reply.

"Have you caught anything?" she asked.

He shook his head. "Not yet. I've only just started. I've been into town job hunting," he added pointedly.

"It's very nice here," she said.

He turned to look at her. "Yes," he said.

"I've been to see your aunt. She said I ought to look round the mill."

"I'll show you around."

"I don't want to be any bother."

"Oh, it's no bother," he said. "The fish don't appear to be biting anyway." He laid down the rod. "Come on."

He led her through a door into a large rectangular room. It was very dusty. A number of wooden barrels and empty sacks were scattered about. In the centre of the room on a stone dais was a wood-framed structure. A wooden wheel was attached to the top and a wood trough stood in front of it.

"What's that?" asked Vicky

"A cider press," said George. "The millstones and workings were removed a long time ago so I use this place for storage and for making cider. Follow me."

He led her through a door, switched on a light and took her down a flight of stone steps into a large cellar. A number of racks of bottles filled the room. George selected a bottle from the rack and showed it to the girl. It was labelled 'Cogrill's Old Mill Cider'. "Would you like to try some?" he asked.

She hesitated for a moment and then said, "Yes please."

George uncorked the bottle, walked over to a stone sink, picked up a glass off the wooden draining board and poured out a small measure of amber liquid. He handed it to Vicky. She took a sip, then suddenly flushed as a warm glow spread over her. Her eyes sparkled and her legs quaked. "It's lovely," she breathed. "Do you sell it?"

"Oh no," said George, "it's too good to sell. You can take the bottle with you if you like but go careful with it. It's very strong."

"Thank you," she said and drained the rest of the glass, George took it from her and rinsed it out in the sink before returning it to the draining board. Then carrying the re-stoppered bottle she followed him back up the steps. He led her up a wooden staircase to the floor above. There were four large rooms, all but one of which were empty and they were all very dusty. The room that was in use contained a wooden bench and was full of fishing tackle. The bench contained a tray of feathered fishing flies together with more hooks and pieces of feather, the ingredients to make additional flies.

"Do you do a lot of fishing?" she asked.

"A fair amount," said George. "This water contains the best trout fishing for miles and they're very tasty."

"It certainly is a lovely place," said Vicky. "Downstairs would make a lovely studio and up here would make a lovely flat. The cellar would convert easily into a darkroom."

George frowned. "Is that what you plan to do?" he asked and then added, "I suppose the mill must be half yours anyway.

"Oh, don't worry," she said, "I'll leave plenty of room for your cider and fishing things. I won't need your cottage. Now I've got plenty of money I want to expand my photography business and this mill will make a lovely home." She stopped and noticed the glum look on his face. "Don't worry, I won't spoil it or interfere with your life. Look, if I'm going to expand I'll need an assistant. If you're looking for a job, why don't you come to work for me?"

He regarded her suspiciously. "I'm not sure," he said.

"Well, you can let me know later." She turned and made her way out of the room and back down the stairs. George followed. Back at her car, she put the bottle of cider on the rear seat and then turned to George who was standing by the gate. "Thank you very much for being so helpful," she said. I'll probably call back in a couple of days." She smiled at him. "Good-bye."

George stood and watched the Mini drive off into the setting sun. The girl had an amazing effect on him. He had accepted everything she said without argument. He wondered why. She was very pretty.

He sighed, turned and looked at the mill. It would not do to go against his aunt. He knew from old that she could make life very difficult for him. It was easier to let events take their course and see how things worked out. Whatever it was that lay ahead, he was resigned to the fact that his life and the mill would never be the same again.

At half past seven that same evening, George had packed away his fishing tackle and had finished an early supper. He washed up his dirty saucepans, plate and cup and, leaving them to dry on the draining board, he put on a sports jacket and made his way out into the cool evening air. Once outside his gate he turned left and set off at a brisk walk towards Mucklesbury. He arrived at the village fifteen minutes later, passed the church, the duck pond and the village green then entered the public bar of The Pullet Inn.

It was deserted except for the landlord, Jack Hump, who was leaning over the bar talking to Tom Firkin, Aunt Jane's gamekeeper at Gleefield Manor and someone George had known most of his life. They had been friends from boyhood.

"Well if it baint George Cogrill!" exclaimed Jack. "We don' often see you in 'ere."

"Good evening, Jack," said George. "Hello, Tom."

"'Ow do, George," said Tom.

George approached the bar. "Could I have a glass of cider please, Jack?" he asked.

"Pint or half?" asked Jack.

"A half pint please," George replied.

Jack picked up a glass and turned to a small barrel perched on the corner of the bar.

"I don't know why yer bothering with that stuff, George" said Tom, "t'aint nearly a patch on yer own zider."

"True enough," agreed Jack, "your Old Mill Zider is best I've tasted." He filled the glass and passed it across the bar to George. "That'll be eighty pence."

George gave him the money, took a sip of the cider and grimaced slightly. "Actually, Jack," he said quietly, "I was wondering if you would care to buy some of my cider."

There followed a stunned silence. Then Tom exclaimed, "What? You sell yer zider! George, what ever's up?"

Jack was also astounded. "'I've bin on at yer for years to sell me yer zider. What's 'appened?"

"I ... I need more space at the mill," stammered George, surprised at the reception of his statement.

"But the mill be more than big enough for yer," remarked Tom.

George took a deep breath. "You may as well know now," he said. "It'll be round the village quick enough. The mill doesn't wholly belong to me any more. Half of it now rightly belongs to someone else."

"Who be that?" asked Jack

"A young lady by the name of Victoria Gloam," said George. "Does that name mean anything to you?"

They both shook their heads.

"She's a photographer and wants to use the mill as a studio," he continued.

"Well, well," said Tom shaking his head, "a photographer at yer old mill. What she want to photograph?"

George's face reddened. "I don't know," he said. "She seems to take photographs of nude men."

Jack raised his eyebrows. "Photos of men wi'out clothes?" he asked incredulously.

George nodded, his face now bright red.

"She photograph you, George?" asked Tom.

"Of course not!" snapped George. He hastily changed the subject. "Now, Jack, do you or don't you want to buy my cider?"

"Course 'I do," said Jack. "'Ow much do yer want?"

George thought. "I'll charge you the same as you pay the brewery for your cider."

"All right by me," said Jack.

"I'll 'elp you to deliver it, George," offered Tom. "You can use me van if yer let me 'ave a couple of free flagons."

"Fine," said George, "thanks very much, Tom. Can you call round to the mill tomorrow morning?"

"Yer," replied Tom, "eleven o'clock suit yer?"

"Fine," said George. "Now I'm afraid I must be going." He put his glass down on the bar.

"You 'aven't finished yer zider," said Tom.

"I'm afraid you're right, it's not up to the same standard as mine. You can finish it if you like, Tom. Good-bye."

They watched the door close behind him. "Well, Jack," said Tom, "what do yer make of that?"

Jack scratched his head. "I don' know,' he said, "'E must be hard up fer cash. I 'eard tell that 'e's been looking' for a job."

"'E must be desperate if 'e's gona sell 'is zider."

"Aye, Tom. But that is lovely zider 'e makes. I ain't tasted nothin' like it."

"Aye, it certainly is," remarked Tom. "I only hope 'e can carry on making it."

Outside, George was making his way out of the village and up the hill towards his home. It was dark now but there was a full moon and its pale glow lighted his way. He walked slowly, deep, in thought.

He had sold his cider, which was something he had never dreamed of doing before. He was proud of his cider and shared it freely with friends and acquaintances in the village. 'Cogrill's Old Mill' cider was a commodity greatly sought after in Mucklesbury. Once a bottle came into a villager's hands it was treasured and only opened for special occasions such as Christmas, birthdays and weddings. He really believed, as he had told Vicky Gloam, that it really was too good to sell.

He walked on until he came to his home and opened the gate that led to the mill. Closing it carefully behind him, he walked slowly and measurably to the river bank. There he sat down on the log of a fallen tree. He looked up at the old building and its great wheel, both of which were bathed in moonlight, and wondered what else he might be forced to do.

CHAPTER 3

It was half past eleven on another sunny day a week later and George was weeding his front garden. A shiny brand new Rolls-Royce appeared and drew to a halt outside his gate. He looked up and saw a young dark-haired man get out of the driving seat. The man smiled and walk round to the near-side rear passenger door. It was Justin, the naked man he had seen in Vicky Gloam's studio. This time Justin was clad in a white, open-necked short-sleeved shirt and a pair of tight-fitting dark blue slacks. He opened the door and Vicky Gloam emerged. She was wearing a light green summer dress. A fair-haired stocky man in his early forties emerged from the rear door the other side. He was clad in bright red slacks and a loose-fitting multicoloured shirt. George, who had been bent over a flower bed, slowly straightened up and looked at them in silence.

Vicky was the first to speak. "Good morning, George," she said brightly, "lovely day, isn't it?"

George looked at her blankly. "Yes, it is," he replied slowly.

She continued. "I've brought some friends to look at the mill. I hope you don't mind. This is Justin and this is Sebastian." She indicated her two companions.

"Mr Cogrill and I have already met," said Justin.

"Yes, of course," said Vicky, "I was forgetting. Sebastian knows about interior design. He's going to give me some ideas about converting the mill."

George was downcast but he met her gaze and said quietly, "If you wait one moment I'll get the key". He disappeared through his open front door and emerged a few minutes later. "Follow me," he said and they followed him to the mill where he unlocked the main door and led them inside

"Gosh, Vicky!" exclaimed Justin looking around him, "this is stupendous!"

Sebastian strode to the centre of the room then he turned and spread out his hands.

"Vicky precious," he said, "this definitely has potential!"

George stared at him with a feeling of horror. He tried desperately not to show any signs of emotion. Then he took a deep breath and said, "I'll leave you to look round on your own. Don't worry about the door, I'll lock up later." He turned to go.

"Thank you for your help, George," said Vicky.

"That's all right," murmured George and made his way out through the door.

Once outside he walked briskly back to his cottage and stood in his garden looking helplessly around at his plants. He picked up his fork and began once more to busy himself with his weeding. He had been working for almost an hour when he heard Vicky's voice. "Hello!" she called softly. He straightened up. She was standing once more at his garden gate but she was alone.

"May I come in?" she asked.

"Please do," he said.

She opened the gate and drew closer to him. "You have a lovely garden," she remarked.

"Some say it's a little wild and untidy."

"I think it's enchanting," she said and smiled. "A little wildness adds character."

"Your friends seem to like the mill," said George.

"Yes, they're still looking around. Sebastian is making some notes. I see you've moved some of your cider."

"That's right," said George, "you should have plenty of room for your stuff."

"The cellar is almost bare. I won't be needing all that space for my dark room. I'm sure we will be able to divide it up between us so you won't have to give up all your things. Have you thought any more about the job I offered you?"

"Yes," said George, "I'm afraid I don't know much about photography."

"Oh, I won't require you to do anything too technical," she said, "just help with setting up the equipment and keeping things clean and tidy."

"Well ... I do need a job ..."

"That's settled then. You can start as soon as I move in. We'll shake hands on it." She stretched out her hand

George held out his hand and then noticed it was encrusted with soil but before he could say anything Vicky shook it firmly. "Oh," she said and with a nervous laugh dusted her hands together. "Never mind, a little dirt never did any harm. We plan to stop off for lunch at a local pub. Is there one nearby?"

"There's The Pullet Inn in Mucklesbury," said George.

"Good. Would you care to join us?"

George did not relish spending lunch with Justin and Sebastian. "I'm afraid I can't," he said. "I've got such a lot to do here."

"Oh well, another time. I'll leave you to your gardening. Good-bye, I'll see you again soon."

"Good-bye," said George and watched her leave. She seemed to glide out the gate, her hips swaying gently as she headed back towards the mill.

Five minutes later the three of them emerged. He looked up from his weeding and watched them climb back into their respective places in the Rolls. Vicky waved to him from the back window and the car set off down the hill. George slowly stood up, raised a hand in acknowledgement and stood watching until the car was out of sight. Then he bent once more to continue his work.

The Rolls-Royce wound its way into the village and turned into the car park at the back of The Pullet Inn. "It looks a pretty rum place, Vicky," said Justin as he opened the door for her, "are you sure you want to stop?"

"Yes, I do," said Vicky. "After all, this will be my local."

Sebastian got out the other door and studied the grey building with its dark slate roof. "It's er ... quite charming, Vicky darling," he said, "but it could do with a spot of paint."

Justin tried the door to the lounge. It was locked. The door of the lounge bar was usually locked at The Pullet Inn as hardly anyone ever used it. Sebastian gently nudged open the door to the public bar. "This looks like the way, Justy," he said and they followed him into the room.

Inside, Tom Firkin was leaning against the bar talking to old Joe Thropp, an elderly farm worker, who was perched on a stool. A gnarled walking stick was propped nearby. Jack Hump was behind the bar polishing furiously at a wine glass in his hand but paying more attention to the conversation in front of him. The room was otherwise deserted. Justin let the door swing shut behind him and the conversation stopped.

"Good afternoon," said Vicky. They approached the bar.

" 'Ow do," said Jack. His voice sounded suspicious as though did not trust strangers.

"Are you serving luncheon?" asked Sebastian.

"What's that?" asked Jack.

"You know - food," explained Justin.

"This be a pub not an 'otel or a restaurant."

"Oh dear," said Vicky.

Jack appeared to soften at the look of disappointment that showed on her face. "Well, 'I might 'ave some bread 'n cheese out back if yer like."

"Only bread and cheese ...!" began Justin.

Vicky nudged him. She smiled at Jack. "Bread and cheese will be just fine" she said softly.

"Jolly good show," said Sebastian. "Three Ploughman's Lunches then."

"Ploughman's what?" asked Jack.

"Ploughman' s Lunches. Many public houses serve bread and cheese with a spot of pickle and call it a ploughman's lunch," explained Sebastian.

"What do you call it here?" asked Justin.

"Bread 'n cheese," replied Jack. "I dunno if I got any pickle."

Old Joe Thropp shook his grizzled grey head and remarked, "I were a Ploughman fer over fifty yer an' I never 'ad lunch - but I did 'ave dinner!"

'Could we have something to drink while are waiting?" asked Vicky "What would you like, Justin?"

"I'll have a coke," said Justin, "as I'm driving."

"Sebastian?"

"If you don't mind. I'll have a Campari and soda," said Sebastian.

"Coke ... camp what? Look this be a pub," said Jack exasperated. "I 'ave beer, zider 'n spirits."

"Do you have a medium dry white wine?" asked Sebastian.

"I 'ave white wine," said Jack.

"And a lemonade?" asked Justin.

"Yer, I've lemonade."

"Good," said Vicky, "that's settled then. A white wine and a lemonade. And I would like some cider."

Jack's eyes seemed to light up with approval. "Now yer in luck," he said. "I 'ave just acquired some o' the best zider fer miles." He picked up a glass, turned to a barrel behind him, dispensed some liquid into it and then placed the glass full of bright golden cider on the bar in front of her. "That be Cogrill's Old Mill zider!" he announced.

"Is that George Cogrill's cider?" asked Vicky.

Jack looked impressed. " 'Tis."

"But he told me it was too good to sell."

Tom Firkin turned towards her. 'Times 'ave changed up the Ol' Mill," he said. "Be you by any chance the lady photographer that now owns 'alf of it?"
'That's right."
'Well I be Tom Firkin. Behind bar be Jack Hump and on stool be old Joe Thropp. If yer need someone ter photograph then yer need look no further than Tom Firkin."

CHAPTER 4

Some weeks later George Cogrill was sitting behind the steering wheel of Vicky's Rolls in the car park outside Tidburn railway station. He disliked driving and would never have taken it up if he had not been cajoled into it by his father and Aunt Jane. However, he had not let them persuade him into owning a motor vehicle and preferred to travel by foot or public transport. But now driving was part of his duties as assistant to Victoria Gloam.

A train slowly drew into the station. George looked at his watch. The train was the ten-fifteen from London and it was on time. He got out of the car and made his way to the entrance where he bought a platform ticket from one of the machines and passed through the ticket barrier.

An attractive girl in her early twenties was standing on the platform, holding a small suitcase and looking about her. She was tall, thin with long red hair and was wearing a smart blue rain coat. A white shoulder bag hung from her left shoulder and her right hand held a pair of matching gloves. George approached her. "Miss Miranda Flit?" he asked.

"That's right, Ducks," came the reply.

"Miss Gloam sent me," he continued. "If you will allow me to take your case, I have a car waiting to take you to the studio."

"That's nice, ta." She handed him the case and followed him out of the station. He led her to the car and opened the back door for her. "Corr," she remarked, "a Rolls. Business must be good." She got in and settled herself on the back seat.

George put the case in the boot and got in behind the steering wheel. He had barely eased the car out into the stream of traffic when Miranda Flit began to speak.

"Oh, I do like the country," she said. "I'm a town girl really. Born an' bred in the big city. But I likes the country. Every thing's so ... green. I do like the country. Do you like the country?"

"Yes I do."

"What's your name?"

"George."

"George," she said thoughtfully. "I know lots of Georges. It's ... a nice name George. My names not Miranda. Not really." She leaned forward and almost whispered. "It's...You won't tell anyone, will you?"

George shook his head.

"It's Mable. 'Orrible, isn't it? Oo ever 'eard of a model called Mable. So I 'ad to change it - just 'ad to. Miranda, now that really is a posh name, - Miranda Flit. Better than Mable Flit, isn't it? I thought so anyway, so did my agent. You won't tell anyone, will you?"

George shook his head once more.

"Thanks ever so. I trust you, but you can't be too careful. I don't want people to think that I've got a common name like Mable." She settled back in her seat. "Oh, I do like the country. Every thing's so green."

The drive took approximately twenty minutes. During that time Miranda Flit talked almost non-stop. George mentally switched off and just nodded his head in response to anything she said that remotely resembled a question. When they arrived at their destination, George opened the gate to the mill and then drove up and parked in front of the great door. Then he led the girl inside.

There they found Vicky amongst lights, back-drops, cameras and reflectors. All were set up where once his cider press had been. The walls had been freshly painted a neutral pale blue and the ceiling a dull white.

George announced the visitor. "This is Mable," he said.

Vicky looked up from adjusting a camera on a tripod. "Oh," she said, "I thought we were expecting Miranda Flit."

George flinched. "Sorry!" he said, "I meant Miranda. Mable is ... Mable is the name of my Aunt's ... cat. My Aunt's cat - it was a slip of the tongue, sorry."

"I'm Vicky Gloam," said Vicky. "George, could you show her to the changing room? You'll find the clothes on the rack, Miranda. Could you try the red one on first?"

"Right-oh," said Miranda.

George led her upstairs. "I'm, er, sorry about that," he said.

Miranda sighed. "Men! My mum always said you can't trust 'em. Serves me right I 'spose." She winked at him.

He led her to one of the rooms that had now been freshly decorated and equipped with a clothes rack and dressing table, on which a box of make-up was set out.

"This is nice," said Miranda.

'I'm glad you like it," George replied sullenly. "Just call if you want anything." He left her there and returned downstairs.

"Everything, all right?" asked Vicky. She was fiddling with one of the lights.

"She likes the room," said George

"Good. Sebastian has done a good job in such a short time, don't you think?"

"He's certainly been quick," said George. "I'll be outside if you need me."

Once outside he sat down on the fallen log and gazed thoughtfully up at the mill. Sebastian had been quick but at least he had not touched the outside of the building. George was pleased that he had persuaded Vicky to leave that to him. He told her she could have a free hand with the interior as long as the outside remained his responsibility and it worked. He had, of course, no plans to do anything to the outside despite hints and then grumblings from Sebastian. He liked it the way it was. They had decided to share the main room and had moved the cider press to one side. Most of the room was hers to use as a photography studio. The cellar had been partitioned into two. One half took Vicky's darkroom but George still had use of the other half to store what remained of his cider, most of which had been sold to The Pullet Inn. His room with his fishing tackle was still there unchanged. Although Vicky had use of the majority of the mill, he considered that he had not done too badly out of their arrangement. He reflected that it could have been a lot worse. Vicky had been very nice and reasonable. George had not liked the changed decor but he could see she was pleased with it. He hoped he had not sounded too rude just now – after all, things had not turned out as bad as he had feared they would. He was even enjoying his job.

He eased himself down on to the grass next to the log, placed his jacket against the rough bark and leant his head against it. Perhaps life would not be so bad after all. In a little while he was fast asleep.

The day passed pleasantly. He awoke just before twelve o'clock, sauntered back to his cottage and prepared a light salad lunch for three in the kitchen. The two girls joined him at one o'clock and he served the lunch in his small dining-room. Both women only required a small amount to eat as Miranda kept to a strict diet and Vicky never ate much during the day, and when they returned to the mill at two, he was left with very little washing up.

At five o'clock he drove Miranda back to the station, where she caught the return train to London. He returned to the mill at half past five, picked up Vicky and drove her back to her flat in Tidburn.

"It went very well," Vicky told him from the back of the Rolls. "I should have enough pictures to complete my portfolio. You may be pleased to know there will be no more models visiting the mill, George. Well, not for a while anyway. "

"I didn't mind," said George.

"I'm afraid I've left the mill a bit untidy."

"Don't worry, I'll soon sort it out," said George.

He returned to the mill at half past six and parked the Rolls in one of the out-buildings they had converted as a garage. It took him an hour to clear up. Then he locked the door at quarter to eight and made his way back to the cottage. He paused at the gate and looked back at the old building. It looked beautiful in the evening light. He sighed. He was really quite fortunate. Miranda had been one of a procession of glamorous young women photographed by Vicky recently, but it was the mill that always stole his gaze. He never tired of looking at it.

An idea came into his mind. He hurried back, unlocked the door and went inside.

CHAPTER 5

It had been a bad week for Vicky Gloam. She had been traipsing round the London offices of all the top women's magazines. None had been interested in her portfolio. Consequently, no one was interested in commissioning her for any fashion work. In desperation she had turned to Oswald Goodsake, an old contact of her father's, who ran a picture agency from a small two-room office above a Chinese fish and chip shop in Soho.

She had given him the portfolio the day before, specifying that she was no longer interested in taking nude photographs for 'art' magazines and that she wanted to break into fashion photography as that was where the money was. He had not seemed enthusiastic but said he would look at her photographs and would give her his verdict the next day. Now she was sitting across from his desk while he sat facing her with her portfolio lying closed in front of him.

He was a thin man with a hawk-like face. She knew him to be in his late fifties and guessed that his jet black hair was either false or dyed. He wore a dark pin-striped suit and was holding a closed pair of thick black-framed spectacles, resting them with both hands on the portfolio.

He looked at her seriously and she was nervous. He had been the only person who had taken time to talk to her personally. Most had returned the portfolio through a secretary without comment.

Oswald Goodsake cleared his throat. "I'm afraid your fashion photographs aren't very good," he said.

"Oh."

"I'm sorry," he said, "you obviously spent a lot of time and money on them. Those are top models you've used. I recognise some of them."

'Thank you for looking at the photographs for me, Uncle Oswald," said Vicky, downhearted. "Can I ask what's wrong with them?"

'Technically," he replied, "they are quite good. They're in focus and have good contrast. Unfortunately, they appear rather bland."

"Bland?"

"Yes, they lack life, sparkle. Fashion magazines require pictures that grab the attention. I'm afraid these photos look very ordinary. The models appear in stereotyped poses. I'm afraid nobody is going to commission you to take photographs like these."

"I see."

He smiled. "Don't look too downcast," he said. "In fact, there was one photograph I rather liked."

"There was?"

"Yes." He put on the spectacles, opened the portfolio at the last page and picked up a black and white print. "I found this tucked in the cover. It looks out of place in this portfolio and I wasn't sure whether or not it had slipped in by mistake. But I'm sure I could sell this pic for you."

"Let me see."

He handed it to her. It was a photograph of the mill.

"You've caught the light beautifully. I can see it was taken either early morning or late evening but the composition and the effect of the light are striking. It's a beautiful building and the photograph shows it. Where is it?'

Vicky stared at it, puzzled. "It's an old watermill I use as my studio. It's in Mucklesbury."

"Charming. Look, there is a market for that sort of picture. I could make enquiries for you. But my main advice is, go back to your studio. Try to capture the lighting and composition in your fashion photography that you used for that pic. If you manage it I'm sure you'll be on to a winner."

Vicky continued to stare at the photograph. "Yes," she murmured.

He closed the portfolio and pushed it towards her. "In the meantime I could try and sell that photo for you, if you like.'

Vicky stood up. "I'll think about it,' she said. 'Thank you very much, Uncle Oswald. You have been very helpful.'

She picked up the portfolio and, clutching it and the photograph, hurried out of the building. The tears that filled her eyes were not due to Uncle Oswald's criticism of her fashion photographs or due to the smells emanating from the Chinese fish and chip shop. They were because she had not taken that photograph of the mill.

Two weeks later George was once again driving Miranda Flit to the mill in the Rolls. He showed her into the building where Vicky was again arranging the lighting and cameras. She looked up when they came in.

"Hello, George, Miranda!" she said. "Miranda, you know where the changing room is. I wonder if you could try on the red dress again. I want to repeat our last session but I'll change things around slightly."

"Right you are," replied Miranda and trotted upstairs.

"I'll leave you to it," said George and turned to go.

"Could you stay, George?" asked Vicky. "I might need you to help move the lighting around."

George was puzzled. "You've never needed me for that before," he said.

"I'm trying different lighting set-ups. It would save time if you helped me. You can begin by loading some film into the Hassleblad." She indicated the camera on the tripod in front of him. "The film is in there." She pointed to a metal case on the floor next to the tripod.

George opened the case, found the film and began to feed it into the camera. Vicky watched him. "You're quite an expert," she remarked.

"I've watched you do it," he replied.

"Did you by any chance use the camera to take a photograph of the mill the other week?" she asked in a matter-of-fact voice.

He stopped what he was doing and looked at her. "I saw that there was still one exposure left on the film," he said. "It seemed a shame to waste it. I hope I didn't do anything wrong."

"Oh, no! It's just that it got mixed up with my portfolio, that's all."

"Oh dear!" George exclaimed "I hope it didn't spoil it. Is that why we are repeating these photographs?"

Vicky stared at him in surprise. She was speechless for a few seconds and, then seeing him looking at her with a beseeching expression, hurriedly said, "That's partly the reason."

"I'm extremely sorry, Vicky."

"That's all right. There's no need to worry," she said.

"I'll do all I can to help put it right."

"It's all right, really. I just need your help to move the lights."

George bent once more to the camera and finished loading the film.

A few minutes later Miranda reappeared wearing the red dress. "Where do ya wan' me?" she asked cheerily.

"Can you just assume one of the poses you did last time?" replied Vicky. "George, can you move the lights?"

"Where to?" asked George.

"Oh, just move them to where you like for the moment. I'm going to take a few Polaroids to start with." She changed the camera back to one with Polaroid film

"How's that?" asked George.

She looked up and studied how the modelling lights played the girl's body. "Fine," she said and pressed the shutter release. Two flash bulbs exploded from out of the modelling lights and the resulting light bounced back on to Miranda by way of the attached umbrella reflectors.

Vicky waited the prescribed two minutes before taking out the film and peeling off the protective backing. She could see straight away that even this Polaroid appeared better than the photographs she had taken. "What made you put the lights there?" she asked George.

He shrugged. "Seemed the most obvious place," he replied.

Vicky walked up to the lights and studied them. "Could you check the camera focusing for me while I check these lights?" she asked.

"OK." George walked over to the camera and looked into the viewfinder. "It seems OK to me," he said.

"Can you think of any improvements?' asked Vicky still studying the lighting.

"Well you could try a different angle, particularly if it is the dress you are trying to emphasise."

"Could you do that for me, George?" she asked and before waiting for a reply she said, "Miranda, could you try out different poses while George changes the camera angles?" She walked back to the tripod and changed the Polaroid camera back with the one containing film. Then she attached the remote control cable and returned to her previous position by the light. "Off you go, George," she said. "I'll operate the shutter release from here."

The remainder of the session passed in the same fashion with occasional breaks while the film was changed or Miranda changed into a different dress. They stopped for lunch again at twelve, which George prepared while the girls chatted in the dining room. The afternoon followed the same pattern again and this pattern was repeated with different models over the next few days, during which time Vicky produced enough material for a new portfolio.

CHAPTER 6

A week later at eight o'clock on a Saturday evening George walked into the public bar of The Pullet Inn. As usual Tom Firkin was leaning against the bar next to Old Joe Thropp who was again perched on his favourite stool.
    Tom's voice boomed out in greeting. " 'Ow do, George!" he said. "See yer got your best suit on."
    "Hello, Tom, Joe," said George. "How are things?"
    "Fair ter middling'," replied Joe
    "Going' somewhere special?" asked Tom
    "I may be," George replied and noticing Jack Hump was missing from his usual place behind the bar inquired, "where's Jack?"
    "'E be out back," Tom replied and then bellowed, "Jack, customer!"
    A few moments later Jack appeared. " 'Ello, George, " he said amiably. "You be looking' smart. What can I get yer?"
    "I'll have a pint of my cider please, Jack," replied George.
    Jack picked up a glass and walked over to a barrel. "Seems strange selling yer your own zider," he remarked. "'Ave this one on the 'ouse."
    "No, Jack. I sold that cider to you for a good price. I insist on paying. And have a drink on me while you're at it." He looked at his two companions. "I dare say Tom and Joe could do with another too."
    Tom drained his glass. "Aye, thanks, George," he said handing it to Jack.
    "Ta, George,' said Joe and followed suit.
    "Zider all round is it?" asked Jack.
    "Arr," muttered Joe, "tis a good drop o' cider of yorn, George."

"Thank you, Joe," George replied and passed Jack a five pound note.

Jack poured a glass of cider for George and then refilled Tom and Joe's glasses. "You going ter tell us why you be so smart, George?" he asked as he passed them their drinks.

"I've been invited to a party," George replied.

"Where's this then?" asked Joe.

"At the mill."

"What at your old mill!" exclaimed Tom. "Why weren't we invited?"

"It's not my party," George replied. "To tell you the truth I'm not sure I'm going. It's not really my thing."

"Why be that then?" asked Jack as he handed George his change.

George pocketed the money without checking it and then replied. "It's all friends of Vicky Gloam's. Most of them are from London."

"You've had some right good dos at the mill yerself, George, when it's zider making' time," Tom remarked.

"Yes," agreed George, "I've had some good parties there with friends from the village. But this party will be much more refined. They won't be drinking my cider."

"What will they be drinking then?" Jack asked.

"Judging by the crates I saw arriving, it looks like champagne."

"Champagne? That be expensive," remarked Tom. "What be they celebrating?"

"Vicky has just received her first large photography commission. I think it's worth a lot of money."

"I ain't never drunk no champagne," muttered Joe

"You 'aven't missed much," said Jack. "Expensive fizzy stuff. Tain't a patch on George's zider."

"Still, I've 'eard a lot about it," Joe continued. "I'd 'ave quite liked ter 'ave tried some before I pops me clogs. Any chance of yer smuggling me out some, George?"

"As I said, I'm not sure I'm going," replied George. "I put on my suit to go and then thought better of it. It's too near my cottage for me to stay at home, so I thought I'd come down here."

Tom slapped him on the back. "That's right," he said. "Stay here with yer mates." He drained his glass. "I'd buy yer a drink myself only I be a little low on funds."

"Never mind," said George. "I know how it is. I'm a wage earner myself now." He paused to finish his drink and then added. "I've been given a bonus this week. We'll have another round of drinks on me, Jack!"

Some hours later, back at the mill, the party was in full swing and Vicky was talking to Uncle Oswald. She was wearing a long, low-cut tight-fitting silver dress which left her shoulders bare and glistening. Uncle Oswald was in a dark evening dress suit. Both were holding glasses of champagne. They were in the main downstairs room. The photography equipment had been cleared away and in its place were the twin turntables and flashing lights of a discotheque which was pounding out the sounds of heavy electro music.

"I must admit I was very impressed with your revised portfolio, my dear," Uncle Oswald was saying. "You certainly seemed to have put my advice to good use and employed the techniques you used in that photograph of the mill. Your father would have been very proud."

"Thank you, Uncle Oswald," Vicky replied.

Uncle Oswald looked around him. "I must say you have a wonderful set-up here," he said. "It is certainly very picturesque. Tell me, have you considered the possibility of opening up an art centre? People would be prepared to come and pay to paint and sculpted etcetera. In such a setting it can be quite lucrative."

"I'll bear it mind," said Vicky,

They were interrupted by Aunt Jane swathed in white feathers. "Hello, Victoria," she said. "I am afraid I'm a little late. Is that nephew of mine around anywhere?"

"I'm afraid he hasn't arrived," Vicky replied. "Have you met my Uncle, Oswald Goodsake, Lady Gleefield?"

"I don't believe I have," Aunt Jane replied, looking Uncle Oswald up and down. "How do you do, Mr Goodsake."

Uncle Oswald's eyes lit up from behind the dark frames of his spectacles. He took her hand. "I'm enchanted, Lady Gleefield, "he said, emphasising the word "lady". "I see you do not yet have a drink. Allow me to find you one." He smiled and led her away.

Justin approached. He was wearing a sky blue jacket with gold sequins and pink bow tie. "I say, Vicky," he whispered hurriedly, "I'm afraid the bubbly is running out."

"It can't be," replied Vicky. "I ordered twenty cases."

"Well you know Sebastian and his friends, they've got through twelve cases between them and your Uncle Oswald has certainly been putting it away. Is there any chance you can open some of that cider you've got in the cellar?"

"It's not mine. It belongs to George."

"I'm sure he won't mind. He works for you anyway. You can always pay him for it later."

"I'm not sure."

"Go on. The party is a great success. A lot of the top fashion people are here. You can't let it fizzle out now. I'm sure I've picked up one or two more commissions for you. Where is George anyway?"

"I don't know. I don't think he's arrived."

"Well, it's bad manners of him not turning up."

Vicky thought for a moment. "All right," she said, "just open one or two bottles."

"Right," said Justin and disappeared.

Miranda approached leading a portly middle-aged American.

"Hi-ya, Vicky!" she called. "This is Hiram, 'e's very big in films."

Vicky held out her hand. "How do you do, Hiram," she said.

Hiram gripped her hand firmly and replied, "Howdy, Mam." He was wearing a dark dinner suit with a broad mauve cummerbund, which encircled his ample waist. The brown hair on top of his head did not quite match that at its sides and looked slightly skewed. "Sure is a nice purdy little ol' place you got here."

"Thank you," Vicky replied,

"Hiram, says 'e can get me into 'Ollywood," Miranda continued.

"Really," said Vicky unconvinced.

Hiram smiled awkwardly. "I have financed the odd production," he said slyly.

"I see," said Vicky.

He grinned and took Miranda's arm. "Come on, sweetheart," he said. "Let's hit the dance floor one more time."

"Sure, Hiram. Bye, Vicky!" They melted away towards the discotheque.

Vicky drained her glass and looked about her. Almost immediately Sebastian was at her side, a bottle and glass in either hand. "Hello, dear heart," he said. "Allow me to fill your glass with this splendid elixir which Justin has just purloined from your cellar."

Vicky held out her glass. "Just a little please, Sebastian," she said.

At that moment the door opened and George stumbled in. He was followed by Old Joe Thropp and Tom Firkin. Jack Hump would have come too but had to stay behind to close up the Pullet Inn. All three were the worse for drink.

George saw Vicky and staggered over to her. "Hello there," he said heartily and in a very slurred voice. "I'm so sorry I'm late. I've ... I've broughth some frienths, I hopes you don' mind."

"No, not at all," said Vicky hurriedly.

George continued, "You thee," he said, "Ol' Joe here hath never had champagne before and Tom says he hathn't had any for a long time so they've both come to try thome."

"That don' look like no champagne, George," Tom remarked pointing at the bottle Sebastian was holding. "That looks like a bo'le of yer zider!"

Sebastian cleared his throat. "I'll just see if anyone else needs a refill," he said and disappeared.

George looked at Vicky. "You're drinking my thider," he said

Vicky flushed with embarrassment. "That's right," she said, "we ran out of champagne. I hope you don't mind."

"I perfers yer zider anyways," announced Tom. "Come on, Joe, let's be getting some," and they both made their way in the direction taken by Sebastian.

"You don't mind about the cider, do you?" asked Vicky once again. "I'll pay you for it of course."

George shook his head. "'Spose not," he murmured. "Don' worry abou' my thider, you've got mothe of my stuff anyway. So why not my thider?" With that he turned and lurched his way back to the main door and out into the dark night.

Vicky stared after him. A pang of guilt went through her. Then after a few moments, she followed him outside.

It was a very dark night. Vicky made her way gingerly along the path towards George's cottage. Suddenly she heard a loud splash. She turned in the direction of the River Muckle. A sudden wild thought went through her mind. She had taken away half George's possessions and now his cider. Had it finally been too much for him? Had he, under the influence of drink, decided to end it all and commit suicide? She ran towards the river. She looked up and down the bank and then saw the pile of clothes. She hurried over to them and looked out across the dark water. She could see a floating shape. She made out the shape of a head.

    She called out. "George! Are you all right?"

    There was no answer.

    "George!" she shouted. "Don't worry, I'm coming!"

She kicked off her shoes, slipped out of her dress, leapt into the water and struck out in the direction of the object. As she drew near she could see it was the body of a man. He was floating, half submerged, face up, eyes closed. It was George. She knew what to do. She had done life saving in the Girl Guides and had obtained her badge. She slipped her arms under his and grabbed him around the shoulders.

    "It all right, George!" she shouted, "I've got you!"

    "What the hell!" exclaimed George and tried to shrug her off.

    "Please don't struggle!" she cried, "there's no need to end it all."

    "What are you doing?" he protested.

    "I'm sure we can work something out."

    "What are you talking about?"

    "Please don't drown yourself!" pleaded Vicky.

    "I'm not drowning myself!"

    "I'll make sure you get credit for the photographs!"

    "I'm not drowning myself!" repeated George louder. "What on earth are you talking about?"

    "Then what are you doing in the river?"

    "I felt like a swim!"

    She let go of him. "You what!"

    "I felt like a swim. I've had a lot to drink. A good dip in the Muckle after a session on the cider sobers me up and prevents one hell of a hangover. I often do it!"

She stared at him. "You often do it?"

"Yes." He stood up. "Look the water here is only four feet deep. I'd hardly try to drown myself in here!"

She stood up still staring at him. "But it's freezing!"

"That's why it sobers you up!"

It was then that she remembered her evening dress was the kind with which she could not fashionably wear a bra and that she was clad only in her panties. Her hands went to cover her breasts. "Oh my God!" she gasped.

She turned and waded hurriedly for the shore. George followed her. She scrambled up the bank, found the dress and pulled it over her wet body. She turned and looked at George who was still in the water.

"Look I know you can't see much in the dark," he said, "and that you are used to naked men. But do you mind awfully turning round while I get out?"

She spun round hastily. George scrambled out and began drying himself on his shirt. He could see she was shivering. "I ... um ... er ... normally jog back to the cottage," he said. "I think it might be a good idea if you followed me back and get warm and dry." He slipped on his underpants, gathered up the rest of his clothes and set off at a brisk pace.

She stared at his departing shadow. Water dripped off her wet hair. She could not go back to the party in her current state. She felt a complete mess. Slowly and sullenly, she followed in his wake.

The door was open when she got to the cottage and the hallway was lighted. George appeared wearing a pair of jeans and a thick woollen pullover. He was carrying a towel. "The bathroom's upstairs," he said. "I suggest you have a hot bath to warm you up. I've put the immersion heater on so the water will be nice and hot."

She took the towel and without a word made her way upstairs. The bathroom light was on and hot water was already running in the bath. Thirty minutes later she emerged wearing a dressing gown she found behind the door. She found George in the sitting room. He had prepared a fire in the hearth and it had just taken light. He turned as she entered.

"Would you like a hot drink?"

She did not reply.

"Will cocoa be OK?"

Again she did not reply.

"Well, I'm having some anyway." He left her alone. She sat down in an armchair and stared at the fire. She was still staring at the fire when he returned with two steaming mugs of cocoa. He handed her one which she took without uttering a sound. He sat down in an armchair opposite her. The fire crackled on the hearth. They both sipped their cocoa.

"What did you mean about me getting credit for the photographs?"

She looked at him for some moments and then said, "I think I've been beastly to you. That's why I thought you were drowning yourself."

"I wasn't drowning myself."

"I know that now! But it was a shock." She took a deep breath. "I'm not really good at subterfuge," she confessed. "It was really you who took the photographs."

"What do you mean? I saw you take them."

"Oh, I pressed the shutter. But you arranged the lighting, posed the models. You even decided what dresses suited them best. They're your photographs. Without them there wouldn't have been any commissions. The ones I had taken before on my own were no good. No one wanted to buy them. It's all down to you. I'm a fraud and I've been cheating you." Tears filled her eyes and she began to cry.

George took a handkerchief from his pocket and passed it to her. She wiped her eyes and then blew her nose loudly. "I don't think you're right," he said gently. "You were there as well. We did it together."

She shook her head. "No, you did it on your own. That photo you took of the mill. It was the only one Uncle Oswald liked. He thought I took it. It was in the portfolio by mistake. He suggested I used the same techniques in my model photos. I tried but it was useless. You deserve the credit and the commissions." She broke off and began crying again.

George stood and took the cocoa from her in case she was going to spill it. He put her mug on the mantelpiece and then left the room taking his mug with him. He opened the front door and went outside. He could still hear the sounds of the party coming from the mill. The party was now sounding much louder and much more raucous. The cider was taking effect.

George stood there in the garden drinking his cocoa and listening to the sounds as they drifted over from the mill. He finished his drink and returned inside. Vicky was asleep in the armchair. Her feet curled up under her. He went upstairs and fetched some blankets from a cupboard and returned to cover her with them. She barely stirred. He sat in the armchair opposite her and stared into the fire until it died down. Then he placed the guard in position and went upstairs to bed.

The next morning, Vicky woke to the sound of a kettle whistling on the stove in the kitchen. She sat up with a start, then went into the kitchen where George was busy making coffee. "Good morning," he said. "Would you like some breakfast?"

She shook her head and sat down at the kitchen table. "Just some coffee, please."

"How are you feeling?" George asked.

"A bit stiff, otherwise I'm fine."

George smiled. "Nothing like a dip in the Muckle to prevent a hangover," he said.

"I'd rather forget about that. You won't mention last night to anyone, will you?"

"Of course not. Do you take milk in your coffee?"

"Yes, please. But no sugar."

He handed her a cup. "Are you sure you don't want anything to eat? I'm going to have some bacon and eggs. Would you like some?"

"No, thank you."

"What about some toast?"

"I really don't want anything to eat, thank you." She stood up. "I think I must be going."

"But you haven't touched your coffee."

"I'm sorry but I really must go. I'll let you have your dressing gown back later when I call back for my clothes."

"There's no hurry, really."

"I'll see myself out," she said. "Good-bye."

"Good-bye," said George.

She let herself out the front door and stepped briskly across the grass to the mill. She opened the door and was confronted by the debris of the party. Empty bottles, glasses, cigarette ends were strewn everywhere. The fetid air stank of stale cigarette smoke and alcohol. She ignored the mess and made her way upstairs to the area she had converted to her flat. There she closed the door, locked it and sat down on the bed.

CHAPTER 7

A month passed. Uncle Oswald parked his Mercedes outside the mill. He got out of the car, walked up to the door and rang the bell. There was no answer. He rang the bell again and then again. Eventually the door was opened by Vicky Gloam. She was wearing a plain ankle-length black dress. Her hair was dishevelled and she wore no make up. "Oh, it's you, Uncle Oswald," she said.

"Vicky, I've been phoning you for days and have got no answer. Whatever's up?"

She shrugged her shoulders. "You'd better come in," she said.

She led him through the main room past the photographic lights and studio backdrops. Uncle Oswald could see the room was now neat and tidy. But it was obvious the equipment had not been used for some time. She led him upstairs to her flat.

"Can I get you anything to drink?" she asked.

"No, thank you." He sat down on the settee. "Vicky," he said, "the completion date for your first commission has passed. The magazine is asking where the pictures are. What's been happening?"

She sat down in the armchair opposite him but said nothing.

"Look, I've risked my reputation in recommending you to these editors. I think you owe me an explanation."

"I'm sorry, Uncle Oswald. But I don't think I can do it any more."

"What are you talking about? Why?"

"I can't explain. It's just that I can't take good pictures."

"What do you mean? Can't take good pictures. The ones for your last portfolio were excellent. Everyone's said so."

She stood up, walked to the window and stood with her back towards him while she looked out over the River Muckle. "I'm sorry. I just can't explain."

Uncle Oswald stood up. "Well," he said, "I suppose there's nothing more to be said. I must say I'm very disappointed with you, my dear - very disappointed indeed. Your father would have been too." He turned and without another word made his own way downstairs and out the front door.

He returned to his car and was about to get in when he noticed George, who had just come from the orchard behind the cottage and was now wheeling a large wooden wheelbarrow full of apples. Uncle Oswald called out to him. "Hello there!"

"Hello," replied George and continued wheeling the barrow towards the gate. Uncle Oswald opened it for him. "Thank you," said George.

"You must be George," said Uncle Oswald. "I've heard a lot about you." He held out his hand. "I'm Oswald Goodsake, Victoria's Uncle."

George set the barrow down and wiped his palm on his stained grey flannel trousers before taking Uncle Oswald's hand. "Pleased to me you," he said.

"Are those apples you've got there?"

George looked down at them. They were quite obviously apples. But he replied politely. "They're cider apples. The last of this year's crop."

"Are they the ones that you make your wonderful cider out of? Dammed fine stuff. I had some at Victoria's party. Strong stuff but wonderful. It had a good kick to it."

"People seem to like it," said George. "But it has to be drunk carefully, particularly if you're not use to it."

"I can imagine," went on Uncle Oswald. "Judging by the effect it had on some of the people at the party. I didn't have much myself as I was driving. But I wouldn't mind buying a couple of bottles off you to take home."

"Yes, of course. Seeing as you're Vicky's uncle. Come with me." George turned and led him along the garden path. After the party a large portion of his cider had gone missing, so George had moved the remainder and most of his new stock to his cottage. He led Uncle Oswald to the kitchen and opened the pantry. Most of which was now taken up by cider bottles, leaving little room for his groceries. He selected two bottles and handed them to him. "This is still last year's harvest. This year's isn't ready to be drunk yet."

"Thank you. How much do I owe you?"

"As you're Vicky's uncle there's no charge."

"I really must insist."

"There's no charge," said George firmly.

"Thank you very much then," said Uncle Oswald. He was about to leave then turned back and, still clutching the bottles in each hand, added, "Tell me, do you know why Victoria has given up taking photographs?"

George shrugged. "I don't know. Perhaps she's decided to take a rest for a while."

"The rest seems to be permanent."

"Is that's what she told you?"

"Yes. It's such a waste. Those photographs in her portfolio were superb. There were magazine editors queuing up to offer her commissions." He shrugged his shoulders. "Well I must be going now. Thank you very much for the cider."

George walked back with him to the gate. He watched while Uncle Oswald got back into his Mercedes and drove off. Then he turned, picked up the handles of his wheelbarrow and set off in the direction of the mill. He wheeled it to the main room and dumped it beside the cider press. Then he climbed the stairs to Vicky's flat and knocked on the door.

It was some moments before Vicky opened it. She was wearing a dark blue sweatshirt, blue denim jeans and white training shoes. "Oh, it's you." she said.

"I haven't seen you for a while," said George. "I was wondering how you were."

"I'm fine."

"Good."

"Is there anything else?"

"Yes. I was wondering if you would like to go for a walk."

"A walk?"

"Yes."

She looked him up and down. His sleeveless pullover, trousers and wellington boots were still covered with mud from the orchard. "Do you mean now?" she asked.

"Yes."

"Dressed like that?"

"Oh, you look fine."

"I don't mean me!" she said angrily.

"Oh yes, of course," said George. "I meant after I've changed."

"No," said Vicky.

"What do mean, no?"

"I mean no. I don't want to go for a walk with you, George."

"Oh." He remained standing there.

"Is there anything else?"

"I suppose not."

"Good-bye, then." She closed the door.

He stood there a moment and then knocked again. She opened the door. "Well?" she asked, clearly irritated.

"I did rather want to talk to you."

"What about?"

"I've just seen your Uncle Oswald. He says you're not going to take any more photographs."

"He's not really my uncle, just an old friend of my father's. It's just that I've called him Uncle since I was a little girl. I don't want to discuss it, George."

"I think you should. Take more photographs that is."

"They won't be any good."

"What makes you think that?"

"I've tried before, remember?"

"Yes, on your own they weren't very good. But with me helping you they were excellent."

"That was you, George."

"How do you know?"

She frowned. "What do you mean?"

"I mean, how do you know it was just me? It might mean that you and I together work well as a team."

She stood in thought for a while.

He continued talking. "We were very successful. Think about it, or at least give it some thought." He turned to go.

She called after him. "Wait a minute! If you ... If you go home and get yourself cleaned up, I'll go for a walk with you, George."

"Good," said George. "I'll be back in half an hour."

Twenty minutes later he returned. He was wearing a brown tweed jacket over a checked shirt and blue sleeveless pullover. Around his neck he wore a dark blue cravat. His trousers were brown corduroy and were tucked into thick grey socks. On his feet he wore thick brown walking shoes. He looked every inch the country gentleman. Vicky on the other hand was wearing the same clothes she had worn earlier. She was carrying a compact 35mm camera. "I always take a camera with me when I go for a walk," she explained. "You never know what you may see."

They made their way out on to the bank beside the Muckle and then followed the towpath downstream in the direction of Mucklesbury. It was now a bright day in early September. The sun was already high in the sky. They felt its warmth on their backs and it was becoming warmer. George took his jacket off and carried it over his arm.

"You really think it might work, George?" said Vicky after a while. "Us working together, I mean?"

"I don't see why not," he replied. "After all, you do seem to have a good business brain. I have never been any good at that sort of thing. And you have a lot of contacts. I think it will work out very well indeed."

"You don't resent me then - taking half your property."

"Let's say I'm getting used to it."

She sighed. "It's a lovely day. You are lucky living in such a lovely spot."

"Yes, I am."

"Where does this path take us?" asked Vicky.

"Well, eventually it will lead down to the sea. But it does take us through Mucklesbury and past The Pullet Inn. We could stop for a drink, if you like."

Vicky thought for a while. "Yes," she said. "I'd like that. It will cement our partnership."

"Partnership?"

"Yes," she said, "if this is going to work, it will have to be as a partnership. We already share half the main asset, namely the mill. We can work together as equal partners."

"Yes, all right," agreed George with mixed feelings. He was still unhappy about sharing his beloved mill with someone else.

An hour later they arrived at The Pullet Inn, hot and very thirsty. Jack was in place behind the bar and old Joe Thropp was perched on his stool. The bar room was otherwise deserted.

"Afternoon, George. Afternoon, Miss," said Jack on seeing them.

"Hello, Jack, Joe!" said George. "You remember Miss Gloam?"

"Arr," muttered old Joe, "that were a mighty fine party of yorn, Miss."

"'T were that," agreed Jack. "What be you both be 'avening.?"

"Oh, let's have some of your cider, George," said Vicky.

"All right," said George. "A pint and a half of cider please, Jack."

"Oh I'd like a pint too please, George. I'm very thirsty."

"Two pints of Old Mill zider coming up," said Jack, "and they be on the house."

"Thanks very much," replied George. "We'll take them outside in the garden if that's all right?"

"I'll bring 'em out to yer," said Jack.

They moved outside to the beer garden and sat down at one of the wooden bench tables. "Oh, it's lovely here," said Vicky.

George looked round at the thistles and dandelions which were scattered about the long grass. "It would be if Jack was a decent gardener," he said.

"But look at the butterflies."

A number of peacock and red admiral butterflies fluttered around them. "You always get butterflies where there are weeds," remarked George.

Jack brought out their drinks, set them down on the table and then went back inside. Vicky picked up her glass and took a sip. "Cheers," she said.

George followed suit. "Cheers." They touched glasses.

"You know this is really fine cider, George. You ought to try marketing it."

"What for?"

"You'd make a lot of money."

"I'm not sure about that."

"Oh yes, people were talking about it to me days after the party."

"Oh, I don't think I could sell it commercially. It would take all the fun out of it."

"Still ... If the photographs don't work out it's worth considering."

All the talk about commercialism made George feel uneasy. But he did find Vicky very attractive and, once they changed subject, extremely good company. They sat there in the sun talking. George explained the history of the surrounding countryside and then they discussed possible outside locations for fashion photography. Ten minutes passed and Jack appeared again carrying two more pint glasses of cider.

"Old Joe says 'e enjoyed yer party so much that 'e would like ter buy yer some zider too," he explained.

"I don't think we should have any more," George told Vicky. "It does have the effect of creeping up on you."

"Oh, we can't offend him, George. Thank him for us please, Jack."

Jack nodded, set the glasses down and went away. Ten minutes later he was back again with two more glasses of cider. "Tom Firkin's been in and 'eard yer were out yer. 'E enjoyed the party an' all and 'e sends these with 'is complements."

They now both accepted the drinks without question. An hour later they felt very relaxed indeed and exceedingly invigorated. They decided to continue their walk. Returning their glasses to the bar, they bade their farewells and made their way back to the towpath beside the Muckle.

"I want to walk to the sea!" announced Vicky happily.

"It's a long way. Anyway I don't think you'd make it. You've had too much to drink."

"Hark at you. You've been staggering all over the place."

"I haven't. Three pints is nothing to me. But, you're certainly not used to it. I think we should be heading back."

"Spoilsport! OK, I suppose we'd better. After all, we have got a lot of work to do."

They set off up back the way they had come.

"Gosh, it is hot!" said Vicky.

It certainly was unseasonably hot. The sun beat down from a clear blue sky. George was regretting his choice of clothing, which he had selected purely because he had thought it would impress Vicky. He was disappointed that she had not remarked on it. He was now sweating freely.

"I know!" announced Vicky. "Let's go for a swim!"

"I don't think that's a good idea. We haven't got any costumes with us."

"That didn't stop you the night of my party."

"That was different. It was dark."

"Come on," she insisted. "There's no one about. It will sober us up. Didn't you say that a dip in the Muckle after drinking your cider helps prevent a hangover?"

George was stuck for a reply.

"I," continued Vicky, "don't like hangovers. I don't want a hangover. It's quite secluded. You go into those bushes over there and take your clothes off and I'll take mine off in the bushes over here." She swung her arms out in opposite directions pointing with her fingers.

George hesitated. But Vicky had already disappeared into her allocated bushes. George reluctantly moved to his bushes and slowly removed his clothing. He emerged gingerly a few minutes later totally naked.

"Smile, George!"

He turned to see Vicky, clad only in bra and panties, aim her camera and take his picture. "What the hell!" he cried.

She put the camera down and leapt into the water. He jumped in after her.

They had chosen the deepest part of the river where the water was nearly ten feet deep. His head broke the surface to see hers laughing at him from only a few feet away. "I didn't mean you to take all your clothes off," she said.

"Oh."

"Never mind, you've got a lovely bottom, George."

He swam after her. She turned and swam away from him. However, he caught up to her and pushed her head briefly under the water. "That's not fair," she spluttered.

"I'm just getting my own back."

"And I was getting my own back for what you did to me the other night."

"All right. Let's call it quits."

"Not quite." She splashed water in his face and then swam away.

"Afternoon, George!"

George turned his head to see Tom Firkin standing on the bank. "Oh ... Er ... Afternoon, Tom," he said.

"Nice day fer a swim!" Tom called back.

"Yes ... Yes it is!"

"I'd join you but I be after seeing to me pheasants. Afternoon, Miss. Enjoy yerselves!"

"Good afternoon, Tom!" Vicky called after him and giggled.

"I think we ought to get out before someone else comes," said George.

"Oh, not just yet. The water's so refreshing." She rolled on to her back and allowed herself to float on the gentle current. "This is heavenly," she said.

George swam back to the shore and clambered out. He found his clothes, and dried himself with his pullover and began to get dressed. He had just pulled on his trousers and was doing up his shirt when Vicky called out to him.

"Can you help me out, George?"

She was in the water by the bank. George went over to her, took her hand and pulled her out. She was glistening wet and close to him. "Have you got anything I can use as a towel?" she asked.

He hastily pulled away, picked up his pullover and threw it to her.

"Thank you," she said. "You're a gentleman, George. Now, can you turn your back?"

George obeyed while she went back into the bushes, dried and then dressed herself. She returned with his pullover rolled up under her arm. "Do you mind if I keep this until we get back? I've got my undies wrapped up inside."

George swallowed hard. "Of course," he said. He picked up his jacket and to his delight she took his arm and they set off again along the towpath.

The sun was beginning to set as they reached the mill. The rosy light cast hazy reflections on the water amongst the shadows of the surrounding trees. "Gosh it's beautiful," said Vicky.

George surveyed the scene in thought. "Yes," he agreed. "The light is good." He had a sudden thought. "You know, it's too good to waste. We should take our photographs here!" he added excitedly.

"But it will be dark soon. We'll never get set up in time."

"I wasn't thinking of tonight. Tomorrow morning, after a day like today, the dawn light will be perfect. We'll have plenty of time to get ready."

"But we haven't time to contact a model."

"You've got the clothes we need to photograph?"

"Yes."

"Then you can model them!"

"What?"

"After seeing you swimming today and remembering how you looked by the river, the night of the party and later on by my firelight, I know you'd be perfect."

"But I'm not sure I want to model. I prefer to be behind the camera or directing operations."

"Then we wait until we hire the models. A pity though, there's no telling whether the light will be the same in a few days time."

Vicky thought for a moment. "Are you sure this will work?" she asked.

"I'm sure," he replied.

CHAPTER 8

"Remarkable!" said Uncle Oswald. "The photographs you finally came up with are remarkable." He was standing in the living room of her flat in the mill. She had just let him in and he had been pacing the room in his excitement.

"I've had editors on the phone to me constantly. Victoria, I knew you were a very pretty girl. But in these photographs you are exquisite. You're really quite beautiful."

Vicky blushed. "Thank you, Uncle Oswald."

"To capture these photographs of yourself and direct the composition. You really are an exceptional talent."

"The photography wasn't me, Uncle Oswald," confessed Vicky. "It never was. It's all down to George."

"George? The man in the cottage?"

Yes. The original photograph you liked, the one of the mill, George took it. Only the ones you didn't like were mine."

"I see." Uncle Oswald thought for a moment and then said. "But you do have talent, my dear. Perhaps not in the way I first envisaged. "Do you realise how much a top model can earn nowadays?"

"No."

"Some won't even get out of bed for less than five thousand pounds a day."

Vicky gave a laugh of disbelief. "You're joking."

"I'm deadly serious. And I understand that there are a number of top photographers queuing up to photograph you. Some of them household names."

Vicky was stunned. "I don't know what to say."

I recommend you join a top model agency. But take care before you sign anything. You can virtually name your own price. If you like I'll act as your agent. I can certainly be your business adviser."

"What about George?"

"His photographs are very good. He has a lot of talent. But he still has a lot to learn technically. You should be photographed by the best there is."

"I'll need to think about it."

"One thing you must realise is that a top model's career is very short. You need to make your money while you're young, while you still have your looks."

"I do know about models, Uncle Oswald. I am a photographer."

"And while you're modelling you can learn from the top photographers. So when you retire you can go back to your own photography."

"I'll still need to think about it, Uncle Oswald."

"Well don't think too long. Now I must be going." She followed him down the stairs to the main door of the mill. He turned and said. "I'm very proud of you, Victoria. I'm sure if your parents were still alive, they would be too." He kissed her quickly on the cheek and was then on his way down the path towards his car.

Vicky followed him to the gate and watched him drive off. Then she turned and looked back at the mill. It had featured in a number of the photographs George had taken of her. She thought back to that morning and remembered how right George had been. The light had been perfect. They had made their preparations earlier while it was still dark, she with the dresses and make-up, he with the cameras, tripods and reflectors. The steamy mist rising from the Muckle had added to the atmosphere. They worked quickly and efficiently so as not to waste the early morning light. It had been an exciting and very enjoyable experience.

She turned and went to look for George. She found him in the orchard. He was raking the fallen leaves from the apple trees into a pile ready to be taken to a bonfire he had prepared at the far end of the field. He looked up at the sound of her approach. "Has your uncle gone?" he asked.

"Yes. The photographs were a great success."

"Well, we both knew they would be."

"They were more than a success. George, they were stupendous!" She flung her arms around him and hugged him.

George was so startled that he slipped and fell backwards, taking her with him into the pile of leaves. "Steady on!" he shouted. "Are you all right?"

She laughed and kissed him. "Of course, I am! George, I'm so happy. Everything has worked out so well."

George was embarrassed by her kiss and by her closeness. He was unsure how to react so he feigned pain. "Ow," he groaned

She immediately let go. "I'm sorry. Have I hurt you?"

He struggled to his feet. "Er ... No! Just a slight twinge, that's all."

She jumped up, concerned, and touched his arm. "I'm so sorry. I didn't mean to hurt you."

George pulled away gently. "It's OK, really," he insisted.

She smiled. "I got a bit carried away."

"I know. I understand."

"Look, I think we ought to celebrate."

George groaned. "Oh, no. Not another party."

"No. The success of the photographs was due to just the two of us. I think the celebration should be between just the two of us. I think we should go out to a really expensive restaurant and order whatever we want."

"Oh," said George.

"Well don't look so enthusiastic. What's the matter?"

"Nothing. I think it's a good idea, us celebrating I mean. It's just that I don't much care for expensive restaurants. Look, I've got a better idea. I'll cook you a really nice meal at my cottage."

She looked at him suspiciously. "Are you a good cook?"

George looked offended. "I certainly am," he said, "and given that we can spare no expense, I will cook you the meal of your dreams."

"All right then," she said, "but no cider."

He smiled. "No cider. We'll have champagne, of course. And you can choose it. Now, when shall we have this meal?"

"What about tonight?"

He looked at his watch. "Well, I should have time to get into Mucklesbury and get some shopping." He looked at her. "Yes, tonight should be fine. What time do you suggest?"

"Eight?"

"Eight o'clock will be fine."

For George the rest of the day passed quickly. The shopping and cooking meant he was very busy. However, at eight o'clock when Vicky knocked on the front door to his cottage, everything was ready.

"Hello," she said. "I hope I'm not too early."

She was wearing a long, deep blue dress. A white silk shawl was draped around bare shoulders. George was wearing a white cotton shirt, black bow tie, black shoes and trousers over which he wore a flowered pattern apron. He led her through to the dining room where the table was set for two. A single candle and a small vase with a single red rose occupied the centre. A bucket of ice containing a bottle of champagne stood on the sideboard.

"This looks lovely," she said, "and that's a lovely smell coming from the kitchen. What is it?"

"Chicken - in my own special sauce. But to start with, fresh trout from the River Muckle."

"Oh, George, you haven't found time to go fishing as well."

"No, these are courtesy of Tom Firkin. They're out of season but the date of the fishing season has never bothered Tom. He is a game keeper, after all."

"It all sounds wonderful."

He pulled a chair out for her and she sat down. "Would you like a sherry or a martini?"

"A martini would be lovely.

He went to the sideboard and mixed her a martini.

"Are you not drinking?" she asked.

"I have a glass of wine which I left in the kitchen." He gave her the drink. "Now if you'll excuse me, I'll go and get the fish."

"Can I do anything to help?"

"No, everything is under control. Though you could help with the washing up afterwards."

She laughed. "All right."

George went through to the kitchen and finished his drink, which in fact was cider and not wine, but he had thought it politic not to tell Vicky. He picked up two plates, each containing a cooked and filleted trout, which had been warming under the grill, and took them into the dinning room. He set them down, lit the candle and turned out the light. He opened the champagne and filled two glasses with the foaming liquid. Then he gave one glass to Vicky, took off his apron and taking the other glass sat down opposite her.

He raised his glass. "To success," he said.

"To success." She touched his glass with hers.

"Actually," he said. "There is something I want to ask you."

"Really, what?"

He grew nervous. "Er ... perhaps not just yet. Let's have the meal first."

She smiled. "All right. I'm intrigued."

The meal passed pleasantly. They talked about photography and modelling. She remarked accurately that his cooking was very tasty. He thanked her and admired her dress. When the meal was over he asked her if she would like coffee and brandy in the sitting room.

"Yes," she said, "that would be nice. I will make the coffee. But first I'll do the washing up."

"There's no need."

"Oh yes there is." She stood up and put on his apron. "We're partners now, George. I also think that we'll get on very well. In fact I think we're very compatible."

"You do?"

"Yes, I do. So don't worry about asking me anything."

She took the dirty plates through to the kitchen. He stood up and took two glasses and a bottle of brandy through to the sitting room. He put another log on the gently glowing fire, lit a candle on the mantelpiece, filled two glasses with brandy, left one on the mantelpiece and settled himself down on the settee with the other. Approximately half an hour later, Vicky came in carrying a tray containing two cups of coffee and a small jug of cream. She set it down on a small table.

"Do you take cream in your coffee?" she asked.

"Yes, please. There's a brandy for you on the mantelpiece."

"Thank you." She poured cream into both cups, took off the apron, picked up her brandy and sat down beside him. "It's been a lovely evening," she said.

"Yes." He took a deep breath. "Look, Vicky, there really is something I want to ask you."

"Yes?"

"My share of the money from the photographs has made me more financially secure, so I think I'm now in a position to make you an offer."

"Yes, George?"

He hesitated. "I've been meaning to ask you this all evening."

"Well, go on."

"Will you sell me your half of the mill?"

"Yes, George ... What did you say?"

"Will you sell me your half of the mill? After all, you'll probably be away travelling quite a lot, what with your modelling and everything."

She stood up abruptly. "Is that what you've been wanting to ask me all evening?"

"Yes."

"Is that why you suggested a romantic meal in your cottage?"

"Romantic? Well I thought it would be pleasant."

"You just thought it would be pleasant?"

"Yes?"

"I think I'll be going home."

"But why?"

"Oh! Work it out yourself." She swept out, made her way to the front door and opened it.

He followed her. "Work what out? What about my offer?"

But she had gone out into the night and back towards the mill.

Next morning at 11 o'clock, George went across to the mill and climbed the stairs to Vicky's flat to suggest that they have a cup of coffee together. He wanted to find out what he had done to offend her and to apologise for whatever it was. He knocked on the door. There was no answer, so he went about the business of pressing the last of his apple crop into cider. The day passed and she still made no appearance. Another day passed and there was still no sign of her.

On the third day he noticed Justin coming out of the mill. George called to him. "Hello there!" he shouted trying to sound hearty.

"Oh, hello," replied Justin.

George approached him. "I haven't seen Vicky for a while," he explained. "I was wondering how she was."

"Oh, she's fine. She's doing some modelling in Paris. I'm looking after her flat for her."

George was taken aback. "Oh, I could have done that. After all, I only live across the way."

"Well, actually she's going to be away for some time so she's asked me to move in for a while."

"Oh."

"Well, I must be on my way," said Justin. "See you around. Bye!"

"Good-bye," said George and stood watching Justin walk down the path, out the gate and down the road towards Mucklesbury. He stood there for some moments, then set off for Mucklesbury himself. However, he took the towpath route that he and Vicky had followed a few weeks earlier.

He reached the village and made for a telephone box by the post office. He opened the door and once inside took a small diary out of his trouser hip pocket, looked up a telephone number from a list he kept on the back page, picked up the receiver, put a pound coin in the slot and dialled.

A female voice said, "Hello, Oswald Goodsake's office."

"Please may I speak to Mr Goodsake?" asked George.

"Who's speaking?"

"George Cogrill."

"Will you hold one moment?"

There was a pause and then Uncle Oswald's voice came on the end of the phone. "Hello, George," he said. "What can I do for you?"

"I'm afraid I haven't got long," said George, "I'm calling from a phone box, but I'd like to contact Vicky."

"If you'd like to give me your number, I'll call you back."

George gave him the number and hung up. A few minutes later Uncle Oswald was talking to him again. "I'm acting as her agent now", he explained, "but I'm afraid she won't allow me to tell you where she is."

"But why?"

"I'm afraid I don't understand either. She said something about you wanting to buy her out and that seems to have upset her."

"I only wanted to buy back her half of the mill. I don't understand why that's upset her."

"Well she's definitely been upset by you, George. Look, just because she's upset with you doesn't necessarily mean that I can't represent you as well."

"In what way?"

"Well, you have talent as a photographer. I could steer some work your way. Not with Victoria, of course. Well not yet anyway."

"I'll think about it."

"Actually, what I'm really interested in is that cider of yours. It went down well with some marketing contacts I tried it on. There's a demand for designer beers and wines and perhaps cider. I think it could really take off."

"I'm not interested in producing it commercially," said George.

"A pity. I believe you could make a lot of money out of it."

"I'm all right financially at the moment."

"Well, if you need any advice on investing your money, let me know."

"Thank you," said George. "I'd better be going now. Good-bye." He hung up and left the telephone box.

" 'Ow do, George!" It was Tom Firkin. He was standing the other side of the road. "I be going for a drink. Do yer fancy coming?"

"Yes," said George, "why not?"

They walked together to The Pullet Inn. Inside, they were greeted by Jack Hump. " 'Ow do lads," he said. "What'll it be? Two pints of zider?"

"Yes, please," replied George, "and have one yourself."

Jack poured the drinks while George looked round the room. In one corner, he noticed Justin with a group of five people. One he recognised as Sebastian, another was Miranda Flit. There was also a dark-haired girl and a sandy-haired young man. He turned back to the bar, collected his cider and paid Jack for the three drinks.

"Cheers," said Tom.

"Good health, Tom," replied George.

"Well, if it isn't George!" Sebastian was on his feet and approaching the bar. "Can I get you a drink?" he asked.

"I've already got one," said George indicating his glass.

"Well join us anyway."

"I'm with a friend."

" 'Ow do," said Tom

"Oh, yes. The fellow from the party. Tim, isn't it?"

"Tom," said Tom.

"Oh, yes - Tom. You must join us too."

George looked at Tom who was already admiring Miranda. "Why not?" said Tom.

Sebastian led them over to the table. "Hello, everybody," he said heartily. "This is George and Tom. George, you know Justin and Miranda. This is Linda and Jonathan." He indicated the other couple at the table.

"Hello," said George. The others muttered their "hellos" in reply.

"Let's pull up more chairs. George, I've got a business proposition for you."

George and Tom set their drinks down on the table and pulled up more chairs. The others pulled their chairs back to make room for them.

"You see, we're setting up a small group of artists to work at the mill," explained Sebastian once they were all seated. Linda is a sculptor. Jonathan is a painter, and Miranda and Justin are both models."

Tom's eyes widened and he stared at Miranda. "Do yer takes all yer clothes orf?" he asked.

She grinned back at him. "You cheeky monkey."

"You look like a handsome specimen of a man, Tom," said Linda. "Would you like to do some modelling?"

"With no clothes on?"

"Yes."

He looked across at her dark eyes. "I don't mind," he said and then turned back to Miranda. "'I do a spot of drawing myself."

"Oh do you?" asked Miranda.

"Oh yer," Tom continued. "Mainly birds, ducks and things, but 'specially birds."

"Tom's a gamekeeper," George explained. He turned to Sebastian. "I'm afraid this sort of business doesn't appeal to me. I don't do any modelling."

"Ah! But you take wonderful photographs," Sebastian replied. "We'd like you to join our group. You too, Tom - if you like."

"We're going to use the mill as a base," said Justin. "Vicky said we could."

"Oh, did she?" remarked George.

"Well, her half anyway," explained Sebastian. "I realise that half of it is yours. However, perhaps if you join us we could use your half too."

"I'll think about it," said George. He looked at his watch. "Goodness, is that the time? I'm afraid I've got an appointment." He stood up and picked up his glass. "I expect I shall see you all around. "Good-bye, Tom. Good-bye, everybody."

"Good-bye," they all said except for Tom who said, "See yer, George," and then turned back to gaze at Miranda.

George walked to the bar, took a long sip of his drink and put the glass down on the bar. "So long, Jack," he said to Jack Hump.

"Bye, George," said Jack and noticing he was not staying to finish his drink added, "zomet wrong?"

"No, I've just remembered an appointment. Good-bye." With that George made for the door and out into the street. He strode briskly towards the towpath and followed it back towards his cottage, feeling guilty about leaving Tom so abruptly. There was no appointment he had to keep but the thought of remaining in the company of Vicky's friends for a moment longer was just too much. She hadn't even seen fit to confide in him – he'd had no idea what she was planning. Head bowed, hands in pockets, shoulders hunched, he slowed his pace and trudged reluctantly home to the emptiness he knew was waiting for him there.

CHAPTER 9

The months passed and it was spring again. A taxi stopped outside the gate to the mill. Vicky got out, paid off the driver and started up the path towards the old building and its paddled waterwheel. She was wearing beige slacks with matching jacket over a white blouse. The main door to the mill was wide open and she walked straight in.

The central room was no longer filled solely with photography equipment. It also contained artist's easels, unfinished canvasses and palettes of paint. In one corner was an unfinished sculpture of a human head. The photography apparatus appeared almost as if it had been discarded completely and was pushed aside into another corner. She climbed the stairs up to what had once been her flat and knocked on the door. It was pulled open by Justin with a great flourish.

"Hi there, Vicky!" he said. "Great to see you." He kissed her on the cheek. "Come in. Everyone else has gone to the pub."

She followed him into the living room. "Can I get you anything to drink?" he asked.

"No thank you. I won't be staying very long. I'm in England for a few days and I thought I'd look in to see how things are going."

"Oh, everything's great. This is certainly a brilliant place to work. Everyone appreciates you allowing them to use the mill."

"Everyone?"

"Well, I'm not so sure about George Cogrill. We don't see him in here much."

"So I heard from Uncle Oswald."

"Everyone else is doing just fine."

"Uncle Oswald says that no one seems to have sold much of their work. He also says that they haven't paid back much in the way of rent."

Justin shrugged. "Well, that's art. It can be quite slow sometimes. Anyway, you'll have to speak to Sebastian about that side of things. I believe he's up in London somewhere."

"But you're looking after my flat and the mill."

"Of course, that's our agreement. I'm living here and keeping an eye on things for you. Everything's fine. Do you want to stay the night?"

"No I have got to get back. Look, if you don't mind I think I'll take a look round."

"Sure. Do you want me to come with you?"

"No. I'll be all right on my own."

"Just as you wish. Come back and see me before you go."

Vicky wandered slowly back downstairs. When she reached the bottom, she decided to make a tour of inspection and looked into all the downstairs rooms and even ventured down into the cellar. She was surprised to find no sign of any cider barrels or bottles. The press was still there, in that part of the main room which had been partitioned off. But everything else that had once belonged to George had now been removed.

She went outside and stood for a while looking at George's cottage. She hesitated and wondered whether to go and knock on the door. But in the end she decided to set off along the towpath towards Mucklesbury. She had not gone far when she spied the gaunt figure of Old Joe Thropp coming towards her.

"Afternoon, Miss," said Old Joe.

"Hello," she replied.

"We 'aven't seen yer in these parts fer a while. Looking for George, are yer?"

"No. I'm on my way to The Pullet Inn."

"Well, 'e don't go in there much now."

"As I said, I'm not looking for him. I'm on my way to the pub."

Old Joe shook his grizzled head. "Tain't the same nowadays," he said sadly. "Full of arty types. George spends most of 'is time in Tickle Woods."

"Where?"

"Tickle Woods." He pointed to an area thick with conifers that bordered on to the towpath. "We calls it Tickle Woods because when we was young. . ." His voice petered out. "Never, mind," he muttered. Then he added, "If you was ter follow the towpath for a few 'undred yards you'll come to a path that'll lead yer right in ter the woods and yer should come across George."

"But as I said, I'm not looking for George."

Old Joe nodded sagely. "Well I be on me way," he said. "If yer sees George give 'im me regards." He gave a wave of his hand and set off.

Vicky stared at his retreating back and started once more to say, "But I'm not looking. . .", but then thought better of it. Instead she continued along her way and soon came to the path mentioned by Old Joe. It led at right angles away from the river and into the woods. She stood for awhile at the junction between it and the towpath and stared in the direction of the woods. She could not see very far as the path soon disappeared amongst a mesh of bushes and trees. Eventually curiosity got the better of her and she started along the path, and into Tickle Woods.

She had been walking for ten minutes when she saw another, this time much taller, younger and more sprightly figure striding towards her. It was Tom Firkin. "'Ow do, Miss," he said breezily. "Are yer looking for George?"

"What makes everyone think I'm looking for George?" said Vicky in exasperation.

"Oh sorry. I just assumed, you and 'im being partners so ter speak and you both being in Tickle Woods."

"Well I was just on my way to Mucklesbury and then I thought I'd take a look at these woods."

"Why's that then?"

"Well ... I've ... heard such a lot about them."

"Well, they do 'ave a certain reputation," remarked Tom.

Vicky hastily changed the subject. "Where is George, anyway?" she asked.

"Is 'e expecting yer?"

"Not especially."

Tom stroked his chin. "Well," he said, "you best come with me."

"Oh, I don't want to put you to any trouble." Vicky was a little concerned. She did not know Tom that well and certainly not well enough to go walking with him in a location with such a dubious name as Tickle Woods.

"Oh it be no trouble. Follow me." He turned and led her along the path deeper into the woods.

After ten minutes walking they came to a small clearing. Tom stopped and pointed to three large bushes in the centre of the clearing. "See those three bushes?" he asked.

"Yes."

"See that one in centre?"

"Yes."

"That be George."

"You mean George's in the bush?" Vicky asked incredulously.

"No. The bush be George."

"What!"

"Well I be off now. Give him my regards," and with that Tom turned and strode off in the direction they had come.

Vicky stood and stared at the 'bush'. But it still looked like a bush to her. Perhaps Tom was playing a practical joke. Perhaps George was hiding in the bush. Perhaps they were both playing a practical joke on her. Still the curiosity which brought her into the woods in the first place led her on and she started walking cautiously in the direction of the 'bush'. Then as she drew nearer she made out the shape of a head amongst the twigs and leaves. Its back was towards her and as she drew still nearer she could see that the 'bush' was indeed the crouching form of a man covered with twigs and leaves.

"George?"

He turned his head. A pair of binoculars was around his neck. In front of him was a camera with telephoto lens on a small tripod.

"Schh!" he hissed.

"Why? What is it?"

"Keep your voice down," he whispered and turned his head back to its former position. "Look over there."

She crouched down beside him. "Over where?" she whispered back.

"There, on the far side of the glade."

"I can't see anything."

He sighed. "Well it's gone now anyway," he said in resignation.

"Typical!" snapped Vicky

He turned to look at her. "What do you mean, typical?"

"I don't believe there was anything there in the first place."

"Well there was and now you've scared it away."

"What was it?"

"It doesn't matter now," he said and rose to his feet. "What are you doing here anyway?" he asked.

"I ... I was on my way to Mucklesbury and I thought I'd take a look at these woods."

"Were you looking for me?"

"Not initially, but I heard you were here, so I thought I'd drop by and see how you were."

"I'm fine. I've been trying to contact you."

"I heard."

"Why did you go off like that?"

She sighed. "You can't figure it out?

"No, I can't. Perhaps you'll explain."

"There's nothing to explain."

He looked at her and shrugged. "I see." He turned, bent down, picked up the camera and tripod, and began unscrewing the camera from the tripod.

"What's all this in aid of?" she asked indicating the equipment.

"Oh, I've been doing some wildlife photography."

"Have you sold any pictures?"

"What makes you think I want to sell pictures? I've been doing it because I enjoy it."

"I'd like to see some of your photographs."

"Why?"

"Because I like photographs and you're a good photographer."

He slung the camera around his neck and looked at her. "I'm heading home now," he said.

"I'm going to The Pullet Inn. Would you like to join me?"

"I don't go there much now."

"I would still like to buy you a drink and we're still business partners."

"I don't think we've got much to discuss. I'm not in a position to buy you out now."

"But you can at least let me buy you a drink. I think we should still talk."

"All right."

They walked back in the direction of the River Muckle. "How's the modelling been going?" he asked.

"It's been good."

"I'm glad."

"Actually," she admitted, "it's been very boring."

"Oh?"

"Yes. It's been very profitable. I've made a lot of money. But I'd rather be back behind a camera."

"You must have picked up some useful tips, working with those famous photographers."

"I hope so."

"Have you taken any photographs yourself?"

"Some."

"I'd like to look at them."

"You would?"

"Of, course I would," he said. They walked on. About an hour later they reached The Pullet Inn.

The Pullet Inn had changed. Gone was the separate public bar. Gone too was the lounge bar that was never used. Instead the divided walls had been knocked down and the interior was now one large carpeted lounge bar with adjoining dinning area. The Pullet Inn now provided food for its customers. Behind the bar were two young busty barmaids, one blonde, one a redhead.

Vicky was quite taken aback by the changes and turned to George. "Have we come to the right place?" she asked.

"I'm afraid so," he replied. "As I said, I don't come here much any more."

"Where's Jack Hump?"

"Oh, he's probably around somewhere, either out the back or upstairs. He doesn't work much behind the bar any more."

"Why's that?"

"Let's get something to drink first and I'll explain." They approached the bar. "What would you like?"

"I would like some of your cider please, George."

George caught the blonde barmaid's attention and said, "Two half pints of Cogrill's cider, please."

"I'm afraid we're right out of Cogrill's," she replied. "I can get you some Somerset. We've also got Cornwall, Kent, or some Normandy or Brittany cider."

"But it's still only spring," said George, surprised. "You can't be out of it already!"

"I'm afraid we are, sir. It has proved to be our most popular cider."

"Look, I'm George Cogrill. I'm sure Jack will have put some aside somewhere."

"Are you really George Cogrill?"

"Yes!"

"Just a minute, sir." She disappeared through a back door. A few minutes later she reappeared with Jack Hump.

"George!" he exclaimed joyfully. "We 'aven't seen yer in here for ages. 'Ow bist?"

"I'm fine, Jack. You remember Miss Gloam?"

"Oh yer! 'Ow do, Miss."

"Very well, thank you," replied Vicky.

"What's happened to all the cider I sold you, Jack?"

"Sold out. Proved very popular it has - brought in customers from miles away. Was the idea of your Uncle Oswald, Miss. I've done very well. Look at all this!" He spread his arms out wide indicating their surroundings.

"Very nice," said George. "But I'm not sure it's an improvement."

"Brings in customers though." Jack lowered his voice. "Look, George, I still 'ave some put by for special occasions." He turned to the blonde barmaid. "Sally, get a bottle of my special Cogrill's."

"Yes, Mr Hump." She disappeared through the back door.

"'Ave yer got any stock left, George?" asked Jack.

"Not to sell, Jack. I have only enough for my own use."

"Shame. Seeing as yer here, would you like something ter eat? We runs a restaurant now."

"What do you think, Vicky?"

"Why not."

"Sit yourselves down and I'll get Sally ter bring you a menu with your drinks."

"Thank you," said George. They moved to a table in the dining area and drew up two shiny new pine chairs.

"'Ello, Victoria, 'ello, George!" It was Miranda Flit. She approached their table. "I thought it was you. I'm over there with Linda and Jonathan." She indicated the couple at the far end of the lounge bar. "We comes 'ere most lunch times. 'Ow are you doing, Victoria. I 'ear you're doing well on the ol' cat walk."

"I am doing well, thank you, Miranda," replied Vicky coolly. "How are things with you?"

"Oh, it's really great 'ere. I've bin doing some modelin' up at the mill. It don't pay that well, but it's good fun. These artist types are really easy going. They does a bit of painting and sculptin', then it's down 'ere for a drink and a bit of a laugh. Why don't you join us?"

"Perhaps later," said Vicky. "Mr Cogrill and myself are going to discuss some business and have something to eat."

"I'll leave you to it then," said Miranda. "Cheerie-bye." She turned and waltzed back to her companions.

Vicky turned to George. "Do you see much of Miranda and her friends?" she asked.

He shook his head. "Not much."

Sally brought their drinks and the menu.

"I see they now do a Ploughman's Lunch," Vicky remarked after Sally had gone.

"They certainly do," replied George, "and a Gamekeeper's Stew and Fisherman's Pie."

"Who does all the cooking?"

"I've no idea. But I bet it's not Jack. What takes your fancy?"

"I think I'll go for the Cowman's Quiche Salad. Do Cowmen around here really eat quiche?"

He winked at her. "I expect so – for breakfast, lunch, tea and supper, probably. I'll think I'll go for the Miller's Sausage and Mash."

Sally returned, took their orders and took away the menus.

Vicky was the first to speak. "Why is it you're no longer in a position to buy me out?" she asked.

George avoided her gaze and studied the cutlery on the table in front of him.

"Well?"

His eyes remained fixed on the table as he answered her quietly. "The money I earned from the photographs we took together has all gone. So too is the money I earned from selling my cider and so has most of my cider. I've only a few bottles left now."

"But you were doing so well."

He looked up and protested. "I've got enough money to live on. I'm just not as well off as I was a few months ago. What about you?"

"Oh, I'm fine. I'm just a bit bored, that's all. The travelling was exciting at first. Now it's become tiring. Everyone wants to take pictures of me. No one will let me behind a camera. I'm just a glorified clothes horse. I'm not sure I really want that despite all the money. I was happiest when I was running my own business. That's what I really miss."

He sighed. "Well, you haven't missed much by not being here. Everything's changed so much. Since our photographs were published, the pub and even the mill have become tourist attractions. I don't know why you had to let out your part of the mill. Your friends have not done much work. They sell a few items to visitors but they spend most of their time down here. The whole atmosphere of the mill, the pub and all of Mucklesbury has changed. I'm not sure I'd like to buy the mill now, even if I could afford to buy you out. How much rent do you charge them, by the way?"

"I don't think that needs to concern you."

He raised one hand in apology. "Sorry, I didn't mean to offend. It's just that it was such a lovely old building. Its character has simply gone."

"It doesn't look much changed to me."

"Outside, perhaps not, but inside - well it makes me shudder. I try and keep away from the place. You should have sold it back to me when I asked."

Vicky lent back in her chair. "That's water under the bridge now," she said. "Perhaps we can do something to make amends."

"What do you mean?" he asked.

"Well, I'm bored and you sound fed up. We ought to get together and do something about it. We worked well as a team before."

He regarded her suspiciously. "I'm not so sure," he said, "I really don't understand why you went off like that. I'm not sure that I trust you or even that I should trust you again."

Sally arrived with their food and they turned their attention to their meals and to eating. When they finished they ordered coffee and while they sipped it Vicky once more brought the conversation back to the possibility of their renewed partnership. "We did work well together," she said. "I really think we ought to work together again."

"And do what?"

"Well," she said, "what I'd really like to do is turn the mill into a form of Arts Centre. We could make it a sort of retreat and invite artists down to spend some time in a quiet rural environment, away from the hubbub of city life. By artists, I mean they could be painters, photographers, writers and poets. We'd charge a fee of course. We could experiment with our photography. You could even continue with your cider making. There appears to be a lot of money in that. There are endless possibilities of what we could do."

A look of horror spread across his face. "Is that why you let your half out to those people over there?" He pointed to Miranda and her companions at the far end of the room.

She followed his gaze. "Partly. I wanted to see if the mill had possibilities as an Arts Centre. I also wanted it looked after while I was away."

"I could have done that for you. I don't think your friends have produced much work or done much in maintaining the upkeep of the property."

"Perhaps not. But I've still made money out of it."

George looked at her quizzically. "Really?"

"Really. Look, I'm staying down here for a couple of days. Think it over and get back to me."

"Where are you staying?"

"With your aunt."

George's look turned to one of disbelief. "With Aunt Jane?" he asked.

"That's right."

"But, apart from her staff, no one stays with Aunt Jane. No one can stand her!"

"Actually, I rather like her." Vicky finished her coffee. "I think I'll be going now," she said. "Please let me know what you decide."

CHAPTER 10

George had drunk too much cider. He had remained at The Pullet Inn long after Vicky had left. Now he was asleep on damp grass under dark trees. He opened his eyes and looked at the branches above him. It was twilight and growing dark. He rose to his feet and brushed loose grass, earth and leaves from his clothing. He could not remember where he was or how he got there. He saw lights ahead of him, walked towards them and made out the shape of a large building. It was Gleefield Manor. He drifted towards the lighted windows and peered in.

He was outside the main drawing room window. Inside he saw his aunt, Uncle Oswald and Vicky Gloam. His aunt and Uncle Oswald were seated in armchairs. Vicky was sitting on the sofa. He could not hear what was being said. He trod carefully round the house to the front door. There he hesitated. Finally he rang the bell.

As usual it was opened by the elderly butler. And as usual Winchester shot out from behind the old man and up at George to greet him. "Hello, Gumage," he said, scratching Winchester behind the ears. "I've come to see my aunt and Miss Gloam."

Gumage nodded sagely. "Come in, Master George," he said. "I will see if they are available."

George followed Gumage into the hall. There Gumage left him and went to find his aunt. He returned and a few moments later showed him into the drawing room.

His aunt, Uncle Oswald and Vicky were still seated as he had seen them through the window. "George!" exclaimed his aunt. "You look disgraceful. What have you been doing? Rolling in the mud?" Gumage made a dignified retreat back to the hallway, silently closing the door behind him.

George ignored her remark. "I wish to speak to Vicky," he said.

"Well," replied Aunt Jane, nodding in the girl's direction, "there she is."

He turned to Vicky. "I've considered your offer," he said. "I accept."

Uncle Oswald rose swiftly to his feet crossed to George and shook his hand. "Congratulations, dear boy," he said, "I hope you both will be very happy."

"Yes, well done, George," agreed his aunt. "I didn't think you had it in you."

George was dumbfounded. "What are you both talking about?"

"Why, your marriage of course," said his aunt. "Vicky has told us all about her plans."

"Marriage!"

"Congratulations!" said Uncle Oswald still shaking his hand. "This calls for a celebration!"

George stood by the door in a state of shock. He looked at Vicky who was still sitting on the sofa. She got to her feet, hurried across to George and took his arm. "I think we ought to talk outside, George," she said.

Nonsense," said his aunt, "you two must stay here. You must have a lot to talk about - arranging the wedding and everything. Oswald, come with me. We will inspect my wine cellar and pick out some vintage champagne with which to celebrate." She called to the dog. "Winchester!" Both she and Uncle Oswald left the room. Winchester reluctantly followed. Aunt Jane shut the door purposefully behind them and leaving George and Vicky alone.

George stared at Vicky. "You didn't mention marriage," he said.

"I know."

"Look, I don't know what to think," he said and began pacing the room. She stood motionless, silently watching him. He stopped and stared at her, unsure of what to say.

She remained silent. He began walking once more. He was confused. His confusion led to panic. He turned, walked to the window, undid the catch, pushed it up to open it and stepped through it and out into the gathering light. Then he began to run.

He ran across the lawn and into the woods. He heard a shout but did not stop. Someone was running after him. He kept on running. Suddenly he tripped over the root of a tree and fell headlong. He was grabbed around the shoulders.

"Come 'ere, you!" cried a voice. He was pulled over on his back. "George!" He looked up to see Tom Firkin standing over him. "What be you doing running through yer aunt's woods. I though you was a poacher!"

"Sorry, Tom," said George breathing heavily. "I just had a bit of a fright, that's all."

Tom helped him up. "You be all right now?" he inquired.

"Fine, thanks."

"What's 'appened?"

"Nothing. Nothing to worry about."

"Look, me cottage is just over yonder. You best comes with me and clean up."

"No, I'm fine Tom, really."

"Come on, George. Yer don't look fine. Come 'ome with I."

"Oh, all right then," said George reluctantly and followed Tom to his cottage, which happened to be only a few hundred yards away.

Tom led him inside. "Yer know where bathroom is," he said. "I'll makes some tea."

"Thanks, Tom."

George went up dusty bare wooden stairs to the bathroom. Took off his jacket and shirt and washed himself down in the sink. He brushed his clothes off the best he could and then went back downstairs. He found

Tom sitting at the kitchen table with two large mugs of steaming tea. He sat down opposite him and picked up the nearest mug. There had been no need to tell Tom how he liked his tea. They had drunk tea, coffee and cider together in each other's cottages many a time.

"You be all right now?" inquired Tom.

"Fine, thanks."

"I was in The Pullet earlier. Jack said that yer left yer camera equipment there."

"Thanks, I'll pick it up later." George stared at his mug and then asked, "Tom, have you ever considered getting married?"

"What me? No. 'I'm like yer. I'm 'appy on me own. Tell the truth, I don't think any one'll put up with me. Mind yer, I've 'ad me moments."

"It's a big step," said George.

"Certainly tis."

"What do you think about the mill becoming an Arts Centre?"

"Well, it be that already, baint it? What with Justin and 'is crowd living there."

"I don't mean just Vicky's part of the mill. I mean the whole thing."

Tom shrugged. "Well it be your mill, George," he said.

"You don't think it'll spoil it? Take away its character?"

"Well, years ago it were used ter grind corn. Then yer father, then you, took it over and used it as a store and ter make zider. I don't see what it matters what it's used fer. It can never be used fer its original purpose fer makin flour ter make bread. T'aint economic. So I s'pose it don't matter what it's used fer now. As long as yer 'appy, George. I can't see that yer will change its character much, nor Justin's friends fer that matter. Yer can't make it any worse than what Jack's done to The Pullet Inn."

"That's a case in point, Tom. The Pullet Inn is now a dreadful place. Do you go there much these days?"

"Of course, it's the nearest place ter drink. But I agrees with yer about it being bad. Makes money though. That's why Jack done it."

"But there's more to life than making money."

"True. But Jack was struggling ter make ends meet afore he decided ter change it. Now people goes there from miles around. T'aint much good running a pub if yer got no custom. It were yer friends at the mill what gave Jack the idea."

"They're not my friends, Tom. And I'm not sure the change has been good for the village."

"Yer got to 'ave change, George. Nothing stays the same. Countryside is changing all the time."

There was a knock at the back door. " 'Scuse me," said Tom and went to open it. It was Miranda. She was wearing a long brown fur coat. George stood up.

" 'Ello, luv," said Miranda and then on seeing George said, " 'ello, George!" and smiled breezily.

Tom ushered Miranda in and closed the door behind her. "Do yer fancy some tea, Miranda?" he asked.

"No, ta. I'll go through to the sitting room, shall I? Is George staying?"

"I'm no' sure. Go through. I'll see yer in a minute."

"Okay, then." She smiled impishly and skipped out the other door.

"Um, Miranda's come to do some modelling," explained Tom. "I've bin doing some drawings of 'er."

"I see," said George. He stood up. "I won't keep you then. Thanks very much for the tea."

Tom showed him out the back door. "Mind 'ow you go," he said.

"Don't worry," George replied, "I'll be fine. Good night and thanks for the tea." Then he set off through the woods in the direction of his own cottage.

The next morning George was woken by a loud banging at his door. He rolled out of bed, crossed to the window and looked out. The first thing he saw was the Triumph motorcycle standing by the gate. The next thing was his aunt, complete with motorcycle leathers, staring up at him through the visor of her crash helmet.

"George!" she shouted. "Come down here. I want to talk to you!"

"Give me a few moments to get dressed, Aunt, and I'll be right down."

"Well, hurry up about it!"

He dressed as slowly as he dared, wondering how he could postpone the impending interview without upsetting his aunt any further. He could see that she was certainly angry - very angry indeed.

He opened the door. Aunt Jane pushed past him, her helmet now tucked under her arm. She made straight for the sitting room and turned to face George, who had followed her. "Just what do you think you are playing at, George!" she demanded.

"Would you like a cup of tea, Aunt?"

"Certainly not! Now please explain your behaviour. Why did you ask Victoria to marry you one minute and then leave suddenly without giving the poor girl good reason? And why did you leave by way of the window? What's the matter with the door? Or is that too civilised for you?"

George drew a deep breath. "I didn't ask her to marry me," he said.

"You proposed to her. I heard you."

"That was a business proposal, Aunt."

"Well it sounded more than that to me."

"I can't help that. It was not meant to be a proposal of marriage. What matters was how it sounded to Vicky. And just how did the idea that it was a proposal of marriage get into your and Oswald Goodsake's heads?"

Now it was Aunt Jane's turn to go on the defensive. "Well ... " she said, "you both seem to get on so well together."

"In what way?"

"The photographs you took together. They were excellent. And although she's become well known as a model, it was your photographs that made her well known. Also no one has since photographed her the way you have. It was your photographs of her that made her look so remarkable."

"I didn't know you were such an expert, Aunt."

"I'm not. But Oswald Goodsake is and even I could see how good those photographs were."

George turned and looked out of the window. "But just because I took nice photographs of her doesn't mean to say that I should marry her," he said quietly.

Aunt Jane went over to him and touched his arm. "Look, George," she said, "you are your father's and my only surviving relative. I would really like to see you marry, inherit Gleefield Manor and benefit from your father's estate. But it would all be a complete waste if you don't marry, have children and pass the inheritance on to your heirs. Don't you see that?"

"But it's not what I want, Aunt."

Aunt Jane became angry once more. "What do you mean, it's not what you want?" she snapped. "We can't all do what we want. Even people who inherit property have a duty to see that it survives. It's time you thought of people other than yourself, George. Particularly if you want to hang on to the rest of your father's estate and inherit mine as well. Think about it!" With that she strode out of the room and out of the cottage. George watched from the window and saw her mount her motorcycle, kick the engine into life and roar off in the direction of Gleefield Manor.

The encounter with Aunt Jane so unnerved George that he was unable to concentrate fully on his routine morning chores of washing, shaving and preparing breakfast. In the end he decided to skip breakfast and opted for a walk. He set off not in the direction of the river or Mucklesbury but through the orchard towards Tidburn.

He had only gone a few yards when he saw a young woman coming towards him from the opposite direction. She had long dark hair and wore a dark blue pullover over an ankle-length green dress. On her feet she wore black wellington boots. She stopped when she reached him.

"Hello," she said and smiled.

"Hello," replied George.

"You're George Cogrill, aren't you?"

"That's right."

"I'm Linda Quilt. I'm staying at the mill with Justin and Jonathan."

Recognition dawned on George's face. "Oh, that's right," he said.

She smiled again. "I thought you didn't recognise me. You own the other half of the mill, don't you?"

"That's right."

"It's a lovely day, isn't it? The apple blossom on the trees is quite beautiful. You should get a good crop of apples for your cider this year."

"You know about cider making, do you?"

"A little. My family were originally from Somerset. Your cider is certainly something special. It's a pity that there's none left."

"Oh, I still have one or two bottles tucked away," said George.

"Really? I wouldn't mind some, if you have any spare."

George smiled. "They're not for sale. I've only enough left to tide me over until the autumn."

"What a pity."

"How are you finding life at the mill?" George asked.

"Good. It has good vibes. We could perhaps do with a bit more space though. I don't suppose you'd like to rent out your half of the mill. We have other friends who would like to make use of the studio and, as I said, it has a very good atmosphere. Very good stimulation for producing good art."

"And what exactly do you do?"

"I sculpt. I do a little painting but sculpting is really my thing."

"It sounds interesting."

"Well come round and have a look if you like. I could always do with selling a few pieces. Bring a few bottles of your cider with you and I could always lower the prices a little."

George laughed.

She continued. "I understand you're a photographer. I saw some of the photographs you took of Vicky. They're very good."

"Thank you. How well do you know Vicky?"

"I met her at art college. In fact that's where we all met, Justin, Jonathan, Vicky and I. Vicky was studying photography. She wasn't much good though. But she was the most organised of all of us. I think she would have done better doing a business course. She makes a good model, though I never managed to get her to pose for me. You must explain how you managed it."

"Are she and Justin very close?"

She laughed. "Do I detect some jealousy?" She shook her head. "I'm afraid you've got it wrong. Justin and Jonathan are what might be called an item. I'm the one who's the odd one out."

"Oh ... I see."

"They've gone to a painting exhibition up in town. Come over this afternoon and, as I said, I'll show you some of my work, if you're interested."

"Yes. All right," replied George.

She smiled a last time. "I'll see you later then."

"Thank you," said George, "good-bye."

"Bye." She started on her way, walked a few paces and then called back, "And don't forget the cider!"

George continued his walk and as he walked he could not help thinking about her. She was certainly very attractive and very different to Vicky. He found himself wondering how she might photograph. It was then that he remembered that his camera equipment was still at The Pullet Inn. He immediately changed direction and set off towards Mucklesbury. As he walked his mood brightened. He was looking forward to meeting Linda again.

Two hours later, George had retrieved his camera equipment and had returned from his walk to The Pullet Inn. He made himself a snack of coffee and sandwiches and, was washing his plate and mug when there was once more a knock at his front door. He opened it and saw Vicky standing there.

"Hello, George," she said. Can I come in? I would like to talk to you for a moment."

"All right." He nodded his head and stood aside to let her pass. "Go through to the sitting room." He followed her there and she turned to face him. "Please sit down," he said. She sat on the sofa and he sat in an armchair facing her.

"I think there has been some misunderstanding," began Vicky. She was fidgeting with her fingers

"Yes," said George.

"I'm sorry. I was going to apologise last night but you ran away."

George shook his head. "I panicked. I wasn't prepared for it."

"I'm sorry too. I don't know how they got that idea. I don't know what to say."

"Well it's done now," he murmured. "There's nothing more to be said." Then he added, "Unless you thought I was proposing marriage to you."

"No, I didn't."

"Well, that's all right then. No harm done."

"Do you still accept my business proposal?" she asked.

George rested his hand on his chin. Finally he said, "Yes, all right then. I don't see why not. As long as it is just a business proposal."

"That's all it was, George, honestly."

He nodded in reply.

Vicky continued. "I'll draw up a contract, if you like."

"Fine."

She stood up. "I'll drop it round in a few days then."

"All right." George followed her to the front door

Outside, she turned and faced him. "I really am sorry, George."

"Let's forget it," George replied. "I'll see you in a few days."

"Yes, good-bye."

"Good-bye."

He watched her walk to the gate, her body straight and regal. The walk of the model she had become. She might have been on the cat walk. There was no car outside. She opened the gate and stepped out in the lane. Then without looking back, she set off in the direction of Gleefield Manor.

An hour later, he made his way across to the mill and knocked on the front door. He had his own key and it felt odd that he should be knocking at his own door. However, he was sure it was the correct thing to do. The door swung open with a flourish and there was Linda.

"Hello," she said breezily and noticed that he was holding a bottle of his cider. "Come in," she added and showed him into the main downstairs room, closing the door behind him.

"What do you think?" she asked.

The room was set out in an orderly fashion. Gone were the half-finished canvasses on easels, pallets of unused paint, discarded paint tubes and unfinished sculptures. Instead framed paintings adorned the walls, completed sculptures sat on plinths and each item was bathed by spotlights. The room had been freshly decorated and the walls painted white to show off the paintings. Everything was clean and tidy.

"It looks like you're going to have an exhibition," he remarked.

"That's right. We've decided to show people we can make this place pay its way. While Justin and Jonathan are at the exhibition in town, they're going to make contacts with collectors and artists, and advertise our work here. Hopefully people will drop by to view and we can sell some pieces. At the same time we'll try and tempt other artists to join us here. That is ... if you agree to allow us to use the whole mill."

George gazed around him and scanned the exhibits. "I've just been speaking to Vicky and I've agreed," he said.

Her eyes lit up. "That's really good! This calls for a celebration. I'll get some glasses." She disappeared leaving George to study the exhibits more closely. He walked over to the pictures first. There were some landscapes and two paintings of the mill. There was one nude and George recognised that it was Miranda Flit. He looked at the printed card beside the picture and to his surprise saw that it was by Tom Firkin who was described as 'A local Artist.'

"Your friend Tom's very good," said Linda, returning with two glass tumblers. "He also speaks very highly of you. We could exhibit some of your photographs if you like. I'm told there's one very good one of the mill. Would you like me to open the cider?"

"No, it's okay, I'll do it." He took a pocket knife from his trouser pocket, pulled the cork with corkscrew attachment, and filled both glasses which she held out to him. Then she handed him a glass, took the bottle from his hand and put it down on a small table.

"Cheers," she said and raised her drink towards him.

He raised his glass to hers and said, "Good health."

She took a sip of cider and sighed. "You know, this is really good stuff."

He nodded in reply and looked around him once more. "Which of this work is yours?" he asked.

"All of the sculpture and those two paintings over there." She pointed to the pictures of the mill.

George walked over to the paintings. One was a close-up of the mill with the River Muckle behind it. The other was a view from across the river, with the river in the foreground; the mill still dominated but in the distance, to the left of the building, was his cottage with the orchard behind it. "I like this one," he said indicating the latter picture.

"It's yours."

George raised his eyebrows in surprise, then bent and looked at the card beside the picture. "But it says here it's worth five hundred pounds."

She shrugged. "Art is something it's very difficult to price. It is your mill after all, without it there would be no picture."

"It's now only really half my mill."

"Let me live in your half of the mill and knock off some rent."

He thought for a while and then said, "I'm not sure that makes good business."

"You can always sell the picture."

He looked at it once more. "All right," he said, "done."

He walked over to one of the sculptures. "Where exactly are you living in the mill now?" he asked

"In Vicky's flat. I have one bedroom, Jonathan and Justin the other. It's not a very big flat."

"I know."

He looked down at the sculpture, which was on a low plinth raised just above the floor. It was hewn out of stone and was smooth and polished. It was circular in form and looked as though it had scales and a tail. The card next to it read 'MillFish'.

"What's a Millfish?" He asked.

"What do you want it to be?" she asked.

"I'm afraid that's beyond me," he said and looked at the card again. "Gosh, you're asking three thousand for it."

"It took a long time to complete." She moved closer to him and said, "If what I heard said of you is true then I don't think interpreting the meaning of a piece of art is beyond you."

They were now standing only a few inches apart. George began to feel uncomfortable. "What do you mean by that?" he asked.

"I hear your photographs are very good. Your cider is certainly excellent. You don't really care about making money. And you care about the mill. All that leads me to think you're a very sensitive and imaginative man. I had been looking forward to meeting you. I think you can help me with my work."

"In what way?"

"You share similar feelings to this place as I do. I'm sure we could work well together."

George drained his glass and moved away. "Doing what exactly?"

"Why, me with my sculpting and painting and you with your photography and cider making."

"Cider making. Is that really an art form?" he asked.

"Your cider certainly is."

"I've already made one business contract with Vicky. I'm not sure I'm in a position to make another."

"You'll think about it though?"

"Yes, I'll think about it." He walked over to another sculpture. It was another abstract form in smooth stone. The card read simply 'Mind' and listed the price as two thousand pounds. "I'll be interested to see if you sell any of these," he remarked.

"Come to the exhibition when it opens and you'll see."

"Thanks", said George, "I will."

CHAPTER 11

The lane outside the mill was lined with parked cars. George regarded them ruefully as he made his way along his garden path. It was two weeks after his meeting with Linda and he was on his way to the exhibition at the mill. He showed his invitation to a man at the door and was ushered inside. The main downstairs room was crowded. People were milling around the exhibits and talking loudly. Someone thrust a glass of champagne into his hand. It was Sebastian.

"Glad you could make it, dear hart," he said and before George could reply he had disappeared back into the heaving crowd from which he had merged, clutching a champagne bottle and looking for more glasses.

George took a sip of the fizzy straw-coloured liquid, grimaced at its taste and left it on a side table. He edged towards the far wall in an effort to get a glimpse at one of the exhibits. He found himself in front of Tom's nude painting of Miranda Flit and looked for a price tag. There was none.

"What do yer think, George?"

He turned at the sound of the voice. "It's ... er ... very detailed, Tom," George replied.

"Arr, it be that," said Tom. "She be a fine figure of a woman, Miranda."

"I can see that. There doesn't appear to be a price tag."

"That's cause it tain't fer sale. It be my best picture of 'er. I couldn't sell 'er. Justin asked if 'e could exhibit 'er. 'E said it would do good to show an example of all the work done at the mill. I've 'ad quite a few offers for 'er though."

"How much?"

He puffed his chest out. "As much as eight thousand."

"Eight thousand pounds!"

"Naw. Eight thousand dollars. American dollars."

"That's still a lot of money."

Tom nodded sagely. "Yer," he agreed, "but I still can't sell 'er."

"Is Miranda here?"

"No. She fell out with Vicky and when she 'eard that Vicky was coming she decided to stay away."

"What did she fall out with Vicky over?"

"Some Yank, called 'Irem somebody, was going to offer Miranda a part in a film. 'E decided to offer it to Vicky instead."

"And she accepted?"

"Think so."

"Well, he might change his mind once he's seen this painting," George remarked.

"I don't think so. 'E barely glanced at it. 'E be upstairs with Vicky, Justin and Jonathan in the flat. They be 'aving a sort of party within a party. I was up there earlier but tain't the same with out Miranda. 'Spect you'd be wanting ter go up there too."

"Not especially."

"Vicky caused quite a stir when she arrived. Press photographers everywhere. She's a much bigger name in the modelling world now than Miranda. That's why she got the part I 'spect. I still prefers Miranda though."

"Hello, George."

George looked round to see Linda gliding towards him in a royal-blue blue one-piece trouser suit.

"I'm glad you could make it," she said and then turning to Tom said, "Tom, there's been another offer for your painting. That Italian gentleman over there."

"'Ow much be 'e offering?"

"Ten thousand."

"Lira, I suppose," said George.

"No," said Linda, her eyes twinkling mischievously, "pounds."

"I'll go and talk ter 'im," said Tom, "I like's ter see their faces when I turns 'em down."

"Have you sold any pieces?" George asked Linda after he had gone.

"A few. The paintings of the mill proved most popular. I've sold both and also the 'MillFish'. But it's the work of your friend Tom who's proved the most popular. It's a pity he won't sell." She paused and shrugged her shoulders. "But perhaps he's simply trying to drive the price up," she added.

"Somehow, I doubt it," remarked George. Then he frowned. "I thought you promised one of those paintings of the mill to me."

"Oh, well you know how it is, an opportunity came up that was too good to miss. A girl has to live." She took his arm. "You must come upstairs with me, meet some people. Vicky's there."

George allowed himself to be led upstairs to the flat, which he entered to find Vicky, Uncle Oswald, Justin and the American known as Hiram in the sitting room. Vicky and Uncle Oswald were sitting on the sofa; Justin and Hiram were seated in armchairs. They were all holding glasses of champagne. The men got to their feet when Linda and George entered.

"Hello, everyone," said Linda. "George, I think you know Oswald Goodsake, Justin and of course Vicky. But do you know Hiram Cornslinger?" She indicated the portly American.

"I'm afraid not," said George. He offered his hand to the American and said, "How do you do?"

"Great," replied the American shaking the offered hand vigorously, "great to meet you. I heard a lot about you."

"Would you like some champagne?" asked Justin.

"Yes please," replied Linda. "George?"

"Yes, thanks," said George. Although he had not like the taste of the drink he had been offered earlier, he felt it expedient not to refuse.

Justin walked over to the side table where bottles and glasses were set out, took a bottle from an ice bucket and began pouring.

Hiram spoke to George. "I hear you're some photographer," he said.

"I hear you're a film maker," said George in reply.

"That's right. And Vicky here is gonna star in my latest movie. Howa about that? I've seen the photographs you've taken of her. I think you'll agree that she'll sure look swell on the big screen."

"I'm sure she will," said George.

"She's bound to," broke in Justin. "Here." He handed George and Linda their drinks.

"Good health," said George and took a sip of champagne. It tasted a good deal better than what was on offer downstairs. He nodded towards Vicky. "Congratulations, Vicky," he said.

Vicky stood up and walked over to him. "Thank you, George," she replied. "What do you think of the exhibition?"

He studied his drink. "I'm afraid it's not really my thing."

"It's a pity we didn't exhibit any of your photographs," added Vicky, "I'm sure they would have gone down well."

"It's that guy Firkin who's proved to be the biggest hit," remarked Hiram.

"I'm trying to get George to work with us at the mill," said Linda. "He could use the photographic equipment and also make his cider. We could turn it into a really good multi-art cum local craft centre."

"That sounds a good idea," said Vicky. "George, can I have a word with you in private a minute? Excuse us, everyone, will you? I must discuss some business with George. George, we'll go through into the kitchen."

He followed her through into the next room and she closed the door. She stood her back against it and he turned to face her. "Uncle Oswald is going to handle my business affairs while I'm away filming," she said, "I've left the details of the contract with him. I'm sure that's the best arrangement. I don't want there to be any more misunderstandings between us."

George nodded. "As you wish," he said.

"You seem to be getting along well with Linda," she remarked. "Things could work out well for you here. You'll be able to continue working at the mill and the mill will also bring in some income through us letting it out as an Art Centre."

"You seem to be getting on well with Hiram Cornslinger," said George. "Are you going to enjoy acting?"

"I don't know. But it must be more stimulating than modelling."

"I hope you'll be happy anyway," remarked George.

"Thank you. I hope you'll be happy too," said Vicky. There was an awkward silence for a few moments and then Vicky said, "Let's go through and join the others."

They went through to the living room to find that Tom had arrived there and was looking very pleased with himself.

"Guess what?" announced Linda. "Tom's sold his painting!"

"Who to?" asked George.

"The Eyetalian, Gersepi zomet," said Tom

"Giuseppe Spagoni," corrected Justin. "He made Tom an offer he couldn't refuse."

"Well done, Tom," said Vicky.

"I wonder if he might commission me to do a sculpture of Miranda," murmured Linda. "I'll go and find him. Excuse me, everyone." She left the room hurriedly.

"Say, Vicky, how about Tom doing a painting of you?" said Hiram. "I could pay for it. I'm sure it'll be a knock out."

"I don't think so, Hiram," replied Vicky coldly.

Hiram cleared his throat. "I don' mean a nude," he said. "I mean a portrait. Something tasteful, like those photographs George took of you."

"I'd still rather not," said Vicky.

"You can always paint me, Tom," broke in Justin. "I'd love to pose for you."

"Er ... thanks," said Tom, "but I be wanting ter concentrate on my animal drawings. The picture of Miranda was a one off 'cause we've bin getting on well together. Yer should see George's wildlife photos: they be zomet to behold."

"I would certainly like to see them, George," said Vicky.

"They're at the cottage and mostly thirty-five millimetre transparencies," said George. "You'd need a projector and screen to view them properly."

"I'd like to see them too," said Uncle Oswald. "There's a market for good wildlife pictures. They could be profitable."

"Let's have a slide show!" cried Justin. "We must have a slide projector somewhere amongst our photographic equipment. We could hold it when everybody's gone home."

"Perhaps another time," said George. "I'll need to sort them out first."

"Well let me know when," said Uncle Oswald. "There could be money to be made there."

"Let me know too," said Hiram. "I'm always interested where money's concerned. "'Ain't that right, Honey?" he added turning to Vicky.

Vicky ignored the question. "I'd like to see them," she said, "because I know they'd be good pictures."

One morning a few days later, George opened the door to the mill and stepped inside. He found Linda in the part of the main room where he kept his cider press. She was working on a large slab of marble, hammer and chisel in hand; in front of her, bathed by light coming from one of two small windows high up on the wall, stood a naked Miranda.

Georges's face reddened. "I'm extremely sorry," he said and turned to go.

"Don't mind me, ducks," laughed Miranda. "You can stay if you want to."

"No, it's okay," said George. "I'll come back later."

"No, stay," said Linda. "It's time Miranda took a break anyway. Would you like some coffee?"

"Well ... I..." began George.

"I prefers tea meself," said Miranda slipping on a blue silk dressing gown. "Justin's got some up in the flat. I'll see you in a bit, Linda, if that's okay?"

"Yes, of course," replied Linda

"Ta, ta, George," Miranda added with another giggle and made her exit.

Linda walked over to a sideboard on which were a filtered coffee maker, some mugs and a half-full bottle of milk. "Would you like some coffee, George?" she asked. "As you can see, I'm having some."

"Yes, thank you."

"Do you take milk? I'm afraid I've no sugar."

"Milk and no sugar will be fine."

He watched while she poured the coffee and added milk to both cups. "Sit down," she said.

The room was devoid of seats save for two wooden stools. George perched on one of them. Linda handed him his coffee and then sat on the other, holding her mug in her hand. "I got my commission from Giuseppe Spagoni," she said.

"So I see."

"He wants a marble statue of her to put in the garden of his villa by Lake Como. He said it would complement the painting of her he will hang inside. I think he's become besotted with Miranda."

"So has Tom."

"Oh, I don't think so. Superficially maybe, but I think Tom is and very much down to earth. It shows in his paintings."

"Maybe. But I've known Tom a long time and I've never known him to paint a picture of anything other than a pheasant, fox or rabbit. I hope he doesn't get hurt."

"I don't think so. He's pretty level headed. Would it surprise you to know that he says the same thing about you and Vicky?"

"There's nothing between me and Vicky."

"And he says the same thing about himself and Miranda. He also says you're quite a painter yourself and that you and he used to go on sketching expeditions together. You've kept that very quite."

"It's only a hobby. It doesn't compare with your work. You do it for a living. Besides I spend most of my time behind a camera now."

"Tom says you've done a painting of the mill which knocks spots off the two I've done."

"Tom's exaggerated. They don't compare. My painting is just a bit of dabbling I do in my spare time. That was a while ago anyway."

"You're too kind to me, George. I'm well aware of my limitations as a painter. Sculpturing's my thing. I painted those pictures of the mill as I'm quite taken with the setting here. Jonathan persuaded me to put them in the exhibition against my better judgement simply because he hasn't produced much material himself and we were all getting short of money. I would certainly like to see your paintings. They probably explain why your photographs are so good. I'd particularly like to see the one you've done of the mill."

"They're just watercolours. Nothing very special."

"Where are they?"

"They're in the loft in my cottage. When I heard a lot of artists were descending on the mill I got them out of the way. I didn't want them to be shown up."

"You've never shown them to Vicky?"

"No point. She only seemed interested in photography."

"Well I'm interested. Can we go and see them now?"

He shrugged. "If you like," he said. "As I said, they're nothing really special. I hope you won't be disappointed."

"I'm sure I won't be," she replied. "Come on, let's go."

"Can I finish my coffee first?"

"All right but be quick."

A few minutes later they were standing in the loft at George's Cottage. Light was allowed in through a dormer window. Paintings were stacked around the walls. In the middle of the room was an easel on which stood an unfinished landscape. By the easel was a chair and a table on which were palettes of paint.

"You used this as a studio?" asked Linda. "The mill would be much better."

"I used the mill to make my cider. I stored my fishing tackle there and sometimes I let people from the village store things there. Most of my painting is done out in the open air. I like landscapes, you see, and the odd painting of animals. But it's Tom who's really the wildlife specialist. Though lately I've been trying to capture the odd creature on photograph. I never really thought of photography until Vicky showed up."

Linda went over to a stack of canvas leaning against the far wall. She picked them up one by one, set them down so that they rested against the foot of the easel and then stood back to look at them. George stood by the trap door and watched her.

"These are really very good," she remarked. "I told you I wouldn't be disappointed. Why, you've got enough here to mount an exhibition yourself."

"I really don't think so."

"Why not? They're good enough. Where's the painting of the mill?"

"It's downstairs. In the bedroom."

"Can I see it?"

"If you like."

He led her down the wooden steps and along the landing to his bedroom. The room was sparsely furnished. There was a single bed, a wardrobe and a small chest of draws. Over the bed was a souvenir tea towel on which was printed a recipe for making cider. The bedroom window looked out not on to the mill or the River Muckle, but the orchard.

"Very cosy," said Linda. She looked round the room. There beside the door, on the wall opposite the bed, was the painting of the mill. Linda stepped backwards into the room and alongside the bed in order to get a better look at it. The mill was pictured in the early morning light. Mist rose up and around it from the River Muckle. The painting shimmered with silver light. "It's magnificent," murmured Linda.

"Well, it is one of my better paintings," agreed George.

"I can see you like it," said Linda. "Otherwise why hang it in your own bedroom."

"You're right," said George, "I hang it there because I like it. But I'm hardly an art expert. I know what I like. And I also know I'm no professional artist."

"Well. I've been around painters and paintings myself long enough to know you've got talent. I think you should work with us at the mill. I know your paintings will sell. Just wait till the others see these."

"I'd rather not show them to anyone," said George. "And I'd rather not sell. It's a bit like my cider really. The things that I value most I'd rather not sell."

"You can't be serious. You could become quite well off."

"I'm quite well off now. The business arrangement I have with Vicky means that my share of the rent from the mill will be quite adequate for me to live on."

"But you could raise enough money to buy back your share of the mill from Vicky. You'd want that, wouldn't you?"

"She won't sell. I tried before when I made quite a bit of money from fashion photography. She just wouldn't sell."

"But why?"

"I've no idea, you'd have to ask her that."

She turned to the door. "You must be able to get a good view of the mill itself from the front bedroom window. Can I go and look?"

"If you like."

He followed her to the front bedroom. She looked out the window. "I thought so," she said, "you get a lovely view from here. I'm surprised you haven't chosen this room as your bedroom."

George did not want to tell her that indeed this room had been his bedroom and that he had looked out at the mill every morning when he woke up. But, with the mill now inhabited by others, he was saddened every time he looked out. In the end he moved to the back bedroom so that he could look out at his orchard. For, even though his cider had become very popular with his new neighbours, no one had so far sought to take it from him.

Linda turned from the window and looked around the room. A selection of the photographs he had taken of Vicky were on the walls, intermingled with photographs of mammals, birds, insects and wild flowers. On one wall were several rows of shelves containing magazine transparencies. Against another wall was a filing cabinet which he used for storing his negatives and contact prints.

"So," said Linda, "you've given up painting for photography."

"For the time being, yes. It's really Vicky who got me interested in photography."

Linda studied one photograph of Vicky, which was a black and white portrait. "This is really good," she remarked. "Have you ever thought of painting Vicky?"

"No."

"I don't really believe you." She turned back to him. "You ought to paint again, you know. There are many good amateur photographers. Not so many good painters."

"Perhaps I will," George replied. "However, I might take Oswald Goodsake's advice and sell some of my wildlife photographs."

Linda laughed. "What's happened to the man who said his work was too good to sell?"

"Oh," said George, "photographs are different. You only sell the prints and not the negatives and you can copy the transparencies."

"Well, I wish you luck," said Linda. "I hope you continue making your cider though."

"Don't worry about that. It's become quite a money-spinner."

"Well," said Linda. "It certainly is marvellous stuff and should help promote the mill. Speaking of which, I'm giving a talk at an art and crafts conference in a few weeks on the History of Sculpture. It might help promote of our work at the mill still further if you gave a talk too."

"Me? What could I talk on?"

"Oh, I don't know, your photography, painting. . ." She had a sudden thought and broke off. "I know! You could give a talk on cider making. Now that will go down really well, particularly if you took along a few bottles as samples for tasting."

"I don't know," said George hurriedly. "I've never done anything like that before. I'm not sure I'd be very good at it."

"Oh, I'm sure you would be. Now, you'd need some visual aids. Your photography could come in handy there. You could take photographs of the cider press, or equipment, your orchard and of course the mill itself. I could help you."

"I'm not sure."

"Go on. Think how it would impress people like your aunt and Vicky. They will see that you are trying to make a go of the mill as a business enterprise. I'm sure it will be successful."

George thought for a while, remembering how his aunt had said that he had never done anything useful with his life. "All right," he said. "I will."

"Good!" She drew closer to him and looked deeper into his eyes. "But I do wish you'd come and paint with us at the mill as well, and then you'll really become part of the Art Centre."

"Perhaps I will," he replied. "Perhaps I will."

CHAPTER 12

The Frog and Compass was the largest hotel in Tidburn. It was also the grandest, and therefore the preferred venue for many business conferences in the region. Thus it came as no surprise to George when he learned it was to be the setting for the arts and crafts conference mentioned by Linda. He had spent many a long hour, with Linda's help, preparing for the talk he was about to give and he hoped, despite all the misgivings and nervousness he felt, that he was ready.

The conference was to last two days, starting at two p.m. on the first day and ending at one p.m. on the second day. Even though the hotel was in easy daily travelling distance, Linda had suggested that he book in with the rest of the delegates. She explained that the most important business contacts were made at the dinner that had been arranged for the evening on the first day and in the hotel bars before and after dinner. Consequently, he found himself standing at the reception desk, suitcase in hand.

"Can I help you, sir?" asked the thin spotty-faced youth behind the counter.

"Yes, I'm here for the conference," he replied.

"Yes, sir. Can I have your name please?"

"George Cogrill."

The youth opened a folder on the desk in front of him and studied a list of names. "Yes, sir," he said. "You're booked in room 201. Do you have a car?"

"No."

"Fine, thank you, sir. Here's your key. Have a pleasant stay."

George took the lift to the second floor and found his room. It had two single beds, a television and en suite bathroom. He unpacked his suitcase and found the conference programme. It stated that there would be lunch at one o'clock. He looked at his watch. It was twelve thirty so he went downstairs to the bar, where he found Linda.

She was wearing an ankle-length maroon dress. A gold chain hung round her neck and for the first time George noticed she was wearing make-up. Above her left breast she wore a badge that bore the legend 'Linda Quilt, Mucklesbury Mill Art and Crafts Centre.' She saw George and came over to him. She was carrying a glass of white wine and a small back handbag.

"Hello, George," she said. "All booked in?"

"Yes, thank you."

"I've got you a name badge. You'd better put it on." She put the glass down, opened her bag, took out the badge and gave it to him. It read 'George Cogrill' and like hers the words 'Mucklesbury Mill Art and Crafts Centre' were added underneath.

George fastened it to the lapel of his jacket. "Thank you," he said.

"Can I get you a drink?" she asked.

"No, thank you," he said. "Perhaps later, after lunch."

"Come on," she said, "I'll introduce you around."

She led him over to a group of six people who were standing holding drinks and engaged in conversation. One of them was a large grey-haired woman in a grey suit and white blouse. Linda accosted her. "Excuse me, Marion," she said. "This is George Cogrill."

Marion turned to see George and stuck out her hand. "Hello, Mr Cogrill!" she said. "Good of you to agree to talk."

George shook her hand and noticed her badge which read 'Marion Tippleberry. Conference Secretary'. "Pleased to meet you," he said.

"Now just let me know if there is anything you need. According to the timetable you are due to talk first thing tomorrow morning. And you, Linda dear, are giving the last talk this afternoon. Can I get you a drink, Mr Cogrill?"

"No, thank you."

"Well, we'll be having lunch in a moment. Excuse me a moment, there's someone over there I must have a word with." She departed to buttonhole an elderly woman on the far side of the room.

"Hello, George!" George looked round to see Uncle Oswald approaching him with Sebastian in tow.

"Hello," said George. "I didn't know you'd be here."

"Well, Sebastian and I wanted to look in to see if we could pick up some business. We won't be going to all the talks but we we're especially interested to see yours and Linda's."

"I'm flattered," said George.

"Well, we've put in an effort ourselves into developing the business potential of the mill," Uncle Oswald continued. "We'd like to keep an eye on things."

"Quite," added Sebastian.

"I hope you won't be disappointed," said George.

"Oh, I'm sure we won't be," said Uncle Oswald. "I'm sure the cider will definitely be a hit. How many bottles did you bring, by the way?"

"Tom was going to drop off a case of twelve bottles in his van earlier this morning," replied George, "which reminds me, I'd better check that he remembered and that they've been stored safely. Excuse me."

He set off in the direction of the reception desk where he was informed that the bottles had indeed arrived and that they had been stored in one of the kitchen pantries awaiting his instructions. George thanked the receptionist and asked that they be set out on tables at the back of the conference room the following morning. He turned back to the bar just in time to hear Marion Tippleberry announce that lunch was about to be served, so he followed the rest of the delegates into the dining room and he sat down at a table next to Linda.

George found the afternoon a mixed blessing. The programme began with a lecture on pottery from a middle-aged woman from Leicestershire. She was obviously very much an enthusiast, and had a great deal of practical experience, but George found she went in to too much detail and tended to over-elaborate. Next came a talk on wood carving from an elderly gentleman from Norfolk. He'd brought along a number of examples of his own work but his voice was dull and, even with the hotel-supplied amplification system, could hardly be heard. This was followed by a twenty-minute break for tea and then a talk on embroidery by a thin, very nervous, bespectacled, tawny-headed girl in her early twenties. Again she provided samples of her own work and those of the students at the technical college where she taught, but her lecture was so disjointed George could scarcely follow it. Then Linda delivered the final lecture of the day. It was excellent and by comparison the previous talks paled into insignificance.

Her visual aids were particularly well thought out. She included many slides to illustrate sculpture from ancient times, such as that of the fertility goddess known as the 'Venus of Willendorf', to the modern work of Henry Moore. She also included samples of her own work, done at the mill, and gave a brief but vivid description of a sculptor's life at the mill. The audience, including George, were entranced.

When she finished, and the chairman had closed the conference for the day, George went to congratulate her. "That was really good, Linda," he said.

"Thank you," she replied. "You know, no matter how many times I've given that talk, I still get the jitters. I'm sure that your talk will go equally well tomorrow."

"I hope so."

"It will, George. Don't worry."

He helped her pack away her exhibits into boxes and carry them up to her room. It was numbered 202 and next door to his. "Thank you," she said as he put them down on the floor next to the wardrobe. "Jonathan is going to pick them up for me tomorrow morning. I'm going to have a bath now and freshen up. I'll meet you downstairs in the bar at half past seven for a drink before dinner, if that's okay?"

"Fine," he replied. "I'll see you then. I'm just next door by the way."

"I know. I booked the rooms."

George went next door to his room, undressed, showered, changed into his best suit and put on his best black leather shoes. Then he went down to the bar where the first person he met was the man who had spoken on wood carving. The man had been wearing a smart navy-blue jacket, grey slacks and a blue and white striped tie for his talk. Now he was dressed in a pale blue sweatshirt and denim jeans and was wearing white running shoes.

He saw the look on George's face and said, "We usually dress down for dinner."

George retraced his steps and emerged again ten minutes later, this time dressed in a blue cotton shirt, green pullover, blue corduroy trousers and brown suede shoes. At the bar he met Linda who was wearing a plain black, high-necked, long-sleeved dress, cut to mid thigh, black nylon tights and black high-heeled shoes. The same gold chain that she had worn earlier hung from around her neck. He swallowed hard at the sight of so much leg and tried in vein not to gaze at them.

"I've just got here," she said. "Can I get you a drink?"

"Let me get you one," he said, his eyes snapping up from the hem of her dress to the bar. "What would you like?"

"A dry white wine, please."

George caught the barman's eye, ordered the wine and a single neat Scotch whisky for himself. He hoped the strong spirit would help soothe his nerves and help him to appear more nonchalant. He returned with the drinks in either hand to find Linda talking to the pottery woman from Leicestershire.

"Hello, George," said Linda. Have you met Margaret Dibble?"

"No," he replied adding politely, "but I enjoyed your talk." He handed Linda her glass of wine and shook her hand.

"You're too kind, Mr Cogrill," she said, reading the name badge which he had remembered to transfer to his pullover. "Linda's talk was excellent. I was just telling her. I'm looking forward very much to hearing you talk tomorrow."

George shifted his feet nervously.

"I think they're just going into dinner now," said Linda. "Shall we go through? We can take our drinks with us."

The conference delegates were split up amongst a dozen tables in the restaurant. George sat next to Linda at a table with Margaret Dibble, the wood carver, the embroidery speaker and Marion Tippleberry.

"We like to keep our speakers together, to make sure they are looked after properly," explained Marion. "I'm not certain if the cider in this establishment is up to your standard though, George," she added with a cheeky grin.

"I think we'll stick to wine with our meal," said Linda.

"Yes," agreed George. "We'll probably tire of cider after tomorrow."

"Oh, I do hope not," said Margaret Dibble. "I've heard remarkable things about your cider. I'm dying to try it."

They ordered two bottles of house red and two bottles of house white wine to go with the meal, the main course of which consisted of a choice between roast chicken, roast beef or a vegetarian pie. The waitress service was very slow so that the meal took an hour and a half. When it was over George and Linda returned to the bar. There George ordered a glass of white wine for Linda and half a pint of cider for himself. Then they found themselves a small table by the window and sat down, George trying hard not to glance at her legs.

"I didn't see Uncle Oswald or Sebastian in the restaurant," he remarked.

"They're not officially part of the conference," Linda explained. "I think they just called in to keep a check on their business interests." She sipped her wine and then added. "You know I don't really trust those two. They seem too much concerned with the money side of the Arts Centre for my liking. You know that he's not really Vicky's uncle, don't you?

"I know. But she's always referred to him as her uncle so I tend to think of him as Uncle Oswald too. I think he's an old friend of her father's."

"I still don't trust him," said Linda, "and I've always found Sebastian rather shifty. I'm glad they didn't stay for the meal. I see you're trying the house cider. How does it compare with your own?"

He grimaced. "Terrible," he said. "It's not local – it's probably made in France from imported apple juice. I thought I'd try it just in case I get asked about it tomorrow."

"Can I try some?"

He passed her his glass and she took a sip. "You're right," she said. "It's terrible. It doesn't compare with yours."

"Hello, you two!"

They looked up and saw Marion Tippleberry bearing down on them. "Are you going to join in the country dancing?"

"Country dancing?" queried George.

"Yes," she continued. "There's country dancing in the ballroom. It's been laid on for us especially. "You'll join in, won't you, Linda?"

"Yes," said Linda brightly, "rather!"

"Good. We'll see you both inside in a few minutes then." She drifted away to approach some more delegates who were seated at a neighbouring table.

Linda bent her head forward towards George. "Damn," she whispered. "I'd forgotten about that. I'm wearing the wrong sort of shoes. I'd better go and change into some flat heels." George's eyes followed the seductive legs as she rose and stepped across the floor. This time he was confident she would not notice as her back was towards him.

He waited at the table for her return which she did ten minutes later, still wearing the same short black dress and black tights but her shoes now changed to dark blue flat-heeled pumps. The sound of wild folk music was emanating from the ballroom. Linda looked at George and smiled. He rose from his seat and they went into the ballroom together.

"Oh no," said George.

"What's the matter?" she asked.

"You see that man over there playing the fiddle?" George indicated a gangling thirty-year-old, with long thin hair hanging down to his shoulders, clad in a blue denim shirt and dark blue jeans in the centre of the stage at the far end of the room. "That's Jimmy Thropp."

Linda grimaced. "He and his friends are making a terrible noise," she said.

"Well," said George, "he's never been any good at the best of times." He indicated the ensemble who accompanied Thropp, a very short man on concertina, and two men on guitars, one extremely fat and one exceedingly thin. All were scruffy and very hairy. "That's his group, 'The Turnip Thumpers'. They're well known around

Mucklesbury and have been banned from more dance halls than anyone cares to remember. I wonder how they managed to obtain a booking here. I thought they had been banished from Tidburn long ago."

"Well, they're certainly very lively," remarked Linda.

Marion Tippleberry appeared at George's elbow. "Good, aren't they?" she enthused. "I think we were lucky to get them at short notice. Come on now, join in!" Then George watched with amazement as she marched across the dance floor, mounted the stage and announced to everyone that she was to act as dance 'Caller'. But both he and Linda dutifully took to the dance floor and joined in.

As the evening progressed, so did their drinking. George could not bear to drink any more of the cider, but to help shield him from the torment of the music he began drinking neat Scotch. Meanwhile, Linda had moved from wine to neat gin. The strong alcohol helped fuel their energy for the dance and enabled them not to care that the music was not always in tune.

Two hours later, Linda sagged exhausted against him. "I think I'd liketh you to taketh me to my room pleath," she said, her speech now very slurred.

Ten minutes later they stood swaying together outside the door to room 201. "Thankth you ver' much," slurred Linda. "Would you like to come in?"

George shook his head.

"I thaw you looking at my legs. Am I not beautiful?"

He could not reply. He felt ashamed that he had been caught out

She sighed. "Ith Vicky you really want, isthn't it?"

George remained silent. The reason being he failed to understand why he was hesitating. It could not be because of Vicky. He had not wanted marry her.

"She ith a lucky girl. Goo' nigh', George."

Linda opened her handbag and began to search for her key. George put his hand in his own pocket, found his own key and opened the door. "Oh," she said. "Is thith your room? Never mind, thith will do." She went inside, threw herself down on one of the single beds and was instantly asleep.

George closed the door and looked down at her. The dress had risen up, exposing more slender thigh, sheathed in silky black. If it had been Tom here instead, he would not have hesitated. George shook his head undressed, put on his pyjamas and got in the other bed. He tried to imagine Linda's legs circling his waist. Then Vicky's face came into his mind. Her golden hair framed in hasleblad's lens, shining in the morning sun against the bank of the Muckle when he first photographed her. Soon he too was asleep.

It was quarter past nine the next morning and there was a loud knocking at the door. "Mr Cogrill!" It was the voice of Marion Tippleberry. "Mr Cogrill! Are you there? You were due to begin your lecture fifteen minutes ago!"

George turned over in his bed. The other bed was rumpled but empty. There was no sign of Linda. "Oh gosh!" he exclaimed. "I am extremely sorry!"

"We've had to completely reorganise the schedule!" continued Marion through the door. "Mr Stimmings is giving his lecture on dry stone walling now. Your talk will have to take place later. Are you all right?"

"Yes!" he called. "I really am very sorry. I'll be down in a few moments!"

"Do try not to be too long!

He rolled out of bed. His head felt muzzy, his mouth dry and his stomach queasy. He went into the bathroom. Someone had been sick in the toilet. He could not remember feeling ill himself so he guessed it had been Linda and that she must have returned to her room soon after. He flushed the bowl and drank two glasses of water. The sight of his white face and bloodshot eyes in the mirror gave him a start. He did not look or feel at all well. He doused his head with cold water then hastily washed, shaved, dressed, gathered together the materials required for his lecture and hurried down to the conference room.

The lecture was a disaster. Everything that could go wrong did go wrong. The transparency slides were in the wrong order, the slide projector broke down, the projection screen collapsed, he knocked the microphone stand over and he lost his place in his notes at least twice. When his ordeal finally drew to a close, the audience politely applauded and he made his way to the back of the room to sit by Linda, who had come into the room half way through. The saving grace was that his talk had been put to the end of the agenda and many of the delegates had gone. Marion Tippleberry gave a short speech announcing the end of the conference and wished the remaining delegates a safe journey home. She forgot to mention that George had brought along some samples of his cider, which were set out as he requested on the table at the end of the room.

The delegates began to file out and George turned to Linda. "It was a disaster," he said.

She looked at him, her face as pale and sickly as his own. "Better luck next time," she said.

"No," he replied firmly. "Never again!"

CHAPTER 13

It was now October and George was in a window seat aboard a jumbo jet en route to Los Angeles in the United States of America. In the intervening months he had settled down again to a simple life of painting, fishing plus his newly found passion, photography. He found working alongside Linda and Jonathan at the mill enjoyable, although he still felt some resentment at having to share what he had hitherto regarded as his mill with other people. A poet called Frank Witterworth from Tidburn had joined the group and everyone lent a hand when the time came to harvest his apples and make his cider. It was then that the air ticket had arrived from Vicky along with an invitation to attend the première of her first film in Hollywood. At first George was reluctant to go. But the others persuaded him. After all, he was still her partner. Now he was aboard the plane and sitting next to a film cameraman from Peterborough.

"I'm on my way to California to film a commercial for English beer," the cameraman was saying. "I know it sounds strange but the weather is more dependable there than in England."

"What brand is it?" asked George.

"I've no idea. I'm freelance, I don't do this job regularly. I just received a call to fly to Los Angeles, all expenses paid and here I am. I'll do a couple days shooting and then return directly to England. I've no idea of the brand of beer."

"I don't drink beer much myself," said George, "I prefer cider."

"I like the odd glass of cider myself," said his companion. "I tasted some the other day that was simply beautiful. Apparently it's very hard to get hold of. It's called Cogrill's Something, ever heard of it?"

"Do you mean Cogrill's Old Mill Cider?" asked George incredulously.

"That's it! Great stuff, isn't it?"

"I'm George Cogrill. It's my cider. I make it."

"Really? I'm pleased to meet you, George." He stuck out his hand. "I'm Simon Clitterbooth."

George shook the offered hand. "Please to meet you, Mr Clitterbooth."

"Please call me, Simon. I'd certainly be glad if you could tell me where I could get some more of your cider."

"It's not produced on a large scale," explained George. "I make it from apples grown from a small orchard near where I live. The cider is pressed in an old water mill, hence the name. It is very much a home enterprise."

"Well, you should expand. Where is this old mill?"

"Mucklesbury, which is a small village near Tidburn."

"I've heard of it. Isn't there a small Arts Centre down there?"

"That's right. That's in the mill too."

"Cogrill ..." said Simon allowed to himself, "George Gogrill ..."He turned to look at George. "There's a photographer called George Cogrill, took those photographs of the model Victoria Gloam. Is that you as well?"

"That's right."

"I must admit I didn't make the connection between the cider and the photographer. I've admired the photographs of yours I've seen, George. That must be some set-up you've got down there."

"It certainly is," said George, pleased at the compliments that had been bestowed on him. "You must visit us sometime."

The airliner landed at Los Angeles airport at midday. George joined the throng of passengers queuing at passport and then baggage control. He became separated from Simon Clitterbooth in the crowd so that when he emerged onto the pavement outside the terminal he was on his own. Vicky had written in the letter that he would be met at the airport and so he looked up and down the street in search of a familiar face.

"Hi, George!"

He looked in the direction of the voice and saw Hiram Cornslinger coming towards him. "Oh hello, Hiram," he said. "Where's Vicky?"

"She couldn't make it." He stuck out his hand and added, "How're you doing, George? Had a good flight?"

George shook the proffered hand. "Yes, thank you. How are you? How's Vicky?"

"Oh, we're all fine." He indicated George's suitcase. "Is that all yah luggage?"

"That's right."

"You gotta tux in there?"

"A tux?"

"Yeah, a tuxedo. What I believe you limeys call an evening suit?"

"Uh, no."

"Never mind. We'll sort yah out later. Come on the car's waiting." Hiram led him along the street to a blue Toyota. Behind the wheel sat a thin fair-haired youth of about eighteen. "This is my son, Sandy. Sandy, stow George's case in the trunk."

"Sure, Dad." Sandy got out, took the case and went to the rear of the car.

"Sandy is my son by my first wife," explained Hiram. "You'd better ride in front," he said to George, indicating the passenger seat.

George did as he was told and, as Hiram squeezed into the driver's seat beside him, found himself wondering how many wives Hiram had. Sandy finished attending to the luggage and got in behind them.

"This your first visit to LA?" asked Hiram as he swung the car out into a line of busy traffic.

"Yes."

"Good. We've got plenty of time to kill so we thought we'd take yah to look at Beverly Hills. Where all the movie stars live. You'd like that, wouldn't yah?"

"Well ..."

"Good. Lovely day, isn't it? There's usually a lot of smog about but today it's clear and sunny. Hell, we've even got blue sky."

The drive around Beverly Hills did not take long. As they drove Hiram explained who lived in which house. But George was bored and unimpressed. Looking at the outside of large houses was not his idea of an enthralling pastime.

"I know," said Hiram, "let's look round Viscount Studios!"

"Yeah, Dad," agreed Sandy. "We haven't been there fer ages."

"Is that where Vicky is?" asked George.

"Naw," Hiram replied, "Vicky's film is made by Silverseal Studios. Viscount is much larger and does guided tours. It'll be good fun."

And good fun it was. The three of them took a tour which led them through and around old film sets. They saw demonstrations given by stunt men and animal trainers, and demonstrations of special effects. George was entranced and enthralled. He was even more amazed by the antics of the audiences in which he sat at the various demonstrations. They all seemed eager to take part when calls for volunteers were made by the demonstrators and jumped up and shouted in an effort to attract their attention. George was quite certain that such antics would never occur if the displays took place in England in front of an English audience.

At four o'clock they left and drove to a gentleman's outfitters that Hiram knew. There George hired an evening suit. At half past five they dropped him, his luggage and a carrier containing the evening suit at his hotel.

"I'll pick yah up at eight to take yah to the première," said Hiram. "Don't eat too much beforehand as there's a party afterwards and there's bound to be a lot of food." The car pulled away leaving George standing alone outside the entrance to the foyer.

He registered at the reception desk and made his way to his room, which he found lavishly furnished. It contained twin beds and an en suite bathroom. He showered and dressed himself in the evening suit. He was now very hungry. It was half past six o'clock and apart from airline food had not eaten properly since he had left England approximately eight hours previously. Remembering Hiram's advice he decided not to frequent the restaurant and made his way out of the hotel to a pizza parlour a few yards down the road. There he ordered a small pizza and a glass of red wine. As he ate he felt suddenly very tired. He had never been to America before and had been so excited by his trip that he had not slept on the plane. Now, lack of sleep and jet lag caught up with him. He finished his meal and ordered some coffee.

"Would you like cream with your coffee?" inquired the waitress.

"No, thank you. I'd like milk, please?"

To his surprise the waitress looked puzzled. "Milk?" she asked.

"Yes please."

A few minutes later she returned with a cup and a pot of black coffee. "I'm afraid we have no milk," she said.

George was surprised but said, "No matter, I'll have cream then."

She returned with a small sachet and tiny plastic carton, placed them in front of George and then left. George looked at the plastic carton. To his surprise it was labelled 'Milk'. Oh well, he thought to himself, I'll have the cream.

He opened the sachet and tipped it into his coffee. Out fell a small soapy paper towelette. George was tired and confused. He fished out the towelette. What should he do now, order more coffee or drink the soapy coffee? He drank the soapy coffee.

He paid the bill and returned to the hotel. He had barely got to his room when the telephone on the table at the side of one of the beds rang. The voice at the end of the line informed him that Mr Cornslinger was waiting for him downstairs.

He found Hiram in the hotel lobby. He was alone. "Hello, Hiram," said George in greeting. "Where's Vicky?"

"Aw, she'll be going separately. Stars have got to make an entrance, you know. She'll be going with Clayburger."

"Who?"

"Her co-star, Cliff Clayburger. Come on, I've gotta limo waiting outside for us."

George accompanied him outside to the longest automobile he had ever seen. It was black, so too were its windows. A uniformed driver was holding a door open for them. George got in, followed by Hiram who seated himself by George's side. The car set off with only a light purring sound from the engine. Although no one could see in through the blackened windows, George could see out and had an excellent view of the neon-lit streets as they slid by in the gathering dusk.

"Would you like a drink?" asked Hiram indicating the cocktail cabinet in front of them.

"What is there?"

Hiram opened the cabinet. "Scotch, bourbon, cognac, beer," he said.

"I'll have some Scotch, please."

Hiram selected two glasses and poured the drinks from the same bottle. "Ice?" he inquired.

"No, thank you," said George picking up his glass and taking a sip. "This is good," he said.

"Nothing but the best malt," Hiram replied, opening a small freezer compartment in the cocktail cabinet, extracting some ice cubes and placing them in his glass. He raised it to George. "Cheers," he said.

They arrived at their destination, a plush cinema on the outskirts of Hollywood. A throng of press photographers was waiting for them. Uniformed security guards were holding the photographers back outside a cordon which they had formed between the curb and the cinema entrance. Flashlights exploded and the photographers jostled one another as they tried to get a better look.

"Who's that?" George heard one of them ask.

"That's Hiram Cornslinger," replied another.

"I don't mean him. I mean who's that with him?"

"I don't know," came the reply. "Hey, you! Who are you?"

"George Gogrill!" George called in reply.

"Who the hell's George Cogrill?"

"Aw, he's nobody," replied the second photographer, "save yah film."

George followed Hiram into the cinema.

Inside was full of bustle. George looked vainly for Vicky. Someone thrust a glass of champagne into his hand. He became overwhelmed by the noise and chatter. Hiram chatted amiably with everyone he met, introducing George as "Say, this is George, a friend of Vicky's from England." People nodded to George in reply and then resumed their conversations. Eventually they were led into the theatre. Everyone stood while the American national anthem was played. Then they settled down into their seats, the lights went out and the film titles came up on the screen. He saw the title *The English Girl* and then the words 'Starring Cliff Clayburger, Introducing Victoria Gloam.' However, it had been a long day and he was overcome with tiredness. So much so that even before the titles had faded, he was fast asleep.

He woke to the sound of applause and opened his eyes in time to see the credits roll. Then he followed Hiram back down to the foyer only to lose him in the crowd. He felt drained. He certainly did not feel like a party and so he quietly slunk out of the cinema, avoiding the waiting photographers. He walked a few yards down the street and then caught a taxi back to the hotel.

He awoke early next morning feeling much refreshed. It was seven o'clock. He showered, shaved and dressed. Then he made his way down via the lift to the restaurant for breakfast. He was very hungry. He seated himself at a small table in the centre of the room and a waitress approached him almost immediately.

"Good morning, sir. What can I get you?" she inquired.

George quickly glanced at the menu and cheered up. "I'll have the sausage, bacon and eggs," he said.

"How would you like your eggs?"

"What do you mean?" he asked, confused.

"Would you like them fried, boiled or scrambled?"

"Oh, I see, fried."

"Sunny side up, over easy, over hard?"

George was now very confused. "Er ... what do you recommend?"

"It's a matter of personal preference, sir."

"Is it? I see." He did not see but he was stalling for time. "How do you like your eggs?" he asked.

"Oh, I have mine over easy."

"Over easy sounds fine by me," he said.

"Would you like coffee?"

"Oh ... yes ... with cream, of course."

"Orange juice?"

"Yes please."

"Toast, English muffins?"

"Toast, please."

"Jam, marmalade?"

"Jam, please."

She brought him the coffee first and a jug of fresh milk. The meal arrived five minutes later and he inspected the eggs closely. They looked like normal fried eggs to him. However, the meal was delicious and he ate ravenously. The waitress approached him again carrying a pot of coffee. "Can I give you a warm up?" she asked.

"I beg your pardon?"

She indicated the coffee.

"Oh ... yes, thank you."

She poured more coffee into his cup and said, "Let me know if you want any more," and went on her way before he could thank her.

George was half way through his second cup of coffee when he saw a figure wearing a leather jacket, blue denim jeans, leather boots and carrying two crash helmets approach his table. For one horrible moment he thought it was his aunt, but then he saw it was Vicky.

"Hello, George," she said.

He stood up. "Hello, Vicky. Would you like to sit down?" She sat down and placed both crash helmets on the floor beside the chair. "Would you like some coffee?" he continued.

"No, thank you," she replied. "I missed seeing you at the film première last night," she added.

"I missed seeing you as well," he said.

"You didn't attend the party afterwards either."

"I was tired after my flight so I decided to go back to my hotel. How did it go?"

"Oh, it was fine. What did you think of the film?"

"Well ... er," began George hesitantly

Vicky cut in. "It's all right, you don't have to say anything. I know it's not very good. Have you read the reviews?"

"No."

"Well, the critics have slated it."

"I'm sorry."

"Don't be - I half expected it." Tears filled her eyes and she bowed her head. "I could have done with you out here, George, to advise me. I needed someone to tell me where I was going wrong. These last few months have been hell, they really have."

George stretched his hand out and put it on hers. "I'm sorry," he said again.

She lifted up her head and wiped away the tears with the back of her hand. "Anyway," she said, "that's all in the past. I just want to get away from everyone. Come with me, George."

"Now?"

"Yes."

She got up and picked up the two crash helmets, and he followed her out of the hotel. In the courtyard stood a 750 cc Honda motorcycle. She led him over to it and offered him one of the crash helmets and said, "Come for a ride with me, George."

He looked at the motorcycle. It had high curved handlebars, an upright American saddle with a back rest behind the passenger portion. There was an additional forward pair of foot rests so that the rider could lean back and put his or her feet up while cruising the freeway. Behind the rear seat were two large lockable panniers attached to a luggage rack.

"I didn't know you could ride a motorcycle," said George.

"I had lessons from your Aunt Jane when I stayed with her in England. I know that she won't approve as it's not a British bike but I'm afraid this is the only model I could find out here at short notice."

"Couldn't you at least find a Harley Davidson?"

"What's a Harley Davidson?"

"Never mind. Where do you plan on going?"

"I thought we'd go down the coast for a bit. I thought you might like to come with me but it's up to you really."

George looked down at the green sweater, blue cotton shirt, grey flannel trousers and brown suede shoes he was wearing. "But I'm not dressed for it," he said.

"We can stop off and get you kitted out on the way if you like. What do you say?"

"Are you sure you can handle that machine?"

"You'll just have to trust me, George."

George stood deliberating. Then said, "All right, but if you go too fast I'll insist you drop me at the nearest bus or train station so I can get back on my own."

"I can't go too fast, George. There's a fifty-five-mile-an-hour speed limit here. But I'll do as you say. I promise."

An hour later they were on the road. They stopped at a motorcycle shop that Vicky knew. There George acquired a leather jacket, boots and gloves. Then, with George wearing his new clothing, they set off once more. At first he held on tightly to Vicky's waist but as they rode further he relaxed more, eased his grip and allowed his body to flow with the movement of the motorcycle. Vicky too relaxed and once out on the freeway was able to put her feet up on the forward footrests. They made their way on to the coast road and rode southward with the rolling Pacific Ocean on their right-hand side.

At twelve o'clock they stopped at a modest diner by the side of the sea. Vicky had a small bag strapped to the petrol tank in front of her. There was a transparent pocket on top of the bag in which was inserted a map. She unclipped the bag from its harness and they took it into the restaurant with them. They ordered sandwiches and orange juice and spread the map out on the table in front of them.

"How do you feel?" asked Vicky.

"I'm fine," said George. "I'm really enjoying the ride."

"You're not just saying that, are you?"

"No, I really am enjoying myself. You're a careful driver. I used to ride behind my aunt when I was younger. It terrified me. She always rode much too fast. I manage to make excuses whenever she asks me to ride with her now."

"Your aunt told me that she gave you lessons too."

"Yes. And I passed my motorcycle driving test but the lanes are too small and windy around Mucklesbury. I prefer walking a lot more and there's never been a need for me to hurry anywhere."

"You can have a go at driving if you like. Have you got your licence with you?"

"Yes. Just in case I need to drive a car. But I'm happy to leave the driving to you."

They finished their meal and rode further south. Half an hour later they stopped at the State Park and found a quiet spot, not far from the ocean.

They left the helmets and leather jackets on the bike, walked down to the beach and stood looking at the sea.

"It's good to see you again, George," said Vicky. "I'm glad you came."

"It's nice to be here." he replied. "I always wanted to see Hollywood. Well now I have. I've enjoyed the ride too."

"Would you like to stay longer? I could show you around."

"I'm not so sure."

"It can be very beautiful here once you get away from the masses. Let's walk along the beach for a bit."

They walked along the edge of the water towards a rocky outcrop. "I hear it can get quite smoggy out here," said George.

"Yes it can. But I've not noticed any pollution in the sea. But there again I've not had much time to notice anything else other than my work."

"You found time to go zooming along the cost on that motorcycle though."

"I had to find some form of release. The pressure of working in the film industry can be enormous, believe me."

They walked on to the outcrop in silence. Once they got there George looked around amongst the rock pools for signs of pollution. He found none.

"What are you looking for?" she asked.

"Oh just crabs and shellfish. A boyhood habit, I'm afraid."

"Look, George, I've rented a beach house to live in while I've been working over here. It's not too far away. You cooked me dinner once. I'd like to return the compliment. I would also like to show you something."

He turned to look at her. "Show me what?"

"Come with me and see."

"All right."

They returned to the motorcycle, rode north and stopped at Vicky's beach house. It was made of white stone and had its own courtyard, enclosed by a high wall in which was set an iron gate. They dismounted. Vicky unlocked the gate and they pushed the motorcycle inside. She led George into the house and through to the living room. There was a small bar in the corner of the room and glass doors looked out on to a veranda and the sea.

"This is very nice," remarked George.

"It's been rented for me by the studio for the duration of the film. I have an option to keep it on. There's a maid who comes and cleans every day." She indicated the bar. "Make yourself a drink if you like and I'll go and see to the food."

She left him alone. He walked over to the bar and studied the bottles on the shelf but nothing took his fancy. Instead, he opened one of the glass doors, walked out on to the veranda and leant on the balcony admiring the view.

She joined him a few minutes later. "It'll be ready soon," she said, "I'm just warming it up in the microwave. I hope you like Mexican food. It's from a recipe my maid taught me. She's Mexican, you know." She followed his gaze. "Marvellous view, isn't it? We'll eat out here." She indicated the garden furniture set out on the veranda. Then she disappeared back inside and began ferrying items from the kitchen to the table on the veranda, refusing all his offers of help. Twenty minutes later they settled down to eat. The meal was chilli con carne, adorned by a green side salad. They washed the food down with red Californian wine.

They finished the meal and sat drinking the wine in silence. The sky was tinged with pink and the sun became red. The sky reddened as the sun sank into the water on the horizon. It disappeared from view and the sky where it had been burst into a fiery red glow that filled the entire horizon and spread upwards into the darkening sky. They watched in silence as the darkness slowly spread down from above, quenching the fire, putting out the red light so that darkness and starlight took its place.

"This is what I wanted to show you," she said.

"It was certainly spectacular."

"I wish you'd stay in California longer, George. The light and scenery are excellent for photography. That's why the film industry developed here."

"I'll think about it." He looked at his watch. "It's getting late. I'd better be getting back to the hotel. Would you like a hand with the washing up?"

She laughed. "I have a maid, George. She'll do that in the morning. You can stay the night if you like." She saw the look of uncertainty on his face and added, "I have a guest room. It's a long journey back. You're quite welcome to stay."

"All right. Thank you."

He retired to bed, to sleep alone in a luxurious guest room, and the next morning was woken by noises coming from the kitchen. He dressed and went downstairs. There he found the Mexican maid washing up the dirty dishes from the night before.

"Hello!" he called.

There was no reply.

He went through into the lounge and then out on the veranda. Vicky was sitting at the table drinking black coffee.

"Hello," she said, "would you like some breakfast?"

"Just coffee, please." He sat down and she poured him a separate cup.

"Help yourself to milk and sugar," she said.

He took the cup and stirred in the milk and sugar. "Vicky," he said, "I want to go home today."

She sipped her coffee and did not reply.

They sat for a while in silence. Then George said, "I hope you're not too disappointed I'm going. I did enjoy yesterday. It was great fun. Thank you very much for inviting me. It's just that I miss home."

She smiled. "I understand," she said. "You miss Mucklesbury and the mill. I've missed it too. I'm glad you came though. I'll take you to the airport and I'll contact Hiram and get him to go to the hotel and bring the rest of your stuff to the airport. Is that all right with you?"

"Yes. Thank you."

They sat and finished their coffee then went into the next room and Vicky telephoned Hiram.

"It's all fixed," she told him, "Hiram will meet us at the airport with your things. I've managed to book you a flight."

"Thank you. Look, I'm quite prepared to take a taxi."

"Nonsense. I'll give you a ride. Besides there are one or to things I need to discuss with Hiram. I'm glad you came, George. I'd like you to have this." She handed him a brown envelope.

"What is it?"

"It's the deeds to my half of the mill."

"But I can't pay you for it."

"It's a gift. I don't need the money. In fact I'm very well off now and it's been because of you and those first photographs you took. I also know how much the mill means to you."

George looked down at the envelope. "I don't know what to say," he said.

She came close to him and kissed him quickly on the lips. "Don't say anything. I owe you a lot, George."

"Well, thank you," he replied and put the envelope in the inside pocket of his leather jacket."

"Come on," she said turning hurriedly, "let's get you to the airport."

The ride to the airport took only half an hour. They met Hiram in the departure lounge and he handed George his suitcase.

"Well," said George turning to Vicky, "this is good-bye, but please come and see me when next you come to England."

"I will."

He stepped forward and kissed her on the cheek. "And don't worry about the film. I'm sure there'll be others. Better films. Good-bye, Hiram." He shook Hiram by the hand and then turned and walked quickly to the barrier. Vicky and Hiram stood watching him.

"I don't know what he meant about the movie," remarked Hiram, "he slept all the way through it."

"What!"

"Every time I looked at him he was sound a sleep. He couldn't have seen much of it at all. Certainly not enough to make a judgement on how good it was."

Vicky stood and stared in silent astonishment at George's departing figure until he was out of sight. George did not turn once to look at her, but continued on his way with her deed to the mill securely in his pocket.

CHAPTER 14

George looked out of the aeroplane window at the fields of England below and was surprised at how green they were. He had been away for only a few days but after the pale California grass this vivid lushness made him feel he was glad to be coming home.

The plane circled Heathrow Airport for what seemed an eternity before descending slowly to a perfect landing on the runway. The time it took for him to pass through Customs and the baggage handling area added to his impatience but then at last he took the underground train to London and from there the train to Tidburn.

He was very much looking forward to seeing his cottage and the mill again, especially now that it was his own once more. Perhaps he could even return to the carefree life he had led before Aunt Jane made him give away half of his possessions. Although he had still lost a good proportion of the money he had inherited from his father, in recent weeks he had generated a modest income from his paintings and photographs, and of course he could continue to sell his cider. It would indeed be good to have the mill back to himself again. There was the problem of what to do about the other occupants and he pondered on this as the train sped through the countryside. He had become very fond of Linda. She had got him painting again and they had worked well together over the past few weeks. It did not seem right to ask her to leave. And if he let her stay, how would she feel? It was her idea that the poet Frank joined the group. She had also moved in at the same time as Justin and Jonathan and so might be upset if he asked them to move out.

He got off the train at Tidburn station and then took a taxi the rest of the way home. He paid the driver at the gate to his cottage and then as the taxi drove away looked up at the cottage. Somehow he had expected it to have changed while he had been away and he was almost disappointed that it looked exactly the same. He opened his garden gate, walked briskly along the path to the cottage, unlocked the front door and went inside. A few moments later he emerged, minus the suitcase, and made his way to the mill. He opened the door and entered.

The main downstairs room was occupied by all four permanent residents of the mill. Justin, fully clothed in blue jeans and grey T-shirt, sat on a stool. His portrait was being painted by Jonathan who was standing a little in front of him behind his easel. The poet, Frank, was sitting with his back to them at a small table scribbling in a lined exercise book. Linda was at the other end of the room, chipping away at a block of marble in front of her. One of Bach's Brandenburg Concertos played quietly from four speakers positioned in each corner of the room.

Linda looked up at his entry. She put one finger to her lips, indicating that he should be silent, laid down her hammer and chisel, walked over to him, took his arm and led him back outside. She led him over to the bank of the Muckle before she started to speak.

"Sorry to bring you out here," she explained, "but I didn't want you to disturb anybody. Things here have been going very well since you've been gone. Everyone's been working hard and produced a lot of good work. It's been fantastic, it really has. It's good to see you back though. How was the film?"

"It ... er ... got bad reviews."

"Oh dear. How did Vicky take it? Badly, I expect."

George nodded. "She was very upset."

"I thought she would be. I suppose it might not be released in Britain now. A pity, I would have liked to have seen it. You must come and work with us. The atmosphere in the mill these last few days has really been marvellous. It is really a wonderful place to work."

"I'd like to. I'm a bit tired at the moment and a bit jet-lagged. I think I'll go and have a lie down for a couple of hours."

"Of course. Look, come across to the mill later this evening and I'll fix you a meal."

"Thank you but I really don't feel up to mixing with the others just yet. I'd like to spend the evening on my own. Just until I get over the jet lag, you understand."

"Just as you wish. I'll see you in a day or two then," she said. "Good-bye." She turned and went back to the mill.

George stood for a while and regarded the River Muckle, deep in thought. Then he turned, made his way back to the cottage and upstairs to bed where he slept right through the rest of the day until the following morning. He rose at nine o'clock and made his breakfast. He finished eating and was halfway through washing up when there was a knock at the door. It was Oswald Goodsake and the interior designer, Sebastian.

"Good morning, George," said Oswald Goodsake. "May we talk to you for a moment?"

"What about?" asked George.

"We have a business proposition to put to you," continued Uncle Oswald. "It could be to your advantage."

"You'd better come in," said George and led them into the sitting room. "Sit down."

Uncle Oswald sat in one of the armchairs and Sebastian on the sofa. George sat in the remaining vacant chair. "Well?" he asked.

"We've heard that Vicky has let you have her half of the mill," began Sebastian.

"How do you know that?"

Uncle Oswald cleared his throat. "As you know, I have been acting as her agent and business adviser. Vicky told me herself."

"What's this got to do with him?" said George and nodded towards Sebastian.

"Sebastian has been advising the artists at the mill on how best to market their work. We feel that we share similar interests."

"The thing is, dear heart," broke in Sebastian, "the mill has proved a fabulous showcase for artistic talent. The exhibition we had there was an enormous success. They sold lots of paintings and sculptures. We can build on this, invite more artists to come and work there and hold further exhibitions. All for a fee, you understand. I have had a great deal of experience in running exhibitions and advertising the work of artists. Oswald has experience on the contract side of things."

"The mill has provided you and Vicky with a good income already," interjected Oswald. "What with the rent charged for the artists living there and a percentage of the income from the exhibition. I also feel we can generate further income from that marvellous cider of yours. I understand the batch you have produced from this year's crop is again excellent."

"It certainly is," agreed George, "but if the demand is as great as it was last year then I'll soon be sold out. I only have a small orchard and only produce enough for my own consumption. The surplus I have been selling to The Pullet Inn."

"Ah, that's where I can help," said Uncle Oswald. "We can buy in apples and crush them at the mill."

"But they won't be my apples. The point about my cider is that it is made from my apples from my orchard."

"I'm sure it won't make any difference if we get the same variety."

"But they are a special variety and are only grown in my orchard. It's what gives my cider its unique taste."

"Don't worry, darling," interjected Sebastian. "I'm sure that with a little judicious quality control and by adding some flavourings no one will be able to tell. It was a big hit at that party Vicky had and people are already asking me where they can get some more. It will sell well on its reputation alone."

"But I would be able to tell," said George, "and so too would most people in the village. I'd rather not sell any at all than lose the reputation of my cider."

"Well, we'll let you think about it," said Uncle Oswald, "and perhaps consider the matter again another time. Meanwhile, would you still allow us to act for you in promoting the art aspects of the mill?"

George stroked his chin. "I'll think about it."

"Please do," continued Uncle Oswald. "I did put the same proposals to Vicky and I know that she was considering them seriously. She said she'd put them to you when you visited her in America. Obviously all that changed when she made the mill completely over to you."

"She mentioned nothing of this to me," said George.

Uncle Oswald rose to his feet. "Well, think about our offer," he said, "and let us know what you decide." George and Sebastian got to their feet and Uncle Oswald extended his hand to George. "Good-bye," he said.

George shook his hand and also Sebastian's and showed them out the front door. He watched them walk down his front path, open the gate, get into Uncle Oswald's Mercedes and drive off. Then he put on his coat, left his cottage and the washing up, and set off towards his aunt's estate in search of Tom Firkin.

He headed for the part of the estate where Tom kept the pheasant rearing pens. It was halfway through the shooting season and so the pens were empty, but George found Tom in a shed at a makeshift desk working on plans for the forthcoming weekend shoot. "'Ow do, George," said Tom as George rapped on the door and walked in.

"Fine, thank you, Tom. How are you?"

"Fair ter middling," replied Tom and bent back to his writing. "Do yer fancy a spot of beating this weekend?" he asked.

"Yes, maybe I will."

An' 'ow was 'Ollywood?"

"Interesting. What I saw of it. I wasn't there long."

"Did yer see any film stars?"

"A few, but not to talk to."

"Who did yer see?"

"I can't really remember now."

Tom looked at him in surprise. "What, you went all that way and yer can't remember who yer saw? Did you see Vicky?"

"Yes,"

" 'Ow was she?"

"She was fine. She's given me back her half of the mill."

"Well, now that be good news. What yer gonna do with it now?"

"I'd like to return it to the way it was."

Tom shook his head. "Pity. I enjoyed scribbling pictures with Linda and Jonathan. And that Frank - 'e certainly has a way with words."

"You think I ought to let them stay then?"

"Tis your mill, George. Tis up to you."

"I've had a visit from Vicky's Uncle Oswald and that Sebastian. They want to act as my agents and make it more commercial."

"In what way?"

"They want to advertise it as an art centre, hold exhibitions and increase the manufacture of my cider."

Tom nodded in reply and returned once more to his writing.

"What do you think?" George asked him.

"Like I said," said Tom without looking up, "Tis your mill."

Aunt Jane stood in a field on her estate bordering Tickle Woods, a double-barrelled shotgun was broken open and lying under her arm, the black Labrador Winchester at her feet. She was wearing green wellington boots, a calf-length green dress with matching padded jacket and a brown Sherlock Holmes deerstalker hat on her head. She was talking to Oswald Goodsake and Sebastian, both of whom wore brown leather boots, thick woollen socks, plus fours, sports jackets and cloth caps. Uncle Oswald's clothing was of a conservative light brown and that of Sebastian's was multicoloured, resembling more those of a golfer rather than that of the country gentleman he was attempting to imitate. Uncle Oswald also carried a broken double-barrelled shotgun under his arm. Sebastian carried a high-powered .22-calibre rifle, which hung from a strap on his shoulder.

They were approached by Tom Firkin. "The beaters all be ready, my lady," he told Aunt Jane.

"Thank you, Tom," she replied. She indicated her companions. "These two gentlemen are Mr Goodsake and Mr Snyde and are late additions to the shooting party."

"It's all right, Lady Jane," interjected Uncle Oswald, "we've all ready met. Hello, Tom."

"Yes, hello, Tom," said Sebastian. "I understand that Mr Cogrill is among the beaters."

Tom regarded Sebastian suspiciously. "So 'e be," he said and then added sternly, "I'm sorry, sir, I can't allow that gun on my shoot." He indicated the .22 rifle. "'E be too dangerous."

"Oh, I'm sorry," Sebastian replied. "It belongs to my cousin in Devon. He uses it to pot rabbits on his smallholding. As I don't own a gun I asked him if I could borrow it."

"That's as maybe," continued Tom, "but it be far too dangerous on a shoot like this."

"Oh dear," said Sebastian in remorse. "I'm sorry, I didn't know." He turned to the others. "Look, you go on with your shoot and I'll see you back at the house later."

"I'm sure we could find you a suitable gun, couldn't we, Tom?" interjected Aunt Jane.

"There's really no need," said Sebastian, "I'm not sure I know how to use one properly anyway and we don't want there to be any accidents. No, I'll see you all later. Cheery-bye!" They watched as he walked away towards Gleefield Manor.

"You can start the shoot now if everything is ready, Tom," said Aunt Jane.

"Very good, my lady," replied Tom. He moved away several yards, took a large black whistle from his pocket and blew on it shrilly.

Several thousand yards away the beaters stood the other side of the woods. George looked up at the sound of the whistle. He turned to old Joe Thropp who was standing next to him. "Do you hear that, Joe?" he asked.

"Aye, George," the old man replied. "I'm not deaf yet. Come on, lads!" he yelled and the long line of beaters moved steadily into the woods, yelling and beating the trees and bushes with sticks as they went.

Meanwhile, somewhere in the distance, Sebastian was making his way towards them from the opposite direction. After he left the shooting party, he had made sure he was out of sight and then circled back, entering the woods from another direction so that he could remain unobserved. Now he was walking stealthily towards the beaters, crouching as he moved with his rifle held in both hands.

The first pheasants broke from cover. Shots rang out as the shooting party endeavoured to bring them down. Sebastian found a thick wild rhododendron bush on the edge of a small clearing, crept inside and peered out through the leaves towards the sounds made by the oncoming beaters. Thirty minutes later, he saw the line of beaters coming towards him. He made out George in the centre of the line, between Old Joe Thropp and a burly farm worker from the Gleefield estate. He carefully aimed the rifle at George and squeezed the trigger.

A silence enveloped Tickle Woods. The pheasants ceased their desperate flight over the raised guns of the shooting party, and the guns were silent for there was nothing for them to shoot. There was no distant sound from the approaching beaters.

Aunt Jane turned to Tom. "What's happened, Tom?" she asked. "There should be more birds than this?"

"I don' know, my lady. I'll go an' look." "Everybody 'old their fire!" he called and disappeared into the woods. The shooting party broke their guns and waited.

Several hours later, Tom stood at the bar in The Pullet Inn. Two pints of Cogrill's Old Mill Cider were set in front of him. One belonged to Tom and the other to Jack Hump who was in his usual position the other side of the counter. Both were staring glumly into their glasses. Tom was explaining what had happened.

"'E was shot clean through the head," he said. "Killed instantly."

"Well 'least 'e did not suffer," murmured Jack.

Tom nodded sadly.

"'Ow did it 'appen?" asked Jack.

"That Zerbastian bloke brought a two-two to the shoot. Sent 'im packing I did but 'e did not go very far - said 'e decided to shoot some rabbits. Got lost in woods, saw a rabbit and fired. Stupid bugger did not know first thing about guns - should never 'ave allowed 'im ter keep it."

"Yer can't blame yerself," sympathised Jack. "You weren't ter know what would 'appen."

"But I've lost a friend. One of the best a man ever had. It was my shoot therefore it was my fault."

"Don't be daft. If it were anybody's fault, it be that Zerbastian's. I've lost a friend too, yer know. 'E were very well respected."

"Arr, that 'e was," agreed Tom and took a sip of cider.

" 'E were a strange bloke, though," mused Jack. "But I 'spose of all people yer must 'ave known 'im ther best, Tom."

"I don' know about that," Tom replied. "But it do seemed like I'd known 'im all my life, but strange? Nah. I would not 'ave called 'im strange. He was very what you might call down to earth. He could not abide modern things. I would not call that strange, not in these parts. I 'spose you could say that 'e lived life as a simple country man and I think, if you was to ask 'im now if that was what 'e felt he was, I think 'e'd go along with that."

"Aye, but was he happy?"

Tom shrugged. "I 'spose only 'e could tell you that really. But I reckons, all in all, 'e was. After all, 'e lived his life simply, amongst his friends in the country. 'E always said 'e hated big cities. 'E didn't like change. And with modern technology invading the countryside, well 'e didn't like that at all. I don't think he'll miss all these changes that seem to be coming to Mucklesbury."

"Arr," agreed Jack. "Yer be right. 'E did not like change. But 'e were a sound man fer all that."

Tom smiled. "Some might not agree with yer there," he said. "E was a simple man, well respected, but some might say 'e was a little eccentric."

Jack agreed again. "Well, I 'spose thinking about it, living alone the way 'e did, some might find it a little peculiar. But that was 'im though, a little peculiar."

"Yes," said Tom. "I 'spose that sums him up really, a little peculiar."

At that moment the door opened and Linda hurried in. "Tom, I've just heard that there was an accident on the shoot and one of the beaters was killed."

Tom nodded his head. "That's right," he said, "Old Joe Thropp."

"How awful," said Linda.

" 'E didn't suffer though," added Jack, "shot through the 'ead. Can I get yer a drink?"

"Yes please. I'll have a Cogrill's cider. What happened?"

Tom repeated the story that Old Joe had been shot accidentally by Sebastian who had been hunting rabbits in the woods.

"How awful," murmured Linda again when she had heard the tale.

"Tis that," agreed Jack, passing her the glass across the bar. Linda opened her handbag in order to extract her purse. Jack raised his hand. "No need," he said, "The zider be on the house." Before she could reply he continued talking. "Poor Old Joe," he said, "'least 'E died in Tickle Wood. Spent many an 'appy time there 'e did in his youth."

"Or so he kept on telling us," commented Tom.

"Well whatever the case," continued Jack, "I think Joe would've been 'appy knowing that 'is last few moments were spent in Tickle Wood."

"I'm glad he didn't suffer," said Linda.

"Nah," said Tom. " 'E didn't suffer. George were with 'im when 'e died. 'E died in George's arms. George said it were very quick. Ol' Joe couldn't 'ave felt a thing."

"Where's George now?" asked Linda.

" 'E be down at the police station giving a statement," explained Tom.

That day, the day after and the following day, the villagers of Mucklesbury mourned the death of Old Joe Thropp. On the afternoon of the third day, the majority of them crammed into the small parish church for his funeral. The funeral address was given by the vicar, the Reverend Philip Scillage. A thin grey-haired man in his early fifties, he looked down on his congregation from his pulpit and spoke in a singsong voice developed from years of speaking prayers, singing hymns and chanting eulogies.

"Joe Thropp," he said, "was a humble man. Although he was small in stature he stood tall because of the respect he earned from all who knew him. He was a good man, an honest man, a good father and a good grandfather. His knowledge of local history and customs was second to none as he reminded me himself on many occasions, especially whenever I encountered him either inside or outside The Pullet Inn. He will be sadly missed." The vicar paused. "Now," he added, "before we move on, one of our newer parishioners, from the community living at the Old Mill, would like to address us."

The vicar left the pulpit and the poet Frank rose from amongst the congregation and took his place. He withdrew a piece of paper from his pocket and then looked down at his audience. "I know I am very much a newcomer to Mucklesbury," he said, "but in that short time I met and got to know Old Joe. Like the vicar, and indeed in common with many of you here today, we had many a long conversation over a drink of cider at The Pullet Inn. When I heard of his death I, like you, was overcome, and I wrote this poem. With the permission of the Reverend and Old Joe's family, I read it to you now." He looked down at the sheet of paper he was holding and spoke the following lines of verse in a loud clear voice.

>Joe Thropp is dead
>A bullet struck him like lightning,
>through the head
>He died where he stood,
>in Tickle Wood
>Joe Thropp is dead

> Like a strong tree he'd stand
> In our green land
> An oak pillar in our community
> No longer will he be in our county
> No longer in fair Mucklesbury
> Joe Thropp is dead.

Then the party trooped outside to the churchyard where they watched as Old Joe's coffin was lowered into its final resting place in the Thropp family plot. When the funeral was over, the party moved to the church hall. The Pullet Inn had been closed for the day as a mark of respect.

Sandwiches and cakes were laid out on long trestle tables. Two barrels, one of beer and one of cider, stood on a makeshift bar at the end of the room. Lemonade and squash were provided for the children and a tea urn stood between the barrels and the bottles of soft drink. The guests needed no invitation to begin eating and, as soon as they arrived, they immediately set about the food and drink.

George made his way to the bar where he found Jack Hump and Tom Firkin helping themselves to the cider. He picked up a glass and waited his turn.

"Ow do, George," said Jack Hump on seeing him.

"Hello, Jack, Tom," George replied, and seeing they were finished, filled his glass.

"The whole village be giving Ol' Joe a good send off," Tom remarked.

"Yes," George replied, "Old Joe would have been proud. It was a very moving service."

"Aye," agreed Jack, "the Reverend Phil does a good funeral. If Old Joe was 'ere, 'E'd be an 'appy man. I'm not so sure about the poem though."

"What's wrong with the poem?" asked Tom.

"Tain't part of the Mucklesbury tradition," Jack replied.

"Oh, surely you can't begrudge a few of the newcomers paying their respects their own way?" protested George.

Jack took a long sip of cider and thought awhile. "No, s'pose not", he replied. "Old Joe had become quite pally with that Frank bloke. They used ter sit in the bar spouting poetry to each other. Though most of what Joe spouted you couldn't use in polite company."

The food was soon eaten and when it was finished the plates were cleared away and the trestle tables were moved against the wall. Someone produce an accordion and someone else a fiddle. A slow lament was played by both instrumentalists and the mourners joined together in a circle dance which moved in a clockwise direction on the space vacated by the tables.

"Hello, George."

George looked round at the sound of his name and standing there right at his elbow was Linda Quilt.

"Hello, Linda," he said. "Have you been here long?"

"I've been over there with Frank, Jonathan and Justin." She indicated the other end of the room. "We've been talking to the vicar. I saw you come in but it didn't seem right for us to partake of the refreshments. After all, we are hardly local and we weren't officially invited."

"Don't let that put you off," said George. "I doubt whether anyone here was officially invited, as you put it."

"But who provided the refreshments?"

"Everyone will have chipped in with something, I expect. That's the Mucklesbury way."

"I see Jimmy Thropp's over there." She indicated the thin gangly musician now clad in a wrinkled dark blue suit, white shirt and black tie and sawing away mournfully on his fiddle.

"Yes, Jimmy's Old Joe's nephew. He and Jack Hump organised everything. They won't mind who comes as long as long as the cider holds out."

Linda grimaced. "He still makes a terrible noise even when playing solo," she said.

George shrugged. "I don't think you'll find many in these parts who'll disagree with you. Old Joe wasn't much better either, but he could dance a good jig if someone bought him enough cider. That is, until his knees gave out."

"What's that tune called they're dancing to? It's horrible."

"It's called the 'Muklesbury Morn'. It's a traditional slow circle dance, performed only at funerals. If he could hear it, Old Joe would recognise it and approve. And join in, no doubt about it."

Gradually the tune quickened into a fast-moving reel and the villagers of Mucklesbury danced the night away in memory of Old Joe Thropp.

Two hundred miles away, Sebastian sat on a sofa in Oswald Goodsakes' Knightsbridge flat. He was sipping a glass of Campari and soda. Uncle Oswald sat opposite him in a leather armchair and sipped a large brandy.

"The funeral will be over now," murmured Sebastian

Uncle Oswald looked at the clock on the mantelpiece. "Yes, it must be," he said. "Is your conscience bothering you, Sebastian?"

"Certainly not! It was an accident."

"It wouldn't have been if you weren't a better shot."

"I couldn't help it. That old man was jumping around like anything. I can't help it if at the wrong moment he got between me and Cogrill. Anyway, next time ..."

"There won't be a next time!" interrupted Uncle Oswald. "I don't know why I listened to you in the first place!"

"You like the sound of money. That's why," murmured Sebastian. "And when we heard about the shoot it was too good an opportunity to miss. But don't worry; I won't try shooting him again. I'll think of something else." He sighed and then added, "Unfortunate about the old man though."

CHAPTER 15

Two weeks passed and George had not visited the mill since the funeral. Although the inquest had confirmed that the shooting had been an accident, it had seemed to him that the death of Old Joe had meant that the Art Centre had brought bad luck. After all, it had been the prospect of a flourishing Art Centre at the mill that had attracted Sebastian to Mucklesbury, a man with no idea of country ways, particularly in the rules which governed a shoot, and because of this Old Joe had died. Consequently, George made up his mind to close the Art Centre and ask everyone to leave. Frank had left already, on his own account, and had returned to his old life in London soon after the shooting. Linda, Jonathan and Justin remained. However, it was with a heavy heart that George pushed open the main door to the mill, for he wasn't looking forward to telling them of his decision.

He found Linda and Jonathan in the main downstairs room. Linda was surveying a block of marble positioned on a podium in front of her. Jonathan stood in front of an empty canvas mixing his paints. They both looked up when he entered and both seemed pleased to see him.

"Hello, George," said Linda. "It's nice to see you."

"Hi, George," said Jonathan.

"Hello," George replied.

"It's been a long time since you've set foot in here," continued Linda. "Have you come to do some work or is this just a social visit?"

"Neither, I'm afraid." He took a deep breath. "I've come to tell you that I've decided to close the Art Centre."

Neither spoke.

After a while George said, "Well?"

"Well what?" Linda asked.

Jonathan held up his hand. "Actually, George," he said. "We both kind of expected it."

Linda sighed. "Yes, we did," she agreed. "I'm sorry if I sounded rude. It's just that I had high hopes for the Centre. I'm disappointed, that's all."

"I realise that," said George. "I'm sorry. I wasn't looking forward to telling you."

"Well, if you must know," said Jonathan, "I think you're doing us a favour. The spark seems to have gone out of the place. Just look at us. We've both been mooching around here for the last couple of days trying to summon up sufficient enthusiasm to begin some new work but it just hasn't come."

"I think we should try harder," said Linda. "We shouldn't let it go."

Jonathan shook his head. "No, it's gone," he said. "Frank had the right idea. Get out and move on. Justin has gone into Tidburn to look at Vicky's old studio. She still owns it but it has been boarded up since she got involved down here. If it's still in good condition we're thinking of asking her if she'd consider renting it to us. Linda is welcome to join us as well. Perhaps things may get better back here in a few months' time. We could always move back if you'd have us. We've really enjoyed it here. Produced some good work."

"Yes, we have," Linda agreed reluctantly. "I will be sorry to leave. But you must do what you think best, George. It's your mill."

"Thank you both," said George, very much relieved. "I'm glad you've taken it so well."

"You won't give up your painting, will you?" asked Linda. "Or your photography? You really are very talented. It would be such a waste."

"No," said George, "I won't give it up. It's just that I don't want it to be so commercialised."

"When do you want us to move out?" asked Jonathan.

"Oh, there's no hurry," George replied. "You're quite welcome to leave some things here until you get settled. Thanks very much for taking everything so well." He turned to go.

"By the way!" Jonathan called after him. "Are you going to the London première of Vicky's film?"

George stopped and looked at him. "What première?" he asked.

"Vicky's film," explained Jonathan, "*The English Girl*, it's opening in London next week."

"We received invitations to the première this morning," said Linda.

"Oh," George replied thoughtfully.

"Perhaps, because you've seen it before you might just get invited to the party afterwards," continued Linda.

"Yes, perhaps I will," said George and then added, "I thought the film got very bad reviews."

"I think the first reviews were very mixed," said Linda. "However, apparently it's done very well at the box office in America. What did you think of it?"

"Well ... I ... I think it's best you make up your own minds about that," replied George after some hesitation.

"What's it about?" asked Jonathan.

"It's ... It's about this English girl. Look, I don't want to spoil it for you by giving the plot away. Have a good time." He turned to go.

Linda could see he was disturbed. "Your invitation may have been delayed in the post," she called after him. "I expect it may well arrive later on in the week!"

"Yes, it may well indeed," George replied. "Good-bye." He hurried to the door and out into the fresh air.

He set off at a brisk pace along the towpath by the Muckle towards Mucklesbury. As he walked he wondered why he had not heard from Vicky, especially as she was obviously returning to England. He was confused and upset. He reached Mucklesbury and The Pullet Inn. Jack was not behind the bar so George bought a pint of his beloved Cogrill's cider and retired to sit alone at a table in the corner. His thoughts were interrupted by a loud voice.

"Ow do, George!" It was Tom Firkin. George had been so preoccupied with his thoughts that he had not noticed him come in and buy himself a drink. Now he was standing by George's table, a pint of cider in his hand.

"Hello, Tom," he said. "I thought you didn't come here much nowadays."

"I was passing through the village and I saw you come in yer, so I thought I might join yer. You don't mind, do you?"

"Not at all, sit down."

Tom pulled up a chair and sat down opposite him. "I thought you might be still upset about Old Joe," said Tom. "It be no good ter bottle it up, yer know."

"Yes, I know - but it's not just that. I've decided to close the Art Centre."

"Thought you might. 'Ave you told Justin and that crowd?"

"Yes. They took it very well."

"That's all right then." Tom took a sip of his cider. "Actually I had another reason for wanting ter talk to yer. I was wondering whether yer be going ter the London première of Vicky's film."

"Well, no ... Are you?"

"Yer. A pity about you though, I was hoping we'd go together - like we used to when we was boys. I 'spect as yer've seen it already you won't want to see it again."

"These things are by invitation," said George. "Have you received one?"

"Yer and to the party afterwards. 'Aven't you?"

"No."

"Oh, I 'spect it got lost in the post. Vicky's on television tonight, you know, on *The Tony Drogson Show*. I got an invitation to be in the studio audience."

"What? Who invited you?"

"I don't know. Vicky, I s'pose. The invitation arrived a few days ago. But I shan't go. It's up in London and I don't fancy going all that way for a TV show, not when I can see it at home. Now, a film première is different. I doubt whether we'd get to see it round here for some time - and then there's the party afterwards. I should see lots of famous stars."

"Are you taking Miranda?" asked George.

"That's all over. She's gone ter Italy with that Giuseppe bloke."

"You could go with Linda and Jonathan. I understand they've got invitations too."

"Yer, tha's an idea. "Look, why don't yer come over tonight and watch the programme with me? I'll get some beer and zider in."

George remained silent.

"Go on - it'll be like ol' times."

George considered the matter. "All right," he said after a few moments, "what time's it on?"

"Ten thirty."

"Okay, I'll come over about ten."

"Tell me," asked Tom, "what's the film about? Is it any good?"

"Er ... you'd better make your own mind up about that," George replied and hastily took a sip from his cider.

He left the pub an hour later and made his way back to his cottage. He half expected to find an invitation from Vicky waiting on his doormat. But he was disappointed. He considered telephoning Uncle Oswald but decided against it. He spent the rest of the day pottering around his garden and then later the cottage, wondering all the time why she had not contacted him. At ten o'clock, he made his way to Tom's cottage with a bag containing two flagons of his best cider. They settled themselves down in two armchairs in front of the TV with a glass of cider each and a bowl of crisps on a small table between them. The television was switched off as the programme they were there to watch had not yet begun.

George was feeling a lot better. "This is a bit like old times," he remarked. "Do you remember how we used to go to the pictures in Tidburn every Saturday morning?"

"Aye, I do. Old Joe used to run us kids over there in 'is ol' bus. He wasn't as old then of course."

"No, but he was as good a friend to us then as he was when he died."

They were silent for a few moments while they thought of Old Joe. Then George said, "I've always liked the cinema. I can still feel the excitement of waiting for the curtains to roll back to reveal the moving pictures. Do you remember how they used to close it before each feature and how the first item we saw was the censor's certificate projected on the curtains as they drew back? That always added to the excitement, especially later when we managed to sneak in to see X films."

"Yer, but they're pretty tame now by modern standards."

"Oh, I don't know," said George. "Some of the horror ones frightened me more than these modern ones, which seem simply to rely on special effects, blood and gore. I'm affected more by atmosphere." He sighed. "It's all changed now though. The last time I went was to that new multi-screen cinema in Tidburn. It was all very clean because of the smoking ban and the seats were very new. But, there were no curtains on the screen and no atmosphere."

"Least yer can breathe clean air."

"But nobody went to the cinema to breathe clean air. You went to see a good film and for the atmosphere and the dark. Mind you, it made you appreciate fresh air when you came out."

Tom looked at his watch. "Tis time," he said. He got up, switched on the television and sat back in his place.

The opening credits to *The Tony Drogson Show* were fading and the host was standing in front of the camera to the applause of his studio audience. He was dressed in a light grey lounge suit. "Good evening," he said, "and welcome to the show. Our first guest this evening is a young lady who has recently risen to stardom. She has been described as the new Vivienne Leigh and her first film *The English Girl* has met with huge box office success in America. Please welcome supermodel and film actress, Victoria Gloam!"

He held out his arm and Vicky entered to the audience applause. She was wearing a short thigh-length green dress. She kissed Drogson on the cheek and he led her over to the interviewee couch where she sat down crossing her long legs. He sat in the arm chair next to her and picked up a clipboard containing his notes from the low table in front of them.

"Welcome to the show, Victoria," he said when the applause died down. "May I call you Victoria?"

"Please call me Vicky."

"Thank you. Now, Vicky, I understand that you started out as a photographer. Please tell me, how did you end up on the other side of the camera?"

"Well, Tony ... can I call you Tony?"

"Please do."

"Well ... actually it was quite simple really. I was taking some photographs for a magazine and we were short of a model, so I wore the clothes and quite literally stepped in front of the camera."

"And those photographs were an instant hit?"

"Well, yes. When they were published, other editors and photographers saw them and offers of more modelling work came pouring in."

"And from there you moved on to Hollywood and films?"

"That's right. I received an offer from a film producer and it seemed an opportunity too good to miss."

"You've obviously got a face that the camera loves and we can all seem why. Can you give any pointers to the audience on any other reasons for your success?"

"I suppose I must have just met the right people at the right time. But it has really been a lot of hard work. I haven't had a holiday for a couple of years. When the British première is over I hope to take a couple of months off."

"Ah yes, the British première, that's next week, isn't it?"

"Yes, at The Odeon, Leicester Square."

"Well," said Drogson, "I think its time now we showed a clip from the film." The camera zoomed in on him and he spoke directly to the audience. "This scene is the now famous restaurant scene, in which Vicky, as 'The English Girl' in the title of the film, empties her dinner over the head of her co-star, Cliff Clayburger, and then follows this by systematically emptying the meals of adjacent dinners over his head as well."

The television cut to the scene in the film which Drogson had described. The whole thing lasted approximately three minutes during which time Vicky covered her co-star and the floor of the restaurant with half-eaten food. It ended with her walking out of the restaurant, leaving him and their fellow diners sitting amongst the culinary mess.

The audience applauded and the camera cut back to show Drogson and Vicky. "That was certainly quite a scene," Drogson remarked.

"Thank you."

"There has been a rumour that there was a romance between you and Cliff Clayburger. Is there any truth in that?"

"I'm afraid not."

"You seem disappointed."

"He's a very good looking man. But not my type."

"You have of course been romantically linked with the film producer Hiram Cornslinger."

"Hiram is a good friend. Nothing more."

"Just good friends, eh? Well, I promised before the interview not to ask you any questions about your private life. But you must understand that audiences are very curious about the romantic attachments of the stars. Is there a man in your life?"

Vicky smiled. "I'd rather not say," she said.

"A man of mystery, eh!" exclaimed Drogson. "Well, thank you very much, Vicky Gloam!"

"Thank you, Tony," said Vicky.

The audience applauded and Drogson turned once more to face the camera which held him in close-up. "We'll take a break now and then we'll be back with my next guest, writer and poet Frank Witterworth. Don't go away!"

The television screen began showing advertisements.

"Do yer want to watch Frank?" Tom asked George.

"Do you like his poems?" asked George.

"Old Joe liked 'em."

"Old Joe liked anything that rhymed. Did you like them?"

"No. Did yer?"

"No."

"That settles it then," said Tom and got up and switched the television set off. He turned and faced George. "I wonder who this mystery man be," he said.

"So do I," murmured George. "So do I."

A week later Aunt Jane was taking tea at the Ritz Hotel in London when she was joined by Sebastian Snide and Oswald Goodsake. "Sit down, gentlemen," she said as they greeted her. She turned to the waiter who had shown them to her table. "Please can you bring some more cups and plates?" she asked him.

"Certainly, madam," the waiter replied and left to do her bidding.

Sebastian and Uncle Oswald sat down opposite her. "I'm in town for tonight's première of *The English Girl*," she said, "and I thought it would be a good idea if we met for a chat. Are you two going?"

"We both are," Sebastian replied.

"I thought you might be," said Aunt Jane. "I think Vicky has invited practically everyone she knows. Everyone that is except for my nephew, George. I don't suppose either of you know why?"

"There's a rumour that George slept through the Hollywood première," said Uncle Oswald. "Anyway that's what Hiram Cornslinger told me. Apparently Vicky was very upset about it when she found out. I have only briefly spoken to Vicky and she didn't mention it, but as her agent, she supplied me with a list of people who she wished to invite tonight and she specifically stressed that she wanted George excluded."

"I can understand why," said Aunt Jane and sighed. "That's typical of my nephew, I'm afraid." Her eyes suddenly hardened. "The reason I asked you both here," she said, "was that I was unhappy with the explanation given for the shooting of Old Joe Thropp."

"What do you mean? It was an accident!" Sebastian protested.

The waiter reappeared with the cups and plates. "Would you care for some scones or cakes?" Aunt Jane asked them. They both declined. Aunt Jane dismissed the waiter and poured them a cup of tea each. "Do you both take milk and sugar?" she asked.

"Milk and two sugars," replied Uncle Oswald.

"Milk and no sugar," said Sebastian.

Aunt Jane finished pouring the tea and passed them their respective cups. Uncle Oswald picked up a teaspoon and began stirring his cup thoughtfully. Sebastian took a small plastic container from his jacket pocket, opened it, took out two small tablets of artificial sweetener and added it to his cup. Then he too began stirring. All these acts were performed in silence.

After a while Uncle Oswald said, "Both the police and the coroner were happy with that explanation."

"I know," Aunt Jane replied. "But I also know that both of you have been interested in exploiting the business potential of The Old Mill. I think you would be quite please if something happened to my nephew so that ownership would revert to Vicky. You are, Oswald, as you have stated, already acting as Vicky's agent. It is certainly quite a coincidence that George was standing next to Old Joe when he died."

"What are you implying?" asked Sebastian, who was becoming increasingly agitated.

"I think you understand what I am implying," continued Aunt Jane. "I also have an interest in George not re-acquiring the mill and returning it to its former state. I want him to achieve something and also settle down, get married so that my estate can continue to be handed down to subsequent generations. I therefore do not want anything to happen to him. Is that quite clear?"

"I assure you, Lady Jane ..." began Uncle Oswald.

Aunt Jane silenced him by holding up her hand. "Enough!" she said. "I don't want to know more. I would, though, like to assist you in putting pressure on George so that Vicky can regain control of the mill. I had great hopes of a romance between the two of them. It would have been nice if they could marry and she could bear the heirs which would continue the family line. But it appears now that she and George have fallen out. But maybe she is now so fed up with him she might be persuaded to try and take the mill away from him. Or at the very least, force him to make a mark for himself."

"You're right, Lady Jane," said Sebastian. "We are interested in obtaining an interest in the mill. But I didn't mean your nephew any harm. It was a complete accident. I only wanted show you and that gamekeeper I could shoot some game. It was unfortunate about that the old man."

"I said I don't want to hear any more!" snapped Aunt Jane. "However, if I hear that George has been harmed in anyway, the police will be hearing from me." She got abruptly to her feet and said, "Now I must go. No doubt I will see you later tonight and we will speak no more of the matter until such time that George loses control of that wretched mill."

The two men stood and said in unison, "Good-bye, Lady Gleefield," and watched as she sailed out of the restaurant.

When she had gone they resumed their seats. "Well, that complicates matters," remarked Sebastian.

"I don't see why," said Uncle Oswald. "She seems dead set against Cogrill continuing to hold control over the mill. She could be a valuable ally."

Sebastian shook his head. "No," he said, "I don't see him giving it up easily now. Not since he so nearly lost it for good the first time. No, the only way as I see it is for him to meet with a fatal accident, like we first planned, and for the mill to revert to Vicky."

"But you heard what Lady Jane said. She'll mention her suspicions to the police."

"That's right. She knows too much already. She must meet with an accident herself, before anything happens to nephew George. Who knows, the whole estate might eventually pass to Vicky and we will be in control. She'll be so wrapped up in her film star career she won't take much notice." He stopped talking, stroked his mouth and then added, "A pity about Cogrill though. I had just arranged something for him."

"What do you mean? We can't afford to make any more mistakes."

"I've sent him a bogus invitation to Vicky's party following the film première. But it wasn't to the film party at all but to a seedy little club in Soho. An awful lot of unsavoury things can happen there to the unwary. I planned on orchestrating an altercation surrounding him. And this time I planned to get in close with a stiletto blade and make no mistake."

"Good God!" breathed Uncle Oswald.

"Well, we can't have that now. In fact, we can't let anything happen to him or Lady Jane might carry out her threat. Unfortunately, it's too late to stop the invitation. He's probably on his way now and, knowing our luck, something unpleasant's bound to happen to him."

"Good God!" Uncle Oswald repeated. "We can't let anything happen to him!"

"Keep your voice down," hissed Sebastian. "No. That's the irony of it, we can't. We'll probably even have to protect the idiot."

"I know some bodyguards," whispered Uncle Oswald. "We can send them to the club with instructions not to allow anything to harm him. But it'll cost a lot of money."

"Yes," agreed Sebastian. "But we'll recoup it later, don't you fear. When I've arranged the accident for Lady Jane and put paid to Cogrill once and for all."

Uncle Oswald shuddered. "I don't much care for the idea," he said. "And how on earth can you devise an accident that will take care of Lady Jane? She's indestructible"

"We've gone too far now," Sebastian replied in an icy voice. "We've got everything to lose and such a lot to gain. Perhaps at some stage her concern for her precious family line will make her change her mind and shop us to the police. Don't worry about the accident to Lady Jane. I'll take care of her."

CHAPTER 16

George was elated. The invitation to the Film Première party arrived by special courier while he was preparing to spend the evening at home, alone in front of the television set. It had arrived too late for him to contact Tom or Linda and the others. They had already left. Fortunately, he now possessed what Hiram had called a tuxedo which he wore under a dark grey raincoat, to keep it clean. He stepped off the train at Paddington station with a spring in his step. In his hand he carried a hastily packed suitcase. He walked quickly to the taxi rank and, climbing into the first cab in the line, gave the driver the address of the hotel that was printed on a reservation form included with the invitation.

The cab stopped outside a very seedy looking dive. George made no attempt to get out. "This is it!" announced the taxi driver.

George was shaken out of his dream-like thoughts. "This is the Hotel Elsinore?" he asked in disbelief.

"That's right, the Hotel Elsinore, Shadrock Street, just like you said."

George stepped hesitantly from the taxi and paid the driver. He stood on the pavement and looked at the drab building. Then he took out the invitation from his pocket and looked at the reservation. It definitely said 'The Hotel Elsinore, Shadrock Street' and the sign above the door definitely said 'The Hotel Elsinore."

He entered the hotel, suitcase in hand. The lobby was little more than a passageway. In front of him was a green wooden reception desk. To the left of the desk was a flight of stairs leading upwards. To the right was a battered green settee on which sat two of the largest men he had ever seen. One had a florid complexion and was completely bald. The other was a Negro and was sporting a thin black moustache. Both were wearing dark grey lounge suits, white shirts and black ties. In front of them was a small table, on which was a bottle of brown ale. The bald-headed man was holding a bottle of larger in his hand. They stopped talking when George entered and stared at him sullenly.

George walked uneasily up to the reception desk. A fat middle-aged man of Mediterranean origin sat behind the counter. "What do-a you want?" he asked.

George cleared his throat, set down the suitcase and handed the man the reservation form. "I may have made a mistake," he said, "but I believe I have an invitation to stay in this hotel."

The man took the form and studied it. "There is-a no mistake," he said and looked at the open book in front of him. "Mister Cogrill, yes we have a reservation for you. Please will-a you sign-a here?" He turned the book round so that it faced George the right way up and handed him a black biro.

George reluctantly signed the book.

The man handed him a key. "Room-a twelve. It is-a up the stairs, second door on-a left. The bath-a room is-a at the end of the hall."

"Thank you," said George and taking the key made his way up the stairs.

The room was equally dingy. It consisted of one double bed, one wardrobe, one upright chair and one bedside table on which was a single telephone. George was nonplussed. He set the case on the floor, sat down on the bed and looked round at his surroundings.

At first, try as he might, he could not understand why Vicky had booked him into such a squalid hotel. If it was some idea of a joke, then he thought that it was not a very good one. Then, after a while, he thought perhaps it was that Vicky knew he was no longer very well off. That she may have thought it better not to book him in anywhere expensive in case he ran up any expensive bills he could not pay. When this idea occurred to him, he felt very much better. Still she had not needed to book him into something quite so downmarket.

He decided not to unpack his suitcase. He didn't want to stay in that room longer than necessary. And, after all, it was only for one night. He was also already dressed in his dinner suit, so there was no need for him to change. He looked at his watch. It was half past nine. The film première would have started at eight o'clock. He did not want to get to the party too early, so he lay back on the bed, without even taking his raincoat off, and waited.

At half past ten he used the telephone to ring downstairs to reception to order a taxi. Ten minutes later, the Italian receptionist rang back to say that the taxi had arrived so he left the room, leaving the suitcase inside, locked the door and went downstairs. He handed the key in to reception and then went outside where a black London taxi was waiting for him. He opened the rear door and got in the back.

"The Majestic Club," he said to the taxi driver.
"Are you pulling my leg?" the taxi driver replied.
"No."
"You said 'The Majestic Club'."
"That's right. Do you know where it is?"
"Oh, yes! I know where it is all right!" The taxi driver started the taxi, drove a few yards and then stopped. Another car stopped abruptly behind them, barely missing colliding with the rear end of the cab. "The Majestic Club!" announced the driver.

George looked out the window. They had stopped outside the building next door to the hotel. The red neon sign over the door said, 'The Majestic Club.'
"That'll be ten pounds please!" demanded the driver.
George got out the car and handed the driver a ten pound note through the open window. He knew the amount was extortionate but he could see that the driver

obviously felt he was part of a practical joke and was a man not to be argued with. As the taxi drew away, he glanced at the car that had stopped so suddenly behind them. The two large men from the hotel lobby were sitting in the front, both trying to look as if nothing untoward had happened. George turned, and without a second glance, hurried to the club entrance and entered through a glass door into the lighted lobby.

Two more large men stood behind the reception counter. Both had black hair slicked back with hair gel. Both wore dark dinner suits, white shirts and black bow ties. George handed one of them his invitation. "I've come for the film première party," he said.

The man gave George a knowing look and nodded. "Go right in," he said.

George went down some stairs and in to the club. It was dingily lit, except for a stage on which a young lady was divesting herself of her clothes to the sound of disco music. However, George barely noticed and went straight to the bar. The blonde barmaid was topless, a fact that even George could not fail to notice.

"I ... I ... think I may have come to the wrong place," he said, his voice uncertain.

"Can I get you a drink, sir?" the barmaid asked.

"I'm looking for the party from the film premiere," George continued.

"I'm supposed to serve you a drink," insisted the girl.

"Oh ... er ... Do you have any cider?"

"Certainly, sir." She turned, took a quarter litre bottle from the shelf behind her and removed the lid with a bottle opener. "Would you like a glass for this, sir?" she asked.

George looked at the label on the bottle. "Do you have any dry cider?" he asked.

"This is the only cider we do, sir. We don't get much call for it in here."

"Oh."

"Would you like a glass, sir?"

"Oh yes, thank you."

She produced the glass and set it on the bar next to the bottle.

"How ... How much is that?" asked George, his eyes fixed on the bottle, unable to look her in the eyes and unable to look at her any where else.

"You pay when you leave," she said.

George poured some of the cider into the glass. He set the bottle down and still looking at it said, "I ... was asking about the party from the film première."

"What film première is that, exactly?"

"The film, *The English Girl*."

"That's the film with that model in it, isn't it? Victoria Gloam?"

"That's right."

She shook her head. "I'm sorry," she said. "I don't know anything about a party from a film première."

"Oh."

He picked up his glass and turned to face the stage. It was then he realised that the girl on it was performing a striptease, and the only other occupants in the club, apart from four topless waitresses, were all male. He hastily took a sip of his drink. It was warm, sweet and fizzy. The barmaid was still standing there watching him.

"I ... er ... think I must have come to the wrong place," he said and set the glass down on the bar. "I'd better be going."

"Certainly, sir. That'll be fifty pounds."

"Fifty pounds! For one glass of cider?"

"Is there something wrong, sir?" The words were uttered by one of the large men George had met behind the reception counter upstairs. He had suddenly materialised and was standing at George's shoulder.

George was becoming very flustered. He started to speak. "I ... I ... think there must have been some mistake," he began.

The man leaned very heavily towards George. "Oh you do, do you?" he said threateningly. "Well I think you need to think again. What's the problem, Julie?"

"He was complaining about the price of his drink," explained the barmaid.

"Oh, you were, were you?" said the man, leaning ever more threateningly towards George.

"What of it!" The words were spoken by one of the men George had noticed at the hotel. His large dark hand was clamped firmly on George's antagonist's shoulder. The man's bald companion was standing the other side, so that he was sandwiched between them. Both towered over him and all three dwarfed George.

The first man looked up at both of them. "Who are you?" he asked.

"We don't like seeing fellow customers bovered," answered the bald-headed man. "Naw, we're sure that you don' either, so why don' you let the nice gent 'ave the drink on the 'ouse?"

"Yeah," agreed his companion. "Naw that would be nice. It would 'elp us fellow customers feel nice too."

The man looked helplessly from one to the other and then quickly around the room in search of assistance. None materialised. He shrugged, moved away from George and straightened up. "Sure," he said, "have this one on the house."

"And just to be sociable like," continued the bald man, "we'd like a couple of lagers - and make them on the 'ouse too."

"Yeah, 'course. Julie, get the gents two pints of larger on the house."

"That's more like it," said the Negro and watched the man hurriedly make his exit.

George stood by the bar dumbstruck while the barmaid poured the drinks. The men took the drinks and moved to the other end of the bar. George stood there nervously sipping his cider.

"Did you say you were waiting for a party from a film première?" asked the barmaid.

George nodded.

"Well, Cliff Clayburger's just come in."

"Who?"

"Cliff Clayburger. You know - the star of *The English Girl*. The film you were talking about." She nodded in the direction of a table near the stage where four men were taking their seats.

George followed her gaze. All four men were wearing dark dinner suits except for one man who was wearing a white dinner jacket with black trousers. He was in his forties with dark hair, black moustache and very was good looking. Two of the others were very large and looked like bodyguards. The fourth man was Hiram Cornslinger.

George set his glass down on the bar. "Excuse me," he said and made his way across to the table. "Hello, Hiram," he said.

Hiram looked up from where he was sitting next to the man in the white dinner Jacket. "Oh ... Hi," he said. "Hi, George!"

"Who the hell's this?" asked the man in the white dinner jacket.

"Oh, Cliff, this is George Cogrill, a friend of Vicky Gloam's," Hiram replied. "George, you know Cliff Clayburger, don't you?"

"No ... No I don't."

"You must have seen some of his movies," said Hiram irritably.

"No, I haven't. But I recognise you from your pictures in the papers; how do you do?" George held out his hand.

Cliff ignored it and simply nodded.

"Didn't expect to see you here, George," added Hiram.

"I was invited. I'm here for the party."

Cliff Clayburger's face brightened. "Hey!" he said. "What party is this?"

"The film première party," explained George.

All four men seated at the table began to laugh. George stared at them dumbly and began to feel embarrassed.

"There ain't no party here!" laughed Cliff.

"I'm afraid somebody musta bin pullin' ya leg, George," Hiram chuckled. "The party's at the Savoy!"

"But I got an invitation."

"Well," laughed Cliff, "as much as I'd like it to be, the party's not here. The press and my agent wouldn't wear it." He nodded towards the girl on the stage. "This is a clip joint, buddy! The party was a drag; I just wanted outa there. Hiram said he knew of a place where we could catch a live show. Know what I mean?"

"I overheard that guy, Sebastian somethin', and Vicky's Uncle Oliver talkin' ," said Hiram. "They mentioned this place. I thought it must be good, so I mentioned it to Cliff."

"An' it sure looks good to me. Sit down, George. Fellas, get the guy a chair." One of the other two men got up and fetched a chair from another table. Clay indicated the two men with a sweep of the hand. "This is Hank and Bobby," he said. "They kinda look after me."

George sat down at the table. A topless waitress appeared. "What would you like to drink?" she asked.

"Champagne!" said Cliff heartily. "Champagne all round. That okay with you guys?"

Cliff's three companions murmured in agreement. George remained silent.

"George?" asked Cliff.

"Er ... yes. Thank you," said George.

"Bring us four bottles and keep it coming!" Cliff told the waitress. She smiled and left.

The men, with the exception of George, turned their attention to the girl on the stage who was nearing the end of her act. George sat in silence, trying to look anywhere but the stage. The waitress returned with a trolley containing the champagne and some glasses. She poured the champagne and the glasses were handed around the table. Six young women appeared. They were heavily made up and wore tight-fitting dresses.

"Come an' join us ladies!" said Cliff heartily.

More chairs were pulled up. Two of the women sat either side of Cliff, almost on his lap. A redhead sat next to George and fixed him with her smile. The man called Hank passed each of the women a glass of champagne. George felt very uneasy. He wanted to leave.

"Tell me, George," asked Cliff, "how well do you know Vicky?"

"George is the photographer who discovered her," said Hiram.

"Is that a fact?" said Cliff. "Tell me; did she ever come across, George? I mean did you an' her ever…?"

"No!" George replied hurriedly. "We're just friends and business partners."

Cliff waved his hand. "Aw," he said, "I know all too well about that. She certainly likes to keep things on a business level, all right. Tell me, you ever photograph her in the nude?"

"Certainly not!" replied George indignantly.

"Can't say I'm surprised," continued Cliff. "She wouldn't shoot any nude scenes. We had to re-write the whole script. She didn't come across well in the love scenes either; on or off screen. She sure was one tight-ass bitch."

George leapt to his feet. "You'd better be careful what you're saying!" he shouted.

Hank and Bobby got up too. Then Hiram leapt to his feet. "Take it easy, George," he said. "Cliff don't mean any offence. Do ya, Cliff?"

Cliff remained seated. "Not to you, George," he said, "but as you gather, me an' Miss Gloam didn't hit it off too well so to speak, which is why I didn't stay at the party."

"I sill don't think you should be talking about her that way!" snapped George.

Hank and Bobby moved quickly either side of George and took his arms. "I think you ought ta be going now," hissed Bobby menacingly.

At that moment, the bald man and the Negro who had intervened earlier on George's behalf appeared. One went to Bobby and the other Hank, grasped their arms and pinioned them behind their backs.

"We think you ought to leave the nice gentleman alone," said the Negro with quiet menace.

George turned and walked quickly up the stairs and out of the club without looking back. His two rescuers released the surprised Hank and Bobby and followed him. Cliff's face was white. "Christ, Hiram," he said, "you coulda told me George was connected."

Outside, George walked back to the hotel. There he collected his suitcase and then took a taxi to Paddington station. He spent the remainder of the night in the waiting room, seated on a bench next to his suitcase. In the morning he caught the first train back to Tidburn and from there took a taxi home

CHAPTER 17

Two days later George looked out of his front window to see a large van parked outside the mill. Linda, Jonathan and Justin were moving out. He went into the kitchen and made his breakfast. Then he busied himself with his household chores. Finally he looked outside and saw Linda standing by the van, talking to the driver who was about to get into the cab. He opened his front door and went out to them. Linda turned and saw him.

"I was going to come and see you," she said. "We're about ready to go. I was going to return the keys to you. You might as well have them now." She handed him a key ring, on which were four sets of keys.

"Thank you," he said.

"They're all there," she added, "including Jonathan's and Justin's."

"Fine, thank you."

They stood looking at each other for a few moments and then George said, "I haven't seen you for some time. I was wondering. How did the film première go?"

"It wasn't really my sort of film but I can understand why it's been doing so well."

"How was the party?"

"It was not really my sort thing either, but it was okay."

"How was Vicky?"

Linda smiled. "Why don't you go and ask her yourself? She's been helping us move out. She's in the mill."

"Really?"

"Really," said Linda still smiling. She held out her hand. "Well, good-bye, George. I hope we keep in touch. After all, we're only in Tidburn."

George shook her hand. "Yes, of course," he said. "We'll keep in touch."

"When you see Vicky, tell her to hurry up, will you? The driver has got to get his lunch. So have I, for that matter."

"Yes, of course," said George. "Good-bye." And he found himself walking in the direction of the mill.

He found Vicky coming down the stairs from the flat. She stopped when she saw him. "Hello, George," she said and then continued until she joined him at the bottom.

"Hello," he replied.

"I've been helping the others move out," she explained.

"I know. I saw Linda outside. She asked me to tell you to hurry up."

"I've just been having a last look around to see if we haven't missed anything."

"How did the British Film Première go?" He asked.

"It seemed to go okay. Did you read the reviews?"

"Yes. They seemed mixed again."

"That's right."

"Are you going back to London today?"

"No. I'm staying with your aunt again. I've decided to take some time off. I've been doing a tour of the talk shows, publicity for the film. The endless round of late night and breakfast TV has left me quite tired. So I'm taking a rest. Tell me, George, what did you think of the film? I never really asked you before."

George hesitated. "Er ... I liked the restaurant scene," he said.

"The restaurant scene. That's the one they keep showing in TV film clips."

"Is it?"

"That's right."

"Oh."

"What did you like about it?"

"Um. It stood out."

"Do you mean the rest of the film wasn't as good?"

"No ... No!" George felt out of his depth and strove to change the subject. "I did see you on *The Drogson Show*," he added quickly.

Vicky nodded knowingly. "You did."

"That's right. I didn't expect to see Frank Witterworth on there though. I didn't know he was that well known."

"Uncle Oswald is also his agent and asked me if I could get him on. I've known Frank for years. It was the least I could do."

"I didn't think his poetry was that popular?"

"Actually," said Vicky, "it's selling quite well just now. His poem in memory of poor Old Joe Thropp was very well received. He's making quite a name for himself."

"Really?"

"Are you ready, Vicky?" They looked round and saw Linda standing in the doorway.

"Yes," said Vicky. "I'm ready. Good-bye, George."

"Good-bye," said George and watched her follow Linda outside.

Two days later, Aunt Jane opened wide the throttle of the Triumph Bonneville motorcycle and, as usual, it accelerated out of the corner, over the brow of Mucklesbury Hill and downwards at breakneck speed. As usual she began breaking fiercely at the bottom. However, on this occasion the breaks failed to respond. She realised that she was not going to make the drive of Gleefield Manor. She knew also that she would not make the bend opposite. Quite deliberately she opened the throttle still wider.

"Winchester!" she yelled and sailed over the hedge, the opposite side of the road, and over the edge of Mucklesbury quarry. She remained astride the motorcycle until it reached the bottom three hundred feet below.

A quarter of a mile away, Winchester lay in front of the open fire in the drawing room of Gleefield Manor. He opened one eye, closed it again, and went back to sleep without raising his head.

CHAPTER 18

Two weeks later and George was visiting the vicarage at Mucklesbury. He found the Reverent Scillage in the garden raking up dead leaves from under a chestnut tree. "Hello, Vicar!" he called in greeting. "I'm glad I caught you. I thought I'd better tell you that my aunt's headstone will be arriving later this morning."

"Thank you, George," the Vicar replied.

"I also wanted to thank for the service you gave last week. I'm not sure I did so at the funeral."

"Oh, don't worry. I'm sure you had a lot on your mind. It was a quiet funeral. The sort I prefer; Quite unlike that of Old Joe Thropp." The reverent shook his head sadly.

"Yes, I always thought it would be. My aunt didn't make many friends."

"No," agreed the vicar, "she wasn't a regular churchgoer either. Still, she always made regular donations to the church restoration fund and I heard that she also left a large amount to the church in her will."

"She was very practical, my aunt. She wanted to make sure her grave would be regularly tended."

"Yes, that was the condition in her will. And you can be assured that her wishes will be followed to the letter." The vicar cleared his throat and added. "We don't see you much in church either, George. In fact I don't recall you attending Sunday service since you were a choir boy."

"Er ... no, Vicar. I'd better be going now. Good-bye and thanks again."

"Good-bye, George. Oh, by the way, your aunt had more friends than you think. In fact I saw a visitor by her grave this morning. There she is now."

George turned to see a blonde-haired figure in a long navy-blue coat coming out of the churchyard. It was Vicky

Gloam. "Good-bye, Vicar," he said and hurried across the road to greet her. "Hello, Vicky."

George saw her stop and waited for him by the gate as he approached. "Hello," she said. "I was so sorry to hear about your aunt's death, and I was sorry I wasn't able to come to her funeral. I was booked to film some TV adverts and contractual obligations meant I was unable to get out of it."

George nodded in reply.

"It must have been very quick," continued Vicky then paused. "Look," she added, "I'm down here with a friend. I know he'd like to meet you. He's waiting in The Pullet Inn. Why don't you join us for a drink?"

"Oh, I don't think I should really intrude."

"Go on," she insisted. "Apparently he's met you before."

"All right then."

They made their way along the road to the pub and found Vicky's visitor sitting alone at a small table. It was Simon Clitterbooth, the film cameraman George had met on the plane to Los Angeles. He got to his feet at their approach and held out his hand to George. "Hello, George," he said. "It's good to see you again."

George shook the offered hand. "Hello, Simon."

Simon continued talking rapidly. "When I heard that Vicky knew you and was coming down this way, I could not miss out on the opportunity of meeting you again and tasting your wonderful cider, so I offered her a lift in my car. Sit down and I'll get you both a drink. Cider, is it?"

"Yes, please," George replied.

"Yes, thank you, Simon," said Vicky.

They sat down at the table while Simon went to the bar.

They sat in silence for a while. George wanted to say something but was unsure how to begin the conversation. Then Vicky asked, "Have you been keeping well?"

"Yes, thank you", he replied. "Have you?"

"Yes."

"How are things at the mill?"

"Fine."

"I'm glad I saw you," she said. "I was going to drop in and see you. To see how you were."

"How long have you known Simon?" asked George.

"Not long. He was filming the advert I was making. We hit it off right away once he knew I knew you and where to get Cogrill's cider. He's quite a fan of your photography, you know. Says he thinks that you've been underrated."

"That's kind of him."

"He's highly regarded in the film business," she added.

"Really?"

"When I told him about the mill, he said it might be suitable for some location work. For TV adverts and such."

"I see."

"But that's not the main reason I came. I was sorry I missed your aunt's funeral. She was very good to me. She let me stay at her house. And she did teach me how to ride a motorcycle. I also wanted to see how you were. To see how you were coping. I know your aunt was extremely fond of you and you must have been awfully fond of her, seeing as she practically brought you up. I've been very concerned about you."

George noticed Tom Firkin come into the bar. He had Aunt Jane's dog Winchester with him on a lead. Tom looked around, saw George with Vicky, nodded to him and came over to them. "'Ow do," he said and noticing that neither had a drink added," can I get yer both a drink?"

"No, thank you, Tom," replied Vicky. "Someone's already getting us one."

"Oh," said Tom, "see yer la'er then, George." He went to the bar to get himself a drink.

"I had arranged to meet Tom in here," explained George.

"Oh."

Simon returned and put two half pint glasses of cider in front of them. "There you are," he said. "I wasn't sure if you wanted pints or halves, so I bought halves to be on the safe side." He sat down. "Vicky tells me that your aunt has just died, George. I must say I'm very sorry to hear that, especially as I understand that you were her only surviving relative. I believe she left rather a large estate, so you must be very busy right now."

"Not especially," replied George. "The estate's nothing to do with me."

"I thought she was going to leave it to you," said Vicky. "She always talked as if she would."

"Not to me she didn't. The new owner's over there." He nodded in the direction of the bar.

They followed his gaze. "You mean Tom?" said Vicky. "She left the estate to Tom?"

"No. She left it to Winchester."

"To Winchester!" exclaimed Vicky in astonishment.

"Who's Winchester?" asked Simon.

"Winchester is the black Labrador with Tom. He was my aunt's gundog."

An hour later Vicky and Simon Clitterbooth left the pub in Simon's Jaguar sports car and drove in the direction of Gleefield Manor. Ten minutes later they pulled up outside the front door of the great house. They rang the bell and the door was opened by Gumage, clad as usual in his black suit and grey waistcoat.

"Hello, Gumage," said Vicky. "This is a friend of mine, Simon Clitterbooth. Simon very kindly drove me down here today. A solicitor contacted me a few days ago. I understand that Lady Gleefield left something for me in her will."

"That's correct, Miss. If you would like to wait here, I will go and get the key." He withdrew back inside the house, leaving the door open and them waiting on the doorstep.

"This sounds interesting," remarked Simon. "What it is it the old lady has left you?"

"I wasn't told. Her solicitor contacted me through Uncle Oswald a couple of days ago. However I think I can take a guess."

"I hope it's not the key to Winchester's kennel. Fancy her leaving a place like this to a dog. She must have been barmy. And that friend of yours George is barmier still. I couldn't believe it when he said he wasn't contesting the will."

Vicky grew angry. "George is not barmy," she snapped. "He's got what he's only really wanted. He's got the mill." She had a sudden thought and added, "I wonder if she left anything to the cat?"

"What cat?"

"I seem to remember George telling me that she had a cat called Mable. Though I've never seen it." She broke off talking at the sound of Gumage's returning footsteps and added in a whisper, "Shush, he's coming back."

Gumage reappeared and said, "Follow me please," and set off across the gravel drive towards the garages. He opened the double doors. Inside were Aunt Jane's three remaining motorcycles.

"Motorbikes!" exclaimed Simon. "She left you motorbikes?"

"After Winchester, they were her pride and joy," said Vicky softly and tears filled her eyes.

Simon entered the garage and ran his hand over the gleaming black petrol tank of the Norton motorcycle and then stood back and admired the Triumph Bonneville and BSA Goldstar which stood next to it. "They're in good nick," he remarked. "Do you ride?"

"Aunt Jane taught me."

"Do you wish to take any of them away, Miss?" said Gumage. "You can keep them here for the time being if you like. I'm sure his lordship won't mind."

Simon raised his eyebrows. "His lordship?" he inquired.

"Lord Winchester, sir."

"Lord Winchester? The dog?"

"That's right sir. However," he added, "I help make the decisions in the running of the house and look after him while he is at home. Mr Firkin makes the decisions with regard to running the estate and looks after him when he goes for walks. Life here is run much the same as when her ladyship was alive."

"Really?"

"That's right, sir."

"What about the cat?"

Gumage raised his eyebrows. "Cat, sir? What cat is that?"

"Lady Gleefield's cat," interjected Vicky, "Mable."

"Lady Gleefield never kept any cats, Miss. She didn't like them. She much preferred dogs. Perhaps I could arrange to have the motorcycles sold and the money forwarded on to you if you wish."

"No, that won't be necessary, Gumage," Vicky replied. "In fact, I'd quite like to take the Boneville with me now, if that's all right. Do you still have my motorcycle leathers and helmet here?"

"Yes, Miss. They are still in the wardrobe in the guest room where you stayed when you were last here. I will go and lay them out for you and, if you wish, you can change in the room before setting out."

"Thank you, Gumage," said Vicky, "that's very kind of you. I'll just say good-bye to Mr Clitterbooth and join you in a minute."

"Very good, Miss," replied Gumage and retreated in the direction of the great house.

Vicky turned to Simon. "Thank you very much for bringing me down here, Simon. I'm sorry it didn't turn out to be worthwhile."

"Well," said Simon, "it would have been nice if we could have persuaded George to use his mill as a location. But he seemed pretty unmovable." He shrugged his shoulders. "It's just one of those things. At least I got to tasting some of that marvellous cider again. So it wasn't entirely wasted." He changed the subject. "Curious about the cat though," he added. "Are you sure George said she had a cat?"

"Definitely, a cat called Mable. It's not something I'd make up; although, as I said, I've never seen it. I'd quite forgotten about it. It was only when you started talking about Winchester and kennels that I remembered."

"Well, cats are very independent," mused Simon. "They can keep out of the way." He smiled wickedly. "You don't suppose Gumage and Winchester secretly did away with her so that Winchester could cop all the money?"

"Now you're just being silly!"

He sighed. "The whole thing sounds most odd," he said. "Where are you headed now?"

"Tidburn. I want to visit Linda, Justin and Jonathan at my old studio. I'll stay there overnight and head back to London in the morning to see Uncle Oswald. I'd be grateful if you could leave my luggage at the studio. I'll pick it up from there."

"No problem," replied Simon, "but then I must press on home. You'll keep in touch."

"Of course." She kissed him briefly on the cheek. "Good-bye, Simon. And thank you."

CHAPTER 19

Uncle Oswald stood in the hall way of his house waiting for the newspaper boy to arrive. It was eight-thirty in the morning and the boy was late. But that did not dismay Uncle Oswald. In fact, it rather suited his plans. He looked out of the window in the door. It was a dark misty autumn morning. The house was situated in a London suburb and was one of a number of Georgian terraced buildings which lined the street.

He saw the boy mount the steps to his front porch and push the paper through the letter box. He quickly slipped into the sitting room adjacent to the hall, switched on the cassette recorder incorporated in his hi-fi system, then he hurried back out to the hall, picked up the newspaper and swung open the front door.

"What time do you call this?" he demanded.

The boy, a thin dark-haired youth with acne and clad in blue denim, had just descended the last step on to the pavement. He turned in surprise. "What do yuh mean?" he blurted.

"Come here!" snapped Uncle Oswald.

The boy hesitated.

Uncle Oswald brandished the paper he was holding. "Come and look at the state of this," he said.

The boy stood his ground. "What's wrong with it?" he asked.

"If you want to keep your job you'll come and look at this," said Uncle Oswald. He patted the newspaper with his other hand.

The boy advanced slowly and reluctantly up the steps towards him. The sound of scraping and banging came from the sitting room then came the sound of Sebastian's voice asking, "Who are you talking to, Oswald?"

Oswald turned his head briefly back towards the interior of the hall. "The paper boy!" he called. He turned back to the paper boy and softened his voice. "It's my friend," he explained. "He's helping me decorate the house. We're stripping off the wallpaper in the sitting room."

The boy nodded and stopped one step away from Uncle Oswald.

The banging and scraping continued. "Makes a noise, doesn't he?" said Uncle Oswald.

"Who are you talking to, Oswald?" repeated Sebastian's voice.

"The paper boy!" Uncle Oswald called once more and then advanced towards the boy who began backing down the steps towards the street. "Look at this paper," said Uncle Oswald. "Look how creased it is."

"Looks all right to me," said the boy.

"Well just take more care in the future."

The boy shrugged. "Okay," he said and set off down the street.

Uncle Oswald stepped down on to the pavement and watched him go. A smile of satisfaction crossed his lips. Earlier that morning he had accosted the milkman in similar fashion, complaining that he had not delivered the right amount of milk. Later that day he had arranged for groceries to be delivered and he planned to give the delivery man the same treatment. He had been well satisfied with how these encounters with delivery men had gone.

A familiar sound came to his ears. He looked along the street into the mist and saw a motorcycle driven by a white-helmeted, leather-suited rider heading in his direction. His heart stopped. Whoever it was looked just like Lady Jane Gleefield. He turned quickly and fled up the steps into his house. He slammed the door shut and pressed his back firmly against it. His face was white and he was breathing hard. Wild thoughts filled his head. It could not be her. She was dead.

Banging and scraping could still be heard from the next room and Sebastian's voice asked, "Who are you talking to, Oswald?"

Uncle Oswald heard the motorcycle stop outside his house. The sound of the engine stopped and footsteps approached his front door. The doorbell rang. His whole body was now shaking with fear. He had to open the door. Failing to do so would destroy all his best-laid plans. The bell sounded again. He turned slowly and opened the door.

Vicky stood on the doorstep, helmet in hand and her long golden hair falling down on to her shoulders. He breathed a sigh of relief. "Good gracious, Vicky," he breathed, "for one moment I thought you were Lady Gleefield."

"I'm sorry to disturb you, Uncle Oswald," said Vicky, "but I wanted to run through some business ideas with you. I'm planning to go back to America soon and I wanted your views. Your secretary told me that you were doing some decorating at home."

Sebastian's voice from next door once again asked, "Who are you talking to, Oswald?"

Vicky called in reply, "It's me, Sebastian. Vicky Gloam!"

Uncle Oswald was shocked into action. "Is that your motorcycle outside? I'd like to take a look at it if I may."

"It's one of Lady Gleefield's, one of her Triumph Bonneville's. The one she wasn't riding when she died. She left it to me in her will. You must have seen it before."

Uncle Oswald became very flustered. "Yes, yes," he said, "it's a lovely machine. I'd still love to take a look at it though. I've always admired it."

"You've never shown much interest before. Are you all right, Uncle Oswald?"

"Yes, of course ... Although now that you come to mention it, I haven't been feeling too well. Perhaps it would be better if you came back later."

Sebastian's voice sounded again, "Who are you talking to, Oswald?"

Vicky looked at Uncle Oswald suspiciously. "What's going on?" she asked.

"Nothing, really. Sebastian's just helping me with the decorating, that's all." Uncle Oswald turned towards the sitting room, raised his voice and called. "It's all right, Sebastian. It's only Vicky!" He turned back to face her. "Look, perhaps it would be better if you came back another time."

Vicky persisted. "I would really like to talk to you now, Uncle Oswald. There are one or two things that have really been bothering me lately. I won't take up too much of your time, honestly."

Uncle Oswald was now very flustered indeed and was breathing heavily. "Look, Vicky dear, please go!"

"What's the matter? Uncle, you look terrible. You're not going to have a heart attack are you? Stay here, sit down, keep calm. I'll get you a drink of water."

She began to push past him but he caught her arm. "No please," he gasped. "I'm all right."

Sebastian's voice called again, "Who are you talking to, Oswald?"

Vicky pulled her arm free. "This is ridiculous!" she snapped and pushed on towards the sitting room. She pushed open the door and entered. "Sebastian, Uncle Oswald is not feeling very ... Oh!"

She stopped abruptly. There was no one in the room. Indeed everything was neat and tidy. There was no sign of any decorating taking place. The sounds of scraping and banging continued from the hi-fi speakers. Uncle Oswald had followed her into the room. He hurried across to the hi-fi system and switched off the sound. Vicky stood and stared at him. She looked bewildered.

"Uncle Oswald," she asked, "why are you pretending that Sebastian's here in this room?"

Uncle Oswald stood silently looking at her.

She continued talking hurriedly. "You're covering up something, aren't you? What are you up to?"

He did not answer so she continued talking, this time speaking more sharply. "Why were you so upset when you thought I was Lady Gleefield?" She stopped talking and looked at him in horror. "You and Sebastian didn't have anything to do with her death, did you? My gosh! He killed Old Joe Thropp, didn't he? It wasn't an accident, was it? Don't say he killed Lady Gleefield as well."

Uncle Oswald remained standing in silence.

Vicky continued her discourse. "Where is Sebastian now? He's trying to kill someone else, isn't he?"

"Vicky ... " began Uncle Oswald.

Vicky's voice rose shrilly. "Who's he going to kill, Uncle Oswald?" She paused as if waiting for his reply but he could not think what to say. "My gosh! Old Joe Thropp's death was an accident, wasn't it? No one could want to deliberately kill a harmless old man they had never met before. He was standing next to George, wasn't he? Sebastian meant to kill George. Oh my God!"

She dashed from the room as this realisation dawned on her and before Uncle Oswald could stop her. He waited, stunned for a few seconds and then rushed towards the sideboard, pulled open a drawer and took out a revolver. He had bought it from a man in London's East End as he did not wholly trust Sebastian and was concerned for his own protection. He had studied videos of old crime movies and practised a basic stance and aiming the gun every night in front of the bathroom mirror. With the gun grasped tightly in his fist, he ran after Vicky.

He reached the bottom of the steps just as her motorcycle was pulling away. Remembering the self-taught basics he had learnt, he stepped into the road, took up a crouched position and with the gun held in both hands took careful aim. Tears filled his eyes. "Sorry, Vicky," he said to himself. "I'm so sorry, Vicky." Unfortunately, he had forgotten any basics he had learnt about road safety and was struck from behind by a red double-decker bus. He was killed instantly.

Vicky rode onward. She was unaware of what had occurred behind her and rode with her body bent over the petrol tank through the streets of London, aiming for the motorway that led to Mucklesbury. As she rode, she became aware that she might not make it in time. Stopping at a line of phone boxes outside a post office, she dialled George's number but the phone at the other end of the line seemed dead. After tapping the receiver cradle impatiently, she dialled the operator, who told her that there had been a storm in the Mucklesbury area and that some of the lines were down. She remounted the motorcycle and rode on.

Eventually she reached the motorway and was soon following the signposts towards Tidburn. The mist now had turned to fine rain, and as she rode further the rain became harder. It sprayed over her visor, and up from under her wheels. It was as if she was riding under a veil of water like a frogman astride a midget submarine. The wind grew stronger, driving the rain into her, but still she rode onward.

Sixty miles away Sebastian was knocking on the front door of George's cottage. George opened the door and stared out at him through the pouring rain. Sebastian was clad in a long black rain coat and wellington boots. A black trilby hat was pulled down to just over his eyes. The rain cascaded off it and down on to his shoulders.

"Hello," he said. "I was passing ... and I couldn't help noticing ... there seems to be something wrong with your mill."

George stared at him blankly. "What do you mean?" he asked.

"It appears to be unstable."

"What do you mean unstable?" George stepped out of the porch and looked towards the mill. He squinted through the rain, which now began splattering his hair and pullover. "It looks okay to me," he said.

"Perhaps you can't see too well from here," went on Sebastian. "It looked from the road that the river may have undermined the bank and affected the foundations."

"You'd better come in while I put on some waterproof clothing," said George. "Then we'll go and take a look."

Sebastian followed him into the house. "Wait in the hall," said George. "I won't be long." He disappeared out to the scullery to fetch his waterproofs and wellington boots.

Sebastian waited just inside the front door. His right hand was in his coat pocket, his fingers touching the hard shinny surface of a stout wooden cosh.

Fifty miles away Vicky was clinging to the motorcycle as it sped on through the rain. The wind was buffeting her and she struggled to keep the machine upright. She thought about stopping at a service station and again telephoning George, the police, or one of her friends in Tidburn. But, if telephone lines were down it would only serve to waste valuable time. She and the motorcycle sped onward.

Forty-five miles farther on, George, clad in his fishing waterproofs of sou'-wester, oil skins and waders, made his way through the rain towards the mill. Sebastian followed behind. They stopped outside the main door to the mill and George studied the outside of the building. Then he walked round the building, surveying the structure as he went. Sebastian followed.

Ten minutes later, they retraced their steps and arrived back at the main door. "It looks all right to me!" George shouted to make himself heard above the wind, rain and the rushing water of the nearby River Muckle. "I think I'll go and check inside!"

"I'll check the outside again!" Sebastian shouted back to him.

George unlocked the door and went inside on his own.

He checked the ground floor first and then the upstairs rooms, which included Vicky's old flat. Everything appeared in order and there were no signs of any leaks. He returned downstairs and found Sebastian waiting just inside the front door.

"Well," said George, "I can't find anything wrong. This building has been standing for hundreds of years. I think you must have been mistaken."

"I don't think I am," replied Sebastian. "I think you ought to come outside and see what I've found."

"Okay," said George, "lead on and I'll follow."

Two miles away Vicky opened wide the throttle of the Triumph Bonneville motorcycle and the great machine accelerated out of the corner and over the brow of Mucklesbury Hill and downwards at breakneck speed. She applied the breaks fiercely at the bottom and then leant the motorcycle hard over to the left so that it missed the hedge on the opposite side of the road and the edge of the cliff above Mucklesbury quarry where Aunt Jane had died. Then she drove on through the rain and along the road in the direction of the old mill.

George followed Sebastian around the outside of the mill to the point where the great waterwheel reached out over the river. Sebastian stopped and pointed up at the wheel.

"Up there," he shouted above the noise of the rushing water. "Up there. It's unsafe."

George followed his gaze, squinting his eyes to avid the stinging rain drops. "What do you mean, unsafe?" he asked. "I can't see anything."

"I'll show you," replied Sebastian. He stepped out on to one of the wooden spokes that supported the wheel and began to climb. "Come on, follow me."

George shrugged and reluctantly followed him. Sebastian stopped and pointed to the wall of the mill. "There!" he shouted. "That looks most unsteady!"

"I can't see anything wrong!" George shouted back.

"Come round me," suggested Sebastian. "You'll be able to see better."

Sebastian climbed a fraction higher to allow him to pass and George climbed round his legs and edged out further over the rushing water.

"I still can't see anything!" called George scanning his eyes up and down the wall.

"Look down where the wall joins the bank!" shouted Sebastian. As he spoke, his right hand went into his pocket and grasped the cosh.

George looked down. "I can't see anything except for an old rowing boat. It's probably slipped its moorings from somewhere upstream and it looks like it's stuck in the reeds under the wheel. I can't see anything wrong with the wheel though."

Sebastian drew the cosh out of his pocket and struck at the back of George's head.

Vicky reached the gate leading to the mill. It had been left open and was swinging to and fro in the wind. She rode the motorcycle though the gap and in the same instant saw the two men clinging to the great wheel. She saw Sebastian strike and saw George fall. She roared on towards the mill sounding the motorcycle horn and screaming at the top of her voice.

Sebastian looked up and saw her. Fear gripped his entire body as he saw not Vicky, but Aunt Jane coming for him from out of the wind and rain to exact revenge from beyond the grave. He let go of the wheel and fell into the rushing River Muckle.

CHAPTER 20

Later that evening Tom entered The Pullet Inn with Winchester attached to a lead. Jack Hump was behind the bar and nodded gravely to Tom as he approached. "Ow do, Tom," he inquired. "Any news?"

"They fished Sebastian's body out the river just afore dark - drowned. No sign of George though. I'll 'ave a pint of zider please, Jack." Tom gestured down to the dog. "Sit, Winchester," he said and then added as an afterthought, "please, yer lordship."

Winchester sat.

Jack took a bottle of Cogrill's Old Mill Cider from his secret supply in a cupboard underneath the till and opened it and poured it into a glass which he passed to Tom. "Ave it on the 'ouse, Tom," he said and then bent down and took out another bottle. "In fact I think I'll join yer."

"Thanks, Jack." Tom raised his glass. "Cheers," he said and took a long sip of cider.

Jack finished pouring his own drink and took a sip also. "Any chance of findin' George alive?" he asked.

"I really don' know. The river's running quite fast. I took Winchester for a walk along the banks. If anyone could find 'im, 'e could. But even 'e can't smell through water. We'll try again first light, but nobody holds out much hope."

Jack shook his head. "Terrible business. First Old Joe, then Lady Gleefield, naw this. Terrible. 'Ows the young lady?"

"Vicky? She's taken it very badly. Blames 'erself. Says it's all her uncle's and Sebastian's doing. I didn' quite understand what she was on about."

"There was a couple of policemen in earlier," said Jack. "They said that the uncle and Sebastian conspired to kill

Lady Gleefield and George, but it seems they got their just deserts. The uncle got run over by a bus in London."

"Yer don't say?"

Jack nodded gravely. "So they say."

Winchester stirred at Tom's feet.

"Can you get 'is lordship a pack of crisps, Jack?" asked Tom, indicating the dog with a sweep of his hand.

"Sure. What flavour?"

"Smoky Bacon, please."

Winchester wagged his tail at the sound of the last three words. Jack fetched the crisps and tossed them over the bar on to the floor where the dog ripped open the packet and began devouring the contents. "Yes, 'ave these on the 'ouse, yer lordship," announced Jack. "Must cet'ainly be strange ter be workin' for a dog."

Tom took a sip of his cider and nodded. "Strange times indeed," he agreed. "And sad ones too."

Ten miles downstream from The Pullet Inn and eleven miles from the mill, George Cogrill opened his eyes. He was lying in the bottom of the old rowing boat that he had seen just before he had fallen from the mill's large water wheel. He had landed in the boat, which was driven by his sudden weight out from the reeds, where it had been stuck, and downstream, forced by the rush of turbulent water.
The boat was now stuck once more amongst reeds but was not far from the river bank. It was dark, but it had stopped raining. The river still flowed fast but the water was not so turbulent.

He climbed out of the boat. The water came up to the knees of his waders. He paddled slowly ashore and climbed out onto the river bank. The pressure from his bladder was almost overwhelming. He stood on the bank, unzipped his fly and urinated.

"Hey, mind what you are doing!" The voice came from a stout shadowy figure crouched by the waterside and in the process of filling a kettle. The figure straightened and turned out to be male and was wearing a Stetson, but George could not make out his features in the dark. "I was hoping to drink this," the man said, "but I s'pose I'd better go further up stream."

George watched while the figure walked a few yards further on, stooped, rinsed the kettle in the water and filled it. He turned to face George. "It's been a pretty wild day, weather-wise," he said.

George regarded him in silence.

"Do you live near here?"

George did not reply.

The man shrugged, turned his back and set off across a grassy field. George stood and watched him for a moment, then slowly followed.

They walked towards a light coming from the edge of the field. As they drew near it was apparent that the light was coming from the windows of a motor caravan that had pulled off the road and was parked in front of a hedge beside an open five-bar gate. Beyond the hedge and gate was the open road and the intermittent sound of passing traffic. There was writing on the side of the caravan and as he drew near George made out the words "The Tumbleweeds", written in red and yellow against the white-painted vehicle. The colours were pale in the darkened light but were distinguishable as the sky was now clear and the surroundings were bathed in the light of a full moon.

The man climbed a step and opened the side door. Light flooded out and revealed him to be in his late fifties with greying brown hair. He was wearing a brown fringed jacket, checked shirt, blue jeans and brown leather cowboy boots. He turned to shut the door and George saw he had a greying brown moustache. He noticed George standing there watching him.

"This isn't your field by any chanced?" the man asked him.

George stood and stared at him blankly.

The man continued. "If it is, we didn't mean any harm. We only stopped to cook something to eat and brew some coffee. We don't mean any harm."

"Who are you speaking to, Roy?" A woman's voice sounded from further inside the van.

"There's a man here I met by the river!"

"Why don't you invite him in?"

"Would you like to come in?" the man called Roy asked George. He opened the door wider and gestured with a sweep of his arm.

George climbed the step and entered the van.

A small woman, also in her late fifties, was busy putting dirty dishes in a sink in a small kitchen area in the centre of the vehicle. She had blonde hair which looked dyed, also wore blue jeans and a checked shirt, but had pink carpet slippers on her feet. She turned and looked at George. "Would you like some coffee?" she asked.

George stood staring at her in silence.

She grew uneasy. "Well?" she asked becoming impatient.

George nodded his head in reply.

"Have you got that water, Roy?" she asked.

"Yes. Excuse me." George stepped aside, Roy passed him and handed the woman the kettle.

"Would you like to take off your rain clothes and sit down?" she asked George who was still wearing his oilskins, sou'-wester and fishing waders.

George slowly took off the sou'-wester followed by the oilskins to reveal a grey damp pullover and damp brown corduroy trousers.

"Goodness!" she exclaimed. "Your clothes look wet through, and by the way your teeth are chattering you're feeling the cold. You don't look too well either. Roy, take the young man to the room in the back. Get those wet clothes off him and give him something warm to wear or he'll catch his death of cold!"

"Come this way," said Roy and led George to the rear of the motor caravan and into a bedroom partitioned off from the rest of the interior. He found him a towel and a thick blue towelling dressing gown. "Here, dry yourself with this and put the gown on. Come through when you're ready and we'll have a hot drink waiting for you." Then he left him alone and returned to the kitchen area, closing the door behind him.

The woman was placing three cups out on a small dining table. The kettle was sitting on the lighted gas stove next to a filled coffee percolator. "What do you make of him, Pearl?" Roy asked her in a low voice.

Peal answered him in a soft excited whisper. "He reminds me of Johnny," she said. "He has the same look about him. In fact he'd be about the same age as him if Johnny had lived."

Roy nodded. "I thought so too."

"He certainly doesn't look to well. He shouldn't be walking around in those wet clothes." She stood still and stared into space. "He does so look like Johnny," she said.

Roy interrupted her thoughts. "Look, we've got to get to that gig by nine," he said. "We can't afford to hang around here too long."

"But we can't just leave him," she protested. "He doesn't look well. We can drop him off somewhere on the way."

Roy sighed and turned away, poured some of the warm water from the kettle into the washing up bowl in the sink, put the kettle back on the stove to re-heat and began washing the dirty dishes. Pearl picked up a dishcloth and began drying the washed plates which Roy passed to her. A few minutes later George emerged from the back room just as the percolator was spluttering into life. He was wearing the towelling dressing gown.

"Sit down, dear," said Pearl indicating one of four vacant chairs at the table. "The coffee's nearly ready."

George sat down at the table.

"Do you live near here?" she asked looking down at him, the dishcloth still in her hand.

George looked up at her. A look of fear was in his eyes. "I don't know," he said. There was a trace of panic in his voice. "In fact I can't remember anything. I've been trying to remember but I can't remember anything!"

"What do you mean, you can't remember anything?" asked Roy.

George looked down at the table and shook his head as if he was trying to clear it. "I can't remember anything," he repeated.

"What's your name?" asked Pearl.

George looked at her blankly. "I don't know," he said. "I just don't know!"

"What do you mean, you don't remember your own name?" asked Roy.

"Take it easy, Roy," said Pearl. Turning to George, she said gently, "Take your time. There's no hurry. We'll have some coffee in a moment and you'll feel much better."

"Pearl! We've got to be in. . ." began Roy in protest.

"Be quiet, Roy, we have plenty of time!" she snapped.

She put the dishcloth on the draining board and sat down opposite George. "I'm Pearl and that's Roy. We're the Tumbleweeds. It's not our real name of course. We're Country and Western singers. We don't really have a fixed home. We travel around from act to act. We don't stay in any one place too long. That's why we call ourselves the Tumbleweeds after the Western plant that gets blown around by the wind. I used to be a social worker. Roy was a school teacher. We've always liked Country Music. Our only son died in a car crash five years ago. After that we decided to quit the rat race and took to the roads. We've been travelling and singing together ever since."

"It's been a great life," Roy added. "Neither of us has regretted it. Have we, Pearl?"

Pearl looked at him and smiled. "No we haven't," she said.

"I reckon the way we live will be the way most people will have to live in the future," said Roy. "Jobs aren't as secure as they once were. People will have to live by travelling from town to town. And I don't mean gypsies or even the so called 'New Age Travellers'. I mean ordinary middle class folk, like Pearl and I once were."

"We've been very happy these last few years," said Pearl.

"Look, Pearl," said Roy. "We really must get moving soon."

"Right," said Pearl and got up, picked up the percolator and poured the coffee. "Do you take milk and sugar?" she asked George. Then, seeing him struggling to remember, added, "No matter. Have it black and sweet like us. Roy, why don't you go next door and find some of your old clothes for our guest? You're about the same size so they should fit."

Roy disappeared next door and Pearl passed a cup of coffee to George. "Drink up," she said. "I'll make you some bread and cheese. I'd cook you something but as Roy said we have to be moving soon. You can eat while we're travelling and see if your memory comes back. But take it easy, there's no rush."

Roy returned. "I've laid out some clothes on the bed," he said. "Go through and try them on. You can take the coffee with you."

George did as he was told and Roy picked up a cup of coffee and sat down. "Are you sure you know what you're doing?" he asked Pearl.

"Well, we can't just leave him here. He's not well."

Roy lowered his voice. "But he might not have lost his memory at all. He might be on the run from the police or something."

"I don't think so. He reminds me so much of Johnny."

Roy sighed. "This reminds me of the old days, when you were working for social services and bringing home so many waifs and strays."

"It's not like that at all!" snapped Pearl. "Now, go on. You can take your coffee and start the van up, seeing as you're in so much of a hurry."

Roy sighed, took a sip of coffee and moved forward to the driving seat. He set the coffee mug down on a small ledge on the dashboard and started the engine. Then he manoeuvred the motor caravan out through the gate and on to the open road. Meanwhile, Pearl took a loaf of bread from the bread bin, some cheese from a small fridge near the sink and began to make a sandwich for George.

George emerged once more from the back room with the empty coffee mug, which he set down on the table. He was also now wearing blue jeans and a checked shirt. But over the shirt was an old thick green pullover of Roy's; on his feet were thick woollen socks and a pair of red cord carpet slippers.

"Hello," said Pearl. "Why don't you go up front and sit next to Roy and I'll bring you your sandwich. You can eat while we're travelling. I'm sorry we can't hang around but we've got a singing engagement and we can't afford to be late."

George moved forward and sat in the passenger seat next to Roy. Roy glanced at him and nodded, acknowledging his presence. "It's a pity we've got to move on so fast," he said. "This looked like a beautiful part of the country." He reached forward and switched on the radio-cassette player. "Let's have some music. I'm afraid the radio's not working. I think something's wrong with the aerial. The cassette player's working though. Do you like Country music?"

George remained silent as he could not remember.

"Well, never mind," continued Roy. "The tape that's in here is one that Pearl and I recorded as a demo three years ago." He turned up the volume and George heard Pearl and Roy's voices giving a rendition of Dolly Parton's "Joylene" to the accompaniment of acoustic guitars.

Pearl moved into a passenger seat behind George and passed him a sandwich. Roy continued talking above the sound of the music. "Yes," Roy was saying. "It certainly looked a pretty part of the countryside around here. It's a pity we didn't take in much of it because of the rain. We called in a pub back there and had some really nice tasting local cider. Cogrill's something, I think it was called. You ever heard of it?"

George thought long and hard and then shook his head.

"A pity," said Roy. "It was really good stuff."

The next day the storm had completely dissipated and a watery late autumn sunlight shone down on to the mill and the surrounding countryside. It was eleven o'clock in the morning and the police were searching the ground around the mill. The river was not running so fast now and there were police frogmen in the water. They were looking for George's body.

Tom was standing on the bank near the great water wheel with Winchester on a lead at his side. They were both watching the frogmen. An old Austin mini car drew up and parked next to the gate leading to the mill. Out got Linda, Jonathan, Justin and Vicky. They saw Tom and started towards the gate, intent on joining him, but were stopped by a police constable who was stationed there to ward off passers-by and sightseers. Tom turned at the sound of the commotion and walked over to them, Winchester walking at his heel.

"Tis alright, Constable," he said. "This lady be Miss Gloam who reported the incident. I can vouch for the others too."

"I'm sorry, sir," the constable replied. "I have strict orders to let no one through."

"I'll come out then," said Tom, "and we'll go in George's cottage."

"I'm afraid no one is allowed in there either," said the constable.

Tom sighed, opened the gate and went over to Vicky. "Come, Vicky," he said. "We'll walk down the road a-ways."

"Is there any news, Tom?" asked Vicky.

"No, there's no news," he replied.

"We'll go on to The Pullet and wait for you there, Vicky," said Linda.

Vicky nodded in acknowledgement. Linda, Jonathan and Justin got back in the car and drove off. Tom and Vicky watched them go and then set off along the road after them with Winchester, still on his lead, trailing along by Tom's side.

Vicky walked with her head down. "Tell me the truth, Tom," she asked. "What are the chances of finding him alive?"

Tom answered quietly. "The police said you told them that you saw 'im fall in the river."

"Yes."

"Well, the river was running quite fast. They found Sebastian's body - he was well drowned. It would be difficult ter imagine anybody surviving in that torrent. But 'e might have got swept ashore somewhere. I can't understand why we 'aven't found 'im."

Vicky started to cry.

Tom placed his hand on her shoulder and they walked on to the pub in silence. At The Pullet Inn they found Jack Hump behind the bar talking to a uniformed police sergeant. Linda, Jonathan and Justin were sitting at a table by the door.

Tom spoke gently to Vicky. "You join yer friends and I'll bring yer a brandy."

Vicky nodded and went and sat down with the group at the table. Tom approached the bar where Jack passed him a pint glass of cider. He picked it up and took a sip. "Thanks, Jack," he said. "Can you get me a large brandy for the lady?"

Jack nodded and turned to fetch the drink. "Yer knows the Muckle better than anyone," said Jack holding a brandy glass under the appropriate bottle and drink dispenser. "I was just tellin' the sergeant 'ere. What are the chances of not finding George's body?"

"The Muckle's not a deep river. It shouldn't be too difficult."

"What are the chances of the body being caught under a sunken log or something?" asked the sergeant.

Tom took another sip of cider. "It could 'ave 'appened, I s'pose. Anyways we should see things easier when the flood level dies down. The body should come to the surface in a few days' time. I can't see it staying below the surface fer too long."

CHAPTER 21

Eight months had passed and it was June once more in Mucklesbury and the surrounding area. Simon Clitterbooth's Jaguar sports car drew up in the lane by the mill. He got out the car, opened the gate, walked up to the mill and entered through the already open door. The interior of the main downstairs room had once again been converted into a large art studio. Easels, canvasses, pieces of unfinished sculpture were cluttered about. In the midst of this clutter, Linda was working alone on a piece of sculpture, a hammer and chisel in either hand. A Bach concerto was playing from the twin speakers of a hi-fi system.

 Simon announced himself. "Hello," he said.

 Linda looked up. "Hello. You must be Simon. Vicky's expecting you. "You'll find her at the cottage."

 "And you must be Linda," said Simon. "How are things going here?"

 "Oh, fine." She gestured with the hand holding the chisel. "As you can see, the Art Centre is up and running again. We have three painters working here now. Two are in Tidburn at the moment. Shopping, would you believe? The other, Jonathan, is in the flat upstairs. But they should all be around later this afternoon."

 Simon nodded. "Fine," he said, "I'll go and see Vicky then."

 He left the mill and made his way back along the path to the cottage where he knocked on the front door. It was opened by Vicky herself. She was wearing a black tee shirt and blue shorts. Her blonde hair was tied back by a blue band and her hands were encased in bright yellow rubber gloves.

 "Hello, Simon," she said. "Come in." He followed her into the hallway and through to the kitchen. "I hope you don't mind but I'm in the middle of washing up. I had a late breakfast. Are you hungry?"

"No, I'm fine."

"Coffee?"

"Yes, thanks."

"Just give me a moment to rinse these things and I'll be right with you." She indicated a mug and a bowl, and a small china plate in the washing up bowl.

"Can I help?" he asked.

"Oh, no. You can go through to the sitting room if you like. The coffee pot is still warm. It won't take a moment. I think I'll have another cup myself."

"It's okay. I'll wait here, if I'm not in the way."

Vicky rinsed the crockery with the aid of soapy water and a washing-up mop, then put them on the draining board to dry while Simon stood and watched her. Then she took two china mugs from a cupboard, set them on the kitchen table and filled them with coffee from a pot which she took from an electric coffee maker standing on a dresser.

"Sit down," she said. "If I remember rightly, you drink it like me, black with no sugar."

Simon nodded. "Thanks," he said and sat down on one of three wooden chairs pulled up at the table. "You seem well settled in here."

Vicky sat down on one of the other chairs opposite him. "I'm just looking after things for a while," she said.

"For how long?"

"I wish I knew. No one knows what happened to George. His body has not been found. There was no one else to look after the mill or his cottage. I just moved in here temporarily to keep an eye on things until he was found. It seemed only right. After all, I was his business partner. I'm now the nearest thing to the next of kin he's got."

"But he's probably dead. And you've got your own life to lead."

"Maybe so; but it was partly my fault. I could have saved him. I almost did. If only I arrived sooner. If only I realised what my uncle and Sebastian were up to earlier."

Simon sipped his coffee and then put the mug back down on the table. "What's done is done," he said, "but why have you started the Art Centre up again?"

Vicky looked down at her cup. "I sort of drifted into it again," she said. "After a few weeks of tidying up and sweeping out the mill, I simply got bored. Linda, Jonathan and Justin started dropping by to see how I was and if there was any news about George. I don't know which one of us suggested it should happen. It just happened."

"Do you think George is dead?" asked Simon.

Vicky shook her head. Tears began to from in her eyes. "I don't know," she said. "The river was really rough that night. I just kept thinking that he could have got swept ashore, got up and walked away. But he would have been found. Reports saying that he was missing were broadcast on the radio, television and in the newspapers for weeks afterwards. Inquests into Sebastian and Uncle Oswald's deaths made headline news. But we've heard nothing. His body's not been found." She wiped the tears away. "Some of the locals say that he could have been swept into a subterranean cavern. I still keep thinking that any day now he'll come walking back in here, either to the mill or to the cottage."

"You don't think he might have just got frightened and taken off?" asked Simon.

She shook her head. "He would have heard the news reports and come back. I do know one thing though. George loved this place. The mill and this cottage meant the world to him. He spent so much time lately trying to hang on to it. He would never go away and leave it. I just want to look after it for him for a little while longer."

Simon sipped more of his coffee. "I'm sorry. I didn't mean to pry," he said. "Things must have been very hard for you."

She looked at him and smiled. "It's okay," she said. "It's done me good to talk about it. People have been very kind." She picked up her mug and began to drink her coffee.

"So," said Simon, "Why did you invite me here?"

She cradled the cup in her hands. "I want you to make a promotional video of the mill. I thought we'd go ahead with the original plans we put to George. The others thought it would be a good idea to start off with a video to advertise the Art Centre. I arranged for them to meet you this afternoon. I didn't expect you to arrive so early."

"There were a couple of things I wanted to talk about with you first. Alone."

"Oh, what?"

Simon took a deep breath. "Hiram Cornslinger's been in touch with me. *The English Girl* has been a great success. They want you to do the follow up. And knowing the trouble you've been through they've been asking me to sound you out for them."

Vicky shook her head. "Sorry, Simon. No. I didn't like Hollywood or filming. I was happiest most when I was here. I want to stay here and set up a successful Art Centre and enjoy working with creative people; just like I did with George."

"But there are creative people in Hollywood."

"But I didn't have the fun that I had here. And now, just lately, some of it is beginning to return again."

"All right. I'll take your word for it. But I warn you Hiram probably won't take it lying down. Not when there's a lot of potential money at stake. He just might try and fly over to persuade you himself."

"Then he'll get the same answer that I have given you." She took a final sip of coffee and put the cup down on the table. "Come on," she said. "Let's take a look at the mill and you can tell me what you think about my ideas for the video. You can have lunch here and then talk to the others about their ideas this afternoon."

Simon finished his coffee and followed Vicky out the house. She waited for him outside and shut the front door.

They were about to set off along the path towards the mill when a small blue Renault car drew up by the gate. The Reverend Scillage got out of the driver's side and called to them, "Good morning!" He walked to the gate. "I'm glad I caught you," he continued. "I hope you don't mind me dropping in unannounced, but I did rather want to talk to you. May I come in?"

"Of course, Vicar," replied Vicky and opened the gate for him.

He stepped through the gateway. "I won't keep you long, "he said. "I was just driving past when I saw you. I've been meaning to contact you for some days now and when I saw you I just had to stop. How are you keeping, my dear? These past months must have been a terrible strain on you."

"I'm fine, really," replied Vicky. Gesturing towards Simon, she added, "Oh, this is Mr Clitterbooth, a friend of mine from London."

"Hello," said Simon.

"How do you do," said the Vicar. "Look, what I stopped by to say is that George Cogrill was very highly respected in Mucklesbury. Everyone has been so upset by what has happened."

"Everyone has been terribly kind," said Vicky.

"I knew George since he was a small boy," continued the Vicar. "In fact I baptised him, which brings me to the reason why I am here. You see in two weeks time it will be George's birthday and there is a feeling in the village that we should not let this date pass without holding a small service. In fact the whole village feels the same."

"What sort of service?" asked Vicky. "His body ... He is still missing."

The vicar laid a gentle hand on Vicky's arm. "I know that dear. I also know that he might never be found. But we thought, that is the Parish council and myself thought, that if we held a service here on the bank by the mill, near where he disappeared. It might ease the pain of his loss."

Vicky looked at Simon who simply stood there in silence, lost for words.

"It might be that he hasn't been lost, my dear," continued the vicar. "We can pray for his safe return or for his soul wherever he may be. But should he never return a service at this time may help his many friends."

Vicky spoke with tears in her eyes. "I see. Thank you. I think that would be very nice."

"Good," said the vicar. "I'll leave you with your friend now and I will come and see you in a few days time to make the arrangements. In the meantime, if you would like a little chat you can always come and see me at any time."

"Thank you very much," said Vicky.

"No, really," said the vicar. "I'm sure after the service the whole village would wish to thank you."

Later that night in a motor caravan on a campsite by the side of Loch Lomond in Scotland, George Cogrill dreamed a dream. He was fighting a duel in shallow water, in the shadow of a giant castle, on top of a powerful waterfall. He was fighting a fearsome black knight who swung a mighty battle axe, while he had but a small wooden paper knife for protection. Across the water, another knight, a white knight, rode towards him on a black charger, water spraying from its hooves. The white knight yelled a warning. The black knight struck with his axe. George felt a sudden pain in his head and heard the rushing water in his ears. Then he woke up.

He was lying in a sleeping bag in a single bunk, shaking with fear. He sat up, breathing heavily. Slowly he became aware of where he was and his breathing became more even. He sat there for some moments and pulled himself out the sleeping bag. He was wearing a black tee shirt and a mauve pair of boxer under shorts. He pulled on a pair of jeans and a green pullover. Then he searched under the bunk, found a pair of white canvass training shoes, put them on, hastily tied the laces, opened the door and stepped outside.

He walked quickly to the loch side and out on to a tiny coarse sandy beach. There he sat down on flat rock and stared at the dark lapping water. The dream had frightened him. It had been very vivid. He began breathing deeply once more, dragging the cold night air into his lungs. Hoping this would cleanse his tortured mind and drive the demons away. After a time he became calmer. He looked out across the water, struggling to understand what it all meant, trying to remember distant images. For one moment he thought he saw a face reflected in the water. It was the face of a beautiful girl framed with long blond hair. The image was all too fleeting and soon disappeared. He rubbed his eyes in an effort to bring it back but it was to no avail. He got to his feet and returned to the motor caravan. Back inside, he undressed once more and climbed back into his sleeping bag. He tried once more to recapture the image of the girl. But it was gone.

The next morning the sun flooded in through the motor caravan windows. It was nine o'clock. Roy Tumbleweed climbed out of the double bed in the small room at the rear of the vehicle. He slipped a dressing gown over his striped pyjamas and went through to the kitchen-dinning area. Pearl was there, seated alone at the table. She was fully dressed in checked shirt, jeans and cowboy boots. She was drinking a mug of black coffee.

Roy greeted her. "Hi, honey. Where's John?"

"He's gone for a jog along the side of the loch," she replied.

Roy helped himself to a mug of coffee from the pot which stood on the coffee maker and then joined her at the table. "I heard him moving around last night," he said.

"Mmm," murmured Pearl.

"He's been doing a lot of that lately," he continued.

Pearl sipped her coffee and remained silent.

"I don't think it's a good idea we continue on like this. It doesn't seem right. The boy needs help."

Pearl looked at him sharply. "What do you mean?" she asked.

"At first I thought he was on the run from something. I didn't believe he had lost his memory. Either the police or a wife was after him. Well that didn't seem to be so bad, being on the run from society. I've always supposed we are, I mean the two of us are, in some way. And he looked kind of lost and like you I thought he was a lot like Johnny. Well, we were in a hurry and I figured that if he was really bad he would show it in some way. But he hasn't. And I'm sure he isn't bad."

"So?"

"So, I don't think we should regard him like our son. I think he has really lost his memory and probably needs help - medical help in trying to recover it."

"But he likes it here with us. He says so. He treats us like we are his parents. It seems more like it was him who adopted us. We've always said he could leave of his own accord."

Roy spread his hands. "Leave for where? If he's lost his memory, then we're probably the only security he's got."

"But he's part of our family now. He helps with the gigs, sets up the microphones, does the sound checks. He's very useful to have around. And he does care for us."

Roy shook his head. "But he can't play a guitar. He can't sing. He doesn't seem to have any musical sense at all."

"Roy, since when did you need to have a good voice to be able to sing Country music? He can learn. Why, he could join us on stage. That would be something."

Roy grew impatient. "Look," he said. "He's been sleeping badly lately. He's been complaining of bad dreams. If he has lost his memory and we don't help him find it, it's not fair on him. He may well have friends and family looking for him. It was your idea we should come up here and tour Scotland shortly after we found him. And I'm sure the break may have done him good. But it doesn't seem to be doing much good right now. I reckon we ought to return to near where found him and find out the truth one way or the other. If he still wants to remain with us, then fine. But it should be up to him." Roy stood up and added. "When he returns I'll put it to him fair and square. Then it'll be up to him to decide."

CHAPTER 22

Three days later Hiram Cornslinger entered The Pullet Inn. With him was his son, Sandy. They approached the bar where Jack Hump was engaged in conversation with Tom Firkin. Winchester was lying asleep at Tom's feet.

"Good day!" Hiram greeted them heartily. "Can you get me a beer and a Coke here for my boy, as he's drivin'."

"What kind o' beer?" asked Jack.

"Oh, just your regular."

"Pint or 'alf?"

"A pint please."

"A pint o' bitter an' a Coke coming up," said Jack and set about dispensing the drinks.

Hiram turned to Tom. "Hi there," he said. "Tom something, isn't it? I seem to remember meeting you at Vicky's mill."

"It's Tom Firkin," replied Tom. "And it's George Cogrill's mill. Anyways it was at the time."

Hiram ignored the remark. "I'm Hiram Cornslinger," he said. "This here is my boy, Sandy."

The boy Sandy nodded to Tom.

"We're down here to visit Vicky," continued Hiram. "They told us up at the mill that she was down here in this pub, having lunch with you."

"We just 'ad a drink and a sandwich," said Tom. "She's over at the vicarage now talkin' to the vicar. She'll be back shortly."

Jack Hump placed a glass of beer and a glass of Coca Cola on the bar in front of Hiram.

"Thank you kindly," said Hiram and handed him a twenty pound note. "Have one yourself and get Tom another of whatever he's drinking - and keep the change."

"Thank yer, sir," said Jack. "I'll 'ave a pint o' zider. Tom?"

"The same please, Jack," replied Tom.

"Well, what's there to do in the way of entertainment around here?" asked Hiram.

"Well," said Tom. "There used ter be a dart board but Jack took it down when the pub was done out. But I dare say he's still got a crib board, pack of cards and dominoes somewhere behind the bar."

"Naw. I don' mean those sorts of entertainment. I mean singing and dancing. Although I don' s'pose a li'le gambling will come amiss."

"There's no gambling allowed in 'ere," said Jack placing a glass of cider in front of Tom. "And if it's music yer after yer'll 've to go into Tidburn. We don't do singing in 'ere any more. This 'stablishment's fer eatin' and drinkin' only."

"More's the pity," muttered Tom. "But it didn't use ter be that way though."

"No, it didn't but times 'ave changed. Folks come 'ere now from the towns fer a quite meal and drink - and they brings their kiddies too. And they don't want lots of rowdy behaviour, see."

"What's there in Tidburn?" asked Hiram changing what he perceived was an obviously contentious subject. "Sandy and me have booked into a hotel there."

"Which un?" asked Jack.

"The Frog and Compass."

"The Frog and Compass? I believe they 'ave Country and Western singing in there some nights," said Tom.

Hiram shook his head. "We get a lot of that at home," he said. "Don' you have any local folk singers?"

"Well there be Old Joe's nephew, Jimmy Thropp and his Turnip Thumpers," replied Tom. "They use ter perform in 'ere until Jack put on 'is airs and graces. Now they're relegated to the village hall, along with the Mucklesbury Morris Dancers. A great bunch o' lads though."

"They drives respectable folks away," warned Jack, scowling.

"Come off it, Jack, you use ter like them. If they brought the customers in you'd 'ave 'em back like a shot."

Sandy spoke for the first time. "Sounds boring, Dad," he said.

"Naw, it sounds interesting," said Hiram. "When do they next perform?"

"I think they're planning to do somethin' the day after tomorrow at the service for George at the mill."

"Oh, I see," said Hiram. "Well we might just look in, but I have to speak with Vicky first."

Meanwhile, fifteen miles away, the Tumbleweeds' motor caravan pulled into a field beside the River Muckle. George was in the passenger seat, next to Roy who was driving. Pearl was sitting in one of the two passenger seats behind them. They were all dressed in checked shirts, blue jeans and cowboy boots and were wearing Stetsons.

"Well," said Roy, "here we are. Do you remember anything, John?"

George stared out the windows at the surrounding fields but said nothing.

"Let's get out and walk down to the river," said Roy. "Perhaps it will help bring it all back to you. Are you coming, Pearl?"

"Yes, I am," Pearl replied. "Now take things easy, Johnny. Remember that we are with you and we're here to help you."

The three of them got out the motor caravan and walked down across the field to the river. They stood on the bank and looked across the water. An old rowing boat was stuck, rotting amongst some reeds. Otherwise nothing appeared out of the ordinary.

"What do you remember, John?" Roy asked George.

George closed his eyes for several moments. Then opened them and looked about him. "I remember seeing you here," he said, "and following you to the motor caravan. Otherwise nothing."

"You remember nothing before that?" asked Roy.

George screwed his eyes shut and shook his head. "I'm trying hard to remember but I can't remember anything!" he insisted.

Pearl took George's arm. "Take it easy on the boy, Roy. Can't you see he's been trying to remember?"

"Okay, I'm sorry," said Roy. "Come on, let's go. I've booked us a gig at a place called The Frog and Compass in Tidburn, which is not too far away. Perhaps we'll find out something there."

An hour later and fifteen miles farther north, Vicky Gloam was standing in the churchyard in Mucklesbury beside the grave of Lady Jane Gleefield. The sun shone down over her and the blue and white dress she was wearing, and on to the grave nestling against her white high-heeled shoes. A dark blue straw hat sat on her head above her long blonde hair but despite this, and the matching blue jacket she wore over the dress, she felt cold.

She heard a noise behind her and turned to see Tom coming along the path towards her, Winchester on a lead at his side. The dog strained forward to greet her but Tom pulled him back with a jerk on his lead. "Now then, your lordship," he said gently. "Tis only Miss Victoria."

Vicky crouched down beside the dog and stroked his head and neck. "Hello, Winchester," she said. "Tom, why are you being so formal? Both you and indeed Winchester have always known me as Vicky."

"Just trying ter remind 'is lordship some manners fitting 'is new status," replied Tom and then, noticing Winchester trying to paw at Vicky, pulled him back once more and rebuked him sharply. "Yer mind Vicky's nice dress!"

Vicky laughed and stood up. "It's all right, Tom. I'm only wearing this because I've been to see the vicar. That's over now."

"Still, 'e needs to show some manners," insisted Tom.

"Tell me," asked Vicky, "why did Lady Gleefield name him after the cathedral town of Winchester? It's always intrigued me."

Tom laughed. "Yer wrong there. She named 'im after the American repeating rifle. 'E be a gun dog after all and, judging by the way 'e farts, he's been apply named."

"Really," said Vicky and drew back.

This time Tom laughed. "Only joking." He bent and scratched him behind the ear and added, "'E's a good dog really. I can understand why 'er ladyship loved 'im so much."

Vicky turned and looked at the grave. "She was a strange woman," she said, "but I believe that in her own way she loved George just as well."

Tom nodded. "Yes, I believe yer right," he said.

Vicky turned and looked at him once more and tried in vain to hold back the tears in her eyes. "Tom, do you believe he's dead?" she asked.

"Well," replied Tom, "I'm not sure I 'olds with the theory that 'e was sucked into an underground cavern. I 'aven't 'eard of any underground caverns in these parts, 'specially around the Muckle. But there again I can't understand why we never found his body. I can't see him leaving the mill though. Whatever's happened to 'im I don't see 'im coming back. 'E would 'ave returned by now if he was going to. All in all I reckon it's right that folk around here ought ter be able to say good-bye to 'im."

She blinked back the rears and asked, "Are you coming to the service?"

" 'Course. 'E was one of my oldest friends."

"It's a pity you won't rejoin the group at the Mill Art Centre. You produced some good drawings."

He shook his head. "It's not the same with George gone."

"You miss Miranda too. Don't you?"

"Yer, I do. But I s'pose it was ter be 'spected. I can't really compete with rich Eyetalians and luxury villas. I 'spect you'll be off to 'Ollywood again when things 'ere 'ave been settled."

"No. I want to stay and run the mill as an Art Centre, like I did with George."

Tom nodded. "You miss 'im too, don't yer?"

"Yes," replied Vicky, "very much so."

"That Hiram bloke and 'is boy are waiting for yer at The Pullet. I think they want ter speak to yer about going back ter make more films."

"Oh dear, I'd rather not talk to them now."

"Well, if you like yer can walk back along ther Muckle with me and Winchester. That should avoid you meeting 'em. They be staying at the Frog and Compass in Tidburn should you change yer mind and decide to meet 'em later."

Meanwhile, a little farther north, Simon Clitterbooth had finished showing Linda, Justin and Jonathan the promotional video he had made of the Mill Art Centre. All four were gathered round the television set in the upstairs flat at the mill. Simon pressed the off button on the VCR and ejected the cassette. He stood, cassette in hand, facing the others who were sitting opposite him on the settee.

"Well, what do you think?" he asked them.

"Very good," replied Jonathan. "Just the ticket. What did you think, Justy?"

"Yes, it was terrific," agreed Justin. "Pity Vicky wasn't here though."

"Never mind," said Linda. "She couldn't really miss that appointment with the vicar. I'll show it to her later, Simon, if you would like to leave it behind."

"Yes, fine," said Simon. He put the cassette back into its box and handed it to her. "I'll leave you all to discuss it then and contact you later."

Linda stood up and said, "I'll show you out." She and Simon made their way out of the flat, down the stairs and out of the mill.

Linda stopped by the doorway. "Thank you for coming and showing it to us. I'm sure Vicky would have been here to see it for herself, if she could. I hope you weren't too disappointed that we weren't all here."

"No," replied Simon, "I understand. She has a lot on her mind at the moment."

"Listen," said Linda. "You look quite fed up. Where are you staying?"

"At a hotel in Tidburn."

"Well maybe I can drop by this evening and give you an update on what she thought of the video. We could go for a drink or something."

Simon brightened up. "Yes, okay," he said, "or perhaps a meal. I hate dining alone."

"What's the name of the hotel?" she asked.

"It's The Frog and Compass," he replied.

Later that evening Simon walked into The Frog and Compass to find Hiram seated on a stool at the bar next to a glass of malt whiskey. "Hello, Hiram," he said. "I heard you were staying here."

"That's right. Me and my boy Sandy. Came over to call on Vicky – haven't got to see her though."

"She's very difficult to get to meet at the moment," said Simon trying to catch the barman's eye.

"Let me get you a drink," said Hiram and drained his glass. "Barman!" The barman came over to them. "Another Scotch on the rocks for me and something for my friend here."

"I'll have a Scotch too," said Simon, "but with soda and no ice."

The barman turned away without a word and tended to their requests.

"Where's Sandy now?" asked Simon.

"Oh, he's gone to a disco or something. Says there's not enough action for him around here. But I hear there's a Country and Western group on in here later. Might be interesting. What brings you in here?"

"Oh I'm staying here too. I'm meeting someone for dinner. We're dining in the restaurant - Linda Quilt, a friend of Vicky's. You might know her."

"The artist girl, yeah I met her. I had heard that you've been quite close to Vicky lately."

"She's been having a tough time. I've been trying to help her through it."

The barman returned with the drinks and placed both glasses on the bar in front of them. "Thanks," said Hiram. "Put the check on my tab, will you?"

The barman nodded in reply and went away.

"Yeah," Hiram continued, "I heard about that Cogrill fella, can't say that I'm surprised though."

"Why, what do you mean?"

"Well, he did frequent some seedy dives and hang out with some heavy characters. I saw him in a clip joint in London. I was with Cliff Clayburger; we'd gone there after the London Première of *The English Girl*. George was there. He had a couple of heavies with him."

"George had a couple of heavies with him? Do you mean gangsters? That doesn't sound like George."

"Well he sure did. It surprised me too until he picked a fight with Clayburger and his bodyguards. I guess he was use to getting into trouble. Clayburger was pretty shaken. He came off second best and thought George was in some way connected with the Mafia."

"George Cogrill connected with the Mafia?"

"That's right. And Clayburger should know 'cause it's been rumoured that he's had some connections in that area himself. I hear there's some sort of ceremony for George tomorrow."

"That's right, at the mill."

"Might try and catch Vicky there then. You going?"

"Yes." Simon picked up his glass, took a sip of his drink and put the glass back down on the bar. "Look, please don't mention what you told me to Vicky. She's had a hard enough time of it as it is."

"Sure, don't worry, I won't."

"I think you'll have a hard time of persuading her to go back to films," added Simon. "She seems determined to stay and make a go of the Art Centre."

Hiram nodded. "We'll see," he said. "But she don't need to be put off by Clayburger any more. Your friend George has certainly seen to that."

"Hello!" The word was spoken by Linda. Both men turned to see her crossing the floor in their direction. Vicky was trailing in her wake. Both women had recently entered from the outside and were wearing long overcoats. Linda's was black and Vicky's blue.

Linda continued talking once they had both joined the men. "I hope I haven't kept you waiting long, Simon. Vicky's come along because she wanted to talk to you about the video."

"Are you joining us for dinner?" Simon asked Vicky.

"No," she replied. "I've already eaten. I knew Hiram was here and I wanted to talk to him. I also wanted a quick word with you first. Hello, Hiram."

Hi there, Vicky," replied Hiram. "Glad to make contact with you at last."

"I'm sorry I haven't managed to see you or Simon earlier," continued Vicky, "but things have been very hectic lately."

"No problem," said Hiram. "Can I get you both a drink?"

"I'm not sure we have time, have we, Simon?" asked Linda.

Simon looked at his watch. "We ought to be going into the restaurant now," he said.

"You two go ahead," said Vicky, "and I'll stay and have a drink with Hiram. Simon, I've looked at the video and it was great. There are a couple of minor points I have to raise. Linda can explain them to you over dinner."

"You're welcome to join us both after," said Hiram. "There's a Country and Western group on here later. In fact I think the group's setting up over there now." He indicated the other end of the room with a sweep of his arm.

"I'm not sure I really care for Country and Western singing," said Linda. She looked in the direction of the musicians, who were arranging their sound equipment and added, "Goodness, do you see who's with them?" They all followed her gaze.

At that moment a large balding man in a dinner suite approached the microphone. "Ladies and gentlemen!" he announced. "Due to unforeseen circumstances the Tumbleweeds can not be with us. But in their place at short notice, we have a local folk group." He paused for effect and then raised his voice and added, "Jimmy Thropp and his Turnip Thumpers!"

"Oh my goodness," said Vicky, "Jimmy Thropp. I think the whole of Mucklesbury and Tidburn have heard their repertoire many times."

"They any good?" asked Hiram.

"They can certainly be very lively," replied Linda. "Come on, Simon," she said, "let's go and eat. We'll leave the other two to their 'Country' music." "They may even be better than The Tumbleweeds, but there again we'll probably never know."

CHAPTER 23

The next day the Tumbleweeds' motor caravan drew up outside Tidburne station. Roy was in the driving seat and he turned to George who was sitting beside him. "You stay here, John," he said, "and keep an eye on the van. I'll take Pearl into the station and see her off. Come on, Pearl love."

He got out the van and Pearl, who was in the seat behind him, followed. He opened the back door and took out a suitcase. They went into the station, bought a ticket at the ticket office and then made their way to the platform. There Roy set the case down and turned to his wife,

"Have you got everything, Pearl?" he asked.

"Yes, Roy, don't worry. I'll be all right."

"It's really rough luck on Alice, Pete dying right now," Roy continued.

"I know," said Pearl, "but she is my younger sister and she has no other relatives. I have to go to her."

"Of course, we agreed. There's no problem."

"I'm so sorry about last night, but I really could not go on," said Pearl.

"Of course, don't worry. I'll stay here and do the gig solo. That way we'll still get paid. The pub manager was very understanding. There's no need for you to worry about a thing. You go and visit Alice and John and I'll follow on later in the van."

A train approached the platform, slowed down and stopped.

"Take care of yourself now, Roy," said Pearl and kissed him on the cheek. "And take care of Johnny."

"I will, don't worry. But this isn't your train. It's the train from London. Your train is the next one in."

"Oh, of course, how silly of me!"

The carriage doors opened and the passengers began getting out. One of them was Miranda Flit. She was wearing a skimpy black top, short white skirt, white stiletto shoes and carrying a small matching suitcase. She did not know Roy and Pearl and they did not know her either. So she walked past them, along the platform and out of the station. There, she saw George standing by the motor caravan.

" 'Ello, George," she said. "I didn't think anyone knew I was coming. I like the cowboy outfit. If you're going to the mill, be a brick and drop us off at Tom's cottage."

George stood and looked at her dumbfounded.

Miranda became impatient. "Well! Where's the Roller?" she asked.

"Roller?"

"The Rolls-Royce, where's the Rolls?"

George still regarded her blankly. Some memory was tugging at the back of his mind but he was unable to grasp it. To cover his uncertainty, he turned to the van behind him and opened the passenger door.

"This yours, is it?" inquired Miranda. "Well, it's certainly different. Who or what are the Tumbleweeds?" she said reading the writing on the side. "Some idea of Vicky's, I suppose." She gave him her suitcase and got in the passenger seat.

George acted as if he was on autopilot. He took the suitcase to the side door of the motor caravan and stowed it in the back. Then he opened the door on the driver's side, got in the driving seat, closed the door and sat there.

"Well, are we going then?" asked Miranda.

He looked down at the ignition lock, saw the key there, turned it, started the engine, and edged the motor caravan out into the traffic.

"It'll be great to see everyone again," said Miranda. "Catch up on all the news. I've really missed Tom, you know. 'As 'E missed me do you know?"

George did not answer. He could not answer. His mind was trying to remember her and place the names she had mentioned.

She continued talking without waiting for his reply. "Well I don' blame 'im really. But I do want to see 'im. Giuseppe was very nice. But 'e was boring. Italy was very nice. But I missed England, the cups of tea, fish and chips. It's amazing how you miss fings like that. People tell you, you know. You don't believe them, but you really do. Anyway, I really missed Tom. I know I was beastly to 'im but I'll make it up. I think I love 'im. I don't know though. If I did I wouldn't 'ave left 'im, would I? I really don't know? But I really did miss 'im. I missed you too of course, George, but not in the same way. I really did miss Tom."

She paused, took a breath and continued. "I just had enough of Italy. Popped on a plane and 'ere I am. I know it's colder 'ere, but I really felt I 'ad to come."

She continued talking in the same vein, mentioning more names as if he should know them. He looked over at her. She was certainly beautiful. He pictured the face of the beautiful girl he thought he had seen reflected in the waters of Loch Lomond. The face had returned to him again, recently, in his dreams. However, the face of the girl who occupied the seat next to him was not the same. But who was she? And why was she calling him George? He should say something but he had become acutely embarrassed. He did not know what to say, so he sat there silently beside her, driving automatically; to where, he did not know. His passenger, whoever she was, did not appear to notice.

They left the town and were out into the country, Miranda chattering all the while. She spoke about Italy and said how much more beautiful the countryside was in England especially in spring and early summer when the leaves filled the trees and everything was fresh and green.

Suddenly she stopped chattering and in mid sentence said, "My God! We're at the mill!"

George was startled. He shook his head, looked out of the window and saw that they had drawn up outside a gate leading to a large building which looked like a watermill. He had no idea why he had stopped. There were a lot of other cars parked in the road leading up to the gate. A group of about a hundred people stood on the river bank by the mill. Despite the sunny day, all were dressed formally and most were dressed in black.

"You've driven right past Tom's cottage. And I was so busy chatting I didn't realise. Oh! Never mind, that looks like 'im with those people over there. What ever's going on?"

George sat in stunned silence surveying the scene in front of him. Something was familiar. Something tugged at the corner of his mind. Miranda got out the van and George followed automatically. She opened the gate and ran across the field towards the group of people. George stood by the van and stared after her.

"Tom!" she called. "Coo-ee, Tom!"

Tom looked up from where he stood in between Linda and Vicky. "Merander!" he said, startled.

Miranda threw herself into his arms, oblivious of the people around them. "Oh, Tom," she murmured, "I missed you so."

"Merander please!" said Tom firmly and then lowered his voice. "I missed yer too, but there be people 'ere."

The Reverent Scillage was standing facing the group, holding a bible, his back toward the river. He cleared his throat noisily.

"Wha's going on?" whispered Miranda.

"Shh," hissed those around her.

"Tell yer later," Tom whispered to her, extracting himself form her grip but holding on to her arm firmly.

A hundred yards away, George stood by the gate still watching the scene. The building in front of him was familiar. Something again tugged at the recess of his mind. The back of his head ached. He shook his head once more; this time to clear the ache. Slowly, he found himself drawn along the path to the mill as if it was some gigantic magnet. Then, without even pausing to think, he stooped and picked a key out of a small flowerpot next to the main door, unlocked it and went inside. Why he entered, or how he knew the key was there, he had no idea. His actions were automatic as if in response to a distant memory pre-programmed into his brain.

He closed the door behind him and stood still on the stone flagstones. The interior seemed vaguely familiar but there was something different. Suddenly a long dark shape rocketed from out of nowhere and up at his chest. He toppled back in shock and surprise, struck the back of his head against the door and slumped to the floor unconscious. Winchester stood over him and began licking his face.

Outside, the Reverent Scillage was addressing the group by the mill. "At this point," he said, "I would like to call upon a good friend of ours, the writer and poet, Frank Witterworth!"

"What's all this in aid of?" Miranda whispered to Tom.

"It's fer George," he whispered in reply.

"Oo tha's nice," said Miranda.

"I didn't know Frank was that good a friend of George's," whispered Jonathan who was standing in between Linda and Justin.

"He wasn't," Linda whispered back, "but his poem in memory of Old Joe Thropp was so successful he wanted to write something for George."

Frank stepped up, stood next to the vicar and faced the group. He took a piece of paper from his pocket and began reading straight away.

> George Cogrill is gone
> The mill where he stood still stands
> But George Gogrill is gone ...

"Wha' does 'e mean, George Cogrill is gone'?" asked Miranda. "'E's 'ere." She looked round in the direction of the motor caravan. "Well, 'e was a minute ago."

Tom grew exasperated. "Be quiet, Merander," he hissed. "I'll explain later."

Frank had halted at the interruption. The vicar, seeing him hesitate, interjected. "Of course, we all feel George's spirit is still with us, by this mill he loved so much, by his home."

"'E was by the gate a minute ago," said Miranda.

"Shut up, Merander!" snapped Tom.

"But 'e brought me 'ere!"

The whole group now became restless and irritated. Miranda was spoiling what had been up to now a very moving occasion.

"Perhaps it was some sort of Divine Providence which brought her here," remarked Justin.

"Be quite, Justy!" snapped Jonathan.

"'E brought me 'ere in that camper van!" said Miranda emphatically and pointed in the direction of the gate.

"Miranda is this some kind of a joke?" said Linda. "If it is, I don't think it very funny."

Vicky suddenly left the group and began walking hurriedly towards the motor caravan by the gate. The remainder of the group looked at each other and then followed. They reached Vicky, who was standing by the van.

"The Tumbleweeds," said Hiram reading the sign on the van. "Say, ain't that the name of the band we was to see last night at The Goat and Compass?"

A police car pulled up and a constable got out and came over to them. "There's rather too many cars parked in the lane," he said. "I'm going to have to ask you to move them." He stopped and noticed the motor caravan. "Hello," he remarked. "This vehicle has been reported missing. Anyone seen who was driving it?"

Everyone turned to look at Miranda.

"It was 'im!" she insisted.

"Was who exactly?" asked the policeman taking a notebook and pencil out of his pocket.

"She says it were George Cogrill. 'E's bin missing fer some time, presumed dead," replied Tom.

"I see," said the policeman as if this was a common occurrence in that part of the country.

The crowd became silent. The sound of a dog barking came from inside the mill. All eyes turned in that direction.

"That's Winchester," said Tom to anyone who cared to listen. "I shut 'im away in the mill in case 'e made a nuisance of 'is self."

"What about the cat?" asked Simon Clitterbooth.

"And what cat is that, sir?" said the policeman continuing in the same matter-of-fact voice.

"The cat called Mable," explained Simon. "The one that was owned by Lady Gleefield but has since disappeared. I'd question the dog if I were you, Constable, since he's inherited her estate!"

"I've told you, sir," said Gumage. "Her ladyship has never had a cat. I do not know where you got that notion."

"I guess you oughta question the butler too, Officer," interjected Hiram. "There's been some mighty fishy goings-on in these parts. That guy Cogrill had connections with the Mafia."

"There ain' no need," said Miranda. Gumage is righ'. There ain't no cat. George made it up. My proper name's Mable, George made it up about the cat 'cause I didn't want people to know my real name." She stopped talking when she saw everyone looking at her in astonishment. "Well," she added, "Miranda sounds much more posh. Mable is ever so common."

The door of the mill opened and George stood in the opening. His Stetson was a little crumpled but still firmly in place on his head and by his side stood Winchester, tail wagging. On seeing him, the group took a few paces backwards, except for Vicky who ran forward and then stopped a few yards short of the mill entrance and stood staring at the figure in the Stetson.

"I'm sorry, Vicky," said George. "I fell asleep during your film and missed it."

"I know," she replied tearfully and then added, "I love you, George."

"I love you, Vicky," he said.

""Bloody 'ell, George!" called Jack Hump, "yer've ruined yer own funeral!"

THE END

Lightning Source UK Ltd.
Milton Keynes UK
01 June 2010
154952UK00001B/26/P